MARSH MYSTICS

A Miss Fortune Mystery

NEW YORK TIMES BESTSELLING AUTHOR

JANA DELEON

membership, women must never have married or if widowed, their husband must have been deceased for at least ten years.

Sinful Ladies Cough Syrup – sold as an herbal medicine in Sinful, which is dry, but it's actually moonshine manufactured by the Sinful Ladies Society.

CHAPTER ONE

At the sound of metal clanking, I halfway opened one eye to see why my afternoon hammock nap was being interrupted. A couple minutes ago, I'd heard footsteps walking across the lawn and knew it was Carter. That wasn't exactly a spectacular feat as he wasn't trying to sneak, but recognizing his exact footfall among the number of people who might come tromping into my backyard probably wasn't attributable to most people.

And while I could have ignored his letting the back door slam and his heavy-footed walk, the metal clanking was disrupting my sleep. And since the muttering had started up as well, I knew peace was not likely to be restored anytime soon. Deciding the situation needed serious assessment, I lifted my head and opened both eyes. If he only had a couple tools, the situation might call merely for earbuds and a short waiting period. The small toolbox probably indicated a relocation inside until he was done swearing and banging.

When I caught sight of the small toolbox in the bottom of the boat, I frowned. Then I glanced back at the house and realized he'd wheeled his mammoth toolbox from inside the garage and it was now sitting next to the deck. Good Lord, this might call for listing the house and leaving in the middle of the night. Carter rarely stayed frustrated for a long time, but if that giant toolbox was any indication, he was in this one for the long haul.

"Problem?" I asked.

"Sorry. Was I too loud?"

I raised one eyebrow and he sighed. Not as if he hadn't already known the answer.

"What are you doing out here in the middle of the afternoon anyway?" he asked. "I figured you'd be off with Trouble 1 and Trouble 2."

"Gertie and Ronald are at that new spa retreat that opened in Mudbug. They're having a restorative five days of contemplation and yoga."

"And you and Ida Belle didn't want to go? Shocking."

"My restoration consists of a shower and a beer. And taking time to contemplate things usually gets you killed."

"It scares me just a little that I almost agree with that. What about the yoga part?" he asked, continuing to goad me. "That's supposed to be great for physical fitness, balance, flexibility, and all."

In one fluid move, I flipped forward and out of the hammock while pulling my knife out of my pocket and launching it directly at his hand, which was on the side of the boat. He yanked it back just before the knife bounced off the metal and onto the ground.

"I'm good," I said and climbed back into the hammock.

He shook his head. "What if I hadn't moved my hand in time?"

"Then I would have to cook the steaks tonight, given that it was your right hand."

"Sometimes you scare me."

I grinned. "*You* asked *me* to marry you... Which one of us should have our sanity called into question?"

"All men proposing should have their sanity called into question. Just some more than others."

"Touché. Want to go shoot some stuff?"

It always made me feel better.

"No. It's illegal to shoot the things I've got issue with."

"Hmmmm. Got some names?"

"We can start with Celia."

"That's a good place to start...or finish. You know if you were tried locally, a jury would probably let you off."

"Unfortunately, she's already set the wheels in motion, so killing her now would be obvious and futile."

"What has she done?"

"She's convinced the state police to conduct an audit of the sheriff's department."

"Let me guess—she started this campaign after you proposed and moved in with me."

"You got it."

I sighed. "What is it she's claiming you're guilty of? Having a life? Not being a miserable excuse for a human being?"

"Providing civilians with information concerning open police investigations. And ignoring complaints of illegal activity due to my personal connections with the perpetrators."

"So me, Gertie, and Ida Belle."

He nodded.

"But we haven't done anything illegal."

He stared at me.

"Let me rephrase that," I said. "The illegal things we've done are not known to Celia. Or you for that matter. I'm dedicated to keeping things from you for your own good, and lying is definitely my strong suit. Well, maybe after killing people."

"And I appreciate your conviction, but Celia is certain that I'm the only thing standing in the way of the three of you rotting in a jail cell."

I shrugged. "Let them look. I've been watched by the CIA, FBI, DEA, Mossad, MI6, a creepy neighbor with a weird obsession back in DC, and more terrorists than I can count. If they couldn't get anything on me, I hardly think the state police are going to come up with anything."

"I don't either, but that's not the point. An audit alone can call my competence and loyalty into question."

"No one who knows you would question your loyalty or competence."

"That gets me the vote of most of Sinful, but the sheriff's territory is a lot bigger than that. Plenty of people keep to themselves and you know that bad news outpaces good news every time."

"Is there anything I can do?"

"Nothing besides what you're already doing—stay under the radar and keep me out of it," he said, and went back to banging.

I nodded as my cell phone rang. I checked the display and held in a sigh. Time to put that promise into action. It was Gertie.

"I thought you were ditching your cell phone to decompress at that retreat," I said as I answered.

"A woman's dead."

"Did you kill her?"

The banging stopped.

"No. I didn't kill her," Gertie said.

"Is the dead person someone I like? Because I'm totally up for a vengeance thing."

Carter stared at me in dismay.

"You don't know her," Gertie said.

"Did someone I like kill her? Is this a tarp-and-shovels call or one to work-up-alibis?"

Carter dropped his hammer and stalked off.

"It looks like a suicide."

"Then why are you calling me? My skill set has zero to contribute to a suicide situation."

"Because something isn't right, and no one ferrets out when something stinks better than you."

"Hmmmmm. I'll grab Ida Belle and head out there. Since there's a body, I assume Carter will be dispatched for duty as well. You'll have to claim you called me to come get you and Ronald because you're distraught or something."

"Just to have you show up at the retreat?"

"There's a new Celia thing." I hopped out of the hammock and headed for the house.

"Say no more. And I wouldn't be lying anyway. Ronald is having a complete meltdown. You'd think he's never been close to a dead body before—outside of a funeral, I mean."

"Maybe he hasn't."

"He lives next door to you."

"I try not to kill people here, and I definitely don't invite Ronald over to judge my efficiency or their wardrobe when I do."

"Just hurry. All that Zen crap disappears completely when a corpse turns up. People are getting paranoid. I need you to get a read on this before the cops secure it and we're all sent packing."

"On it."

Carter wasn't in the house when I headed inside, but I saw a sticky note next to my keys on the kitchen table.

Caught a situation. Lie low.

I shook my head, knowing good and well his 'situation' was what I was about to drive into. I'm certain he knew it too, hence the 'lie low' comment. Fortunately, I also knew that he knew I was going to ignore it completely. And since that was entirely too much inferred thought in a matter of seconds, I grabbed my keys and hurried out to my Jeep, calling Ida Belle on the way.

Ida Belle was at the curb when I pulled up, looking as though she'd been waiting there all day. She was dressed in jeans, hiking boots, and a tank top with a short-sleeved flannel shirt layered over it. I caught a glimpse of her nine at her waist as she climbed in and knew that bulge in her right boot held a backup piece.

"How do you manage to get outfitted for a case in less than a minute?" I asked.

She stared at me, obviously confused. "I was working on my boat engine. How else are you supposed to dress for that?"

"You were working on your boat engine with two pieces strapped?"

"Wouldn't you?"

I shrugged. Given that I showered with my gun on the shampoo ledge, it was a valid point.

"So what's Gertie done now?" she asked.

"Hopefully nothing, since there's a dead woman."

I filled her in on the call and the Celia situation and she shook her head.

"That's not a lot of information. She didn't even tell you who died."

"Does it matter?"

"Yes. It might have been someone I liked."

"At a yoga retreat?"

"Touché. But Gertie and Ronald are there."

"And you like them?"

She grinned. "You're on fire this morning. I'll go with 'most days.'"

"Well, Gertie didn't sound all that upset, so I'm going with it's not someone the two of you were close to. She had potential-case voice."

"So excited, but it's too rude to phrase it that way since someone died."

"Ronald is upset, if that makes a difference."

She waved a hand in dismissal. "Ronald is upset if you don't moisturize enough or wear summer plaids after Labor Day."

"Well, it's a thirty-minute drive to the retreat, so give me the background on the retreat location, the owner...whatever I need to know to frame what we're headed into."

"The owner is Eleanor Matte-Stout, midforties, born and raised in Mudbug and never left. She has one sibling a year younger. Mildred went off to college and never came back until this past April. Their mother died three months earlier and Eleanor's husband just a week before their mother."

"That's a lot of death in one family in a short time."

"It's the South. Their mother, Dora, had been ill for a long time, but I heard doctors couldn't figure it out. Eleanor had taken on her care. Eleanor's husband, Jasper, died when his boat engine exploded. Eleanor said she'd been on him to make the repairs, but he didn't listen."

"That 'South' thing makes more sense now. What about their father?"

"Been six feet under for ten years at least."

"So are Eleanor and Mildred partners in this yoga thing?"

"I honestly have no idea. My understanding through the gossip train is that the relationship between Mildred and Eleanor wasn't close, which makes sense with Mildred leaving and never even coming to visit. But I don't know either well enough to ask why that's the case or, to be honest, to care enough to ask why. I just know that Mildred turned up in

Mudbug this spring and has been living with Eleanor ever since."

"Maybe they reassessed their relationship when their immediate family was cut in half."

Ida Belle nodded. "That will do it. Anyway, the property the retreat is located on, and all the cabins, belonged to the girls' father, who rented them out. I looked into buying the property when he passed, figuring Dora wouldn't have any interest in running the rentals, but the whole thing was held in trust and Dora had no ability to sell it."

"Their mother's name was Dora Matte? That's unfortunate."

"More like prophetic. Her husband was a real piece of work. No one knows why she married him, much less stayed with him all those years. He was an angry, abusive alcoholic on his best days."

"Maybe she was afraid to leave."

Ida Belle raised one eyebrow.

"Okay, I didn't say *I* get it, but they say that on TV."

"The women the infamous 'they' say that about usually don't have options. Dora did. Family would have helped. Friends in Mudbug and Sinful would have helped. The churches would have helped. It's more likely she stayed put because of religion and stubborn pride. Everyone, including her parents, told her not to marry Bruno, but she swore it was going to work."

I sighed. "Living a miserable life just to avoid people saying 'I told you so' is ridiculous. So moving forward to today, people died, the sisters inherited the cabins through the trust, and Eleanor decided a yoga retreat was needed. I guess I understand the desire for peace after all that and what must have been a rough childhood, plus the past year being a crap show."

Ida Belle frowned. "Maybe."

"Why do you say it like that?"

"It's just that Eleanor was never a peaceful sort. Bruno died when the girls were in their twenties so still plenty of time for her to mature and change into a solid adult, but no one really saw an improvement in her personality. Charitably, she could be called abrupt but more accurately, I'd go with rude."

"Abrupt like you and me when we're telling the truth but no one wants to hear it?"

"No. She seemed to go out of her way to twist the screws in sometimes. Gertie and I worked with her on a couple of charity things and let's just say, she's the last person I would have predicted to take up anything peaceful or self-reflective."

"People who knew me before Sinful would never believe I sometimes wear a dress, have a hairstylist, and am living with a man I'm engaged to and am actually happy about it."

"You still get to kill people occasionally."

"There is that. So other than the sisters and Ronald and Gertie, do you know anyone else at this retreat?"

"No idea. I mean, it's a yoga retreat. Past saying 'absolutely not' when Gertie tried to cajole me into going, I never spoke about it."

I made a turn into the woods at the sign for the retreat. "Well, hopefully it's some attendee who came trying to sort things out and couldn't manage it. Even better, it will be someone from out of town who has no connections to Sinful or Mudbug, and Carter will be completely off the hook, and I won't have to worry about that under-radar nonsense."

Ida Belle's phone signaled an incoming text as I pulled into a parking spot in front of a building designated as the Welcome Center. She checked the text and shook her head.

"I'm afraid we're batting zero. The victim is Eleanor, and I don't believe for a second that woman was suicidal."

GERTIE MUST HAVE BEEN WATCHING FOR MY JEEP BECAUSE she practically ran out the door of the main building before I even put it in Park. Ronald was right behind her, hands flying and mouth running, and I knew he was blathering before I ever opened the door and heard him. At least they both had long T-shirts on over their leotards. I had been afraid we were going to pull up on a butt floss parade, and most people I'd met didn't have the kind of butt built for floss.

Since they were both yelling at a million miles an hour, and Ronald was sniffling at the same time, Ida Belle stuck her fingers in her mouth and let out a piercing whistle that stopped them both.

"They're holding us hostage," Ronald said. "And with that dead woman there and everything."

I stared, a bit confused. Carter's truck was parked in front of the building, which meant he was in control of the scene.

"Carter's holding you all in a building with the body?" I asked.

Ronald turned two shades paler than his already white. "Good. God. No. The body is in the sauna. I don't even know how one disinfects after something like that. I mean there's that body just oozing everywhere with all that heat."

"Oh, there's a ton of ways to get fluids out of things," I said.

Ronald yelped and threw one hand over his mouth. "You mean I might have sat somewhere that a body leaked on before? I need a drink. Scratch that. I need some of Nora's best stuff."

Ida Belle rolled her eyes. "What do you suggest people do —bulldoze every structure that someone passed away in?"

He nodded. "If they're not in a medical facility, then that sounds like a plan."

"A lady died in the Fifth Avenue Bergdorf's last week," Gertie said. "Just keeled over right there in the middle of a shoe display."

Ronald squealed. "Not the shoes!"

"Will you please tell me why you called me here?" I said to Gertie. "I'm already limited as to what I can do because Carter beat me to it."

Gertie glanced back as a man walked toward us from a path in the woods and frowned. "It's not just Carter."

The approaching man had cop written all over him. The reflective sunglasses, the disapproving and slightly bored expression on his face, the deliberate and cocky stride, and the rigid set of his jaw were all I needed to know. And unfortunately, he was locked in on me.

Six foot two. Two hundred twenty pounds, but the muscle was all from the gym. Given his breathing rhythm from simply walking down the sidewalk in the heat, I'd put his cardiovascular health at about sixty years old. Zero threat physically. I doubted he could even draw his gun fast enough to shoot me before I could run away.

"Dorothy's here," Gertie said quietly.

I groaned. Dorothy was Celia's cousin and her biggest supporter in all things stupid. I had no doubt that the first person she'd called was Celia, and now the state police were here to make sure Carter was doing his job. Without interference.

"Miss Redding," he said as he stepped up entirely too close to me.

"Do I know you?" I asked.

"I'm Lieutenant Calahan."

I waited but nothing else was forthcoming.

"Congratulations?" I said finally.

His jaw flexed and he removed his sunglasses to glare at me. When I stared back without any visible response or even blinking, I saw a blush rise up his neck.

"I'm with the state police IA division," he said. "Your boyfriend's methods of operation have come under question. I'm here to ensure he's following the letter of the law."

I wriggled my fingers on my left hand in the air. "Fiancé. And again, congratulations? Why are you talking to me when you're here to shadow Carter?"

"Because the biggest complaint from citizens about Sheriff LeBlanc's policing is that he allows you access to confidential police business."

"I wish he would. It would make my job easier. Look, I don't know what's going on here. I got a call from my friend saying she needed me, so here I am."

I gestured to Gertie, who nodded.

He narrowed his eyes at Gertie. "Needed her for what?"

"She's my emotional support assassin," Gertie said.

"You think that's funny?" he asked, but I noticed he moved back a bit.

"I think it's accurate," Gertie said. "Someone's dead. I'm not interested in joining them, so I called Fortune to come get me and Ronald out of here. Trust me, there's no better protection."

"The woman committed suicide," he said, clearly frustrated. "You don't need protection."

"Is that your official statement?" I asked.

"No." Carter's voice sounded behind me. "It's not his official statement, and he shouldn't be giving you information concerning an ongoing investigation, especially when it's what he just accused me of."

Calahan stiffened, and I didn't bother to hold back a smile.

"Looks like you're going to need to investigate yourself," I said to Calahan, then looked at Carter. "Are they free to go?"

He nodded. "I'll contact them later for their statements."

"You should take the statements here," Calahan argued.

Carter's face flashed with anger. "I'm not holding a bunch of traumatized people here waiting for me to finish with forensics when that will take hours. I've known everyone in that building, save one, since birth. I'm pretty sure I can find them tomorrow and get their statements."

He whirled around and headed inside. Calahan glared at his back, then flashed me a dirty look before following.

"Did they let you pack your things?" I asked.

"Yes," Gertie said. "We all packed our stuff and put it in the lobby."

"Then grab them and let's get out of here," I said. "There's nothing I can do with Calahan here."

Ronald reached under his T-shirt and pulled his keys out of his leotard bottoms. I refused to ponder that one.

"Can you please drive my car?" he asked Ida Belle. "I'm too upset to drive."

Ida Belle stared at the dangling keys, probably wondering where they'd been dangling before and with what, but finally she shrugged and took the keys from his hand.

"It's a Bentley," she said.

CHAPTER TWO

RONALD ELECTED TO RIDE WITH IDA BELLE—IN THE BACK seat like Miss Daisy—but Gertie chose to ride with me. I knew there was zero chance of getting them to wait until we all got to my house to start talking, so I called Ida Belle and put us all on speaker. Then I was sorry I had.

"I can't believe these leggings have a tear," Ronald complained. "Good Lord! All my business is going to be on display if these keep running like cheap pantyhose."

"If you display any 'business' I will shoot it off," Ida Belle said. "I suggest you keep that T-shirt pulled down."

"The shirt isn't all that long."

"Then hunch."

"If you guys are done talking wardrobe," I interrupted, "I'd like to talk about this very un-Zen retreat."

Gertie and Ronald both started talking at once and I couldn't understand a word. Finally Ida Belle whistled again, practically making us all deaf, but it stopped the excited babble.

"One at a time," I said.

"I get to go first," Ronald said. "I was the one invited to the retreat, and Gertie was my plus one."

"The better one, you mean," Gertie argued. "Besides, I'm the detective and you passed out when you heard about it. You didn't even see the body."

"You saw the body?" I asked, and she nodded.

"Okay, lay this out for me from the beginning. Starting with how many people were at the resort and who."

"This part doesn't have a body so it's my turn," Ronald said. "There were eight people total staying there. Eleanor and Mildred, Eleanor's assistant Kim, that witch Dorothy, and two women from Mudbug named Silvia and Lucy. I can't even begin to understand the guest list as no one was competent at even very basic yoga, and that group can't meditate to save their lives. The noise coming from them was so disruptive."

"Silvia hums," Gertie explained, "and Lucy is gassy."

Good. God.

"You forgot that weirdo Zion Gates," Gertie said.

"He wasn't staying at the retreat," Ronald said. "He just came to provide spiritual guidance."

"You're taking spiritual guidance from a man named Zion Gates?" Ida Belle asked.

"I didn't take anything from him," Gertie said. "Nora is more enlightened than that guy."

"Because Nora is so high she's floating up there next to Jesus," Ida Belle said.

"I think he's a not-really-silent partner," Ronald said. "These retreats are his creation. He designed the format, the workshops, and the meals."

"So it's like a franchise?" Ida Belle asked.

"It seemed that way," Ronald said. "But no one explained the business model. He was there to align our body and mind."

"He was there to align Eleanor's back," Gertie corrected.

"Did he do an adjustment?" Ronald asked. "If I'd known he was a masseur, I would have asked for a session. Those dining chairs have my lumbar area all tight."

Gertie snorted. "It wasn't that kind of alignment. Did you really not catch on that he and Eleanor are collaborating on more positions than just yoga?"

"What? You saw them having sexy time?"

"I didn't have to. A woman knows these things. I'm surprised you missed it as you're female-adjacent."

"I'm going to take that as a compliment rather than an insult, but now that you mention it, Eleanor did seem a little smiley, almost giggly around him, which was odd. I'm not certain that centered and joyful were anywhere in her personality makeup."

"I told you she was the last person I could see doing the whole Zen thing," Ida Belle said.

"Well, I guess now we know the reason for her odd choice of business to open," I said. "So was Zion there when Eleanor died?"

"No," Gertie said. "He left after yoga class."

"Okay, let's shelve Zion for later. Tell me about the last time you saw her up until the time she was discovered deceased. Where were all of you during that time and what were you doing?"

"We had a yoga class down by the bayou, led by Zion, followed by cooldown and recentering," Ronald said. "That ended at two o'clock, and we all headed back to our cabins to shower because the humidity down there by the water was extra. We were supposed to meet at the Welcome Center for smoothies at three fifteen. The attendees, I mean. Mildred was at the main building, which is where the offices are, with Eleanor's assistant Kim, when we headed to class.

"Did Eleanor go to her cabin as well or straight to the sauna?"

"Both," Ronald said. "The sauna is located in Eleanor's living quarters. Eleanor claimed she always used the sauna after class."

"No one else went with her?"

"Good God no," he said. "First off, it was so hot doing yoga, we all looked like we'd been swimming. I can't imagine taking on more heat. Second, the sauna is only open to guests in the morning for two hours and another hour after dinner."

Gertie nodded. "I wouldn't sit in there until maybe December."

"Sounds miserable," I agreed. "So why would Eleanor want to sit in it?"

"Probably trying to take off a few pounds," Gertie said. "She could stand to lose about twenty."

"Twenty is generous," Ronald said. "But if she's chasing the hottie yoga guy, then I guess it would have been a start."

"Are you sure everyone went to their cabins?" I asked.

"Not sure, no," Ronald said. "We all walked up the path together, but the cabins are spaced out. I could only see Gertie's and Dorothy's from mine. They both went inside, but so did I. I wouldn't know if either of them left after or if the other two ladies even went to theirs."

"Or if Mildred and Kim were still in the main building," Ida Belle said.

"But why does it matter where everyone was?" Ronald asked. "She committed suicide."

"Gertie's not convinced that's the case."

Ronald yelped. "What? You never told me that."

"Why the heck do you think I asked Fortune to come?" Gertie asked. "I could have driven us back. I was hoping she could get a peek at the sauna before the cops got here. I didn't know that Carter would beat her there or that the state police would be in tow. Now do you understand why I'm the one who needs to be telling this story?"

"I can't take you people anywhere," Ronald said. "It's like a death cloud hangs above you."

"Look on the bright side," I said. "We're not the ones who commit the murders."

I looked over at Gertie. "I'll get to you in a minute, but first I want to back up to something Ronald said about the invitation. How were the attendees chosen? Ronald, did you know Eleanor?"

"Barely. But she clocked my Gucci boots the last time I ran into her at a charity event and then followed me out and asked a bunch of questions about my car. That was about a month ago, and she told me about this yoga retreat she was going to be opening. She wanted to do a test run with hand-selected guests before opening up registration to the public and asked if I'd be interested."

"But she never asked if you enjoyed that sort of thing? And the others didn't seem all that adept at yoga, correct?"

"No, she didn't ask, and those people definitely don't do yoga on the regular. Maybe never."

"It was a money thing," Ida Belle said. "She figured if Ronald liked it, he'd tell his other rich friends."

"Dorothy isn't rich," I said.

"But she's one of the ringleaders of God's Wives," Ida Belle said. "If she told them to go, they'd all be stealing their husband's beer money to cover the cost."

I nodded. "And she told you that you could invite someone else?"

"No, I asked if I could bring someone," Ronald said. "No way I was going to some cabin in the woods without protection. I've seen *Deliverance*. I've also seen the things Gertie carries in her purse. I knew there was no way I'd get you or Ida Belle there, so I asked if Gertie could attend."

"And Gertie is one of the ringleaders of the Sinful Ladies, so a lot of potential customers there," I said. "Those picks make sense from a business perspective. What about the other two ladies?"

Gertie shook her head.

"I don't know anything about them," Ronald said. "There are eight cabins total for attendees. Dorothy and I had the two smaller cabins with queen-size beds. The others were larger with twins so they could hold two attendees, but everyone had their own. My understanding was that they weren't quite done remodeling the last three, so this was a smaller run of guests to work out any kinks. No pun intended."

I frowned as I pulled onto Main Street. It sort of made sense, but given my understanding of the major players, I could see why Gertie felt something was off. The whole thing seemed odd.

"Let's continue this at my house," I said. "I want to start making some notes."

Ida Belle pulled into Ronald's garage and by the time they'd hurried over, Gertie had iced tea and cookies on the kitchen table.

"Okay, so let's move on to the body," I said, opening my laptop. "Walk me through it."

"I took my shower and was pulling out my new leotard when I heard a gunshot," Gertie said. "I didn't think anything of it, really. I mean, we were in Mudbug. People could be hunting, poaching, practicing, shooting a lock off a shed door—"

"Is that why your shed door has a hole in it?" Ida Belle asked.

"Not relevant," Gertie said. "Besides, that was a fluke."

"So you didn't go outside and look," I said.

"I was naked."

"That's never stopped you before," Ida Belle said and turned to Ronald. "What about you?"

"Being naked almost always stops me from going outside," he said. "But I didn't look because I didn't hear anything. I had my earbuds in and Taylor Swift cranked all the way up. I'm thinking about learning to twerk so—"

"What happened after you got dressed?" I interrupted.

"I walked outside about five minutes after I heard the shot and saw Kim on the trail that goes to Eleanor's cabin," Gertie said. "She looked perturbed, so I asked her if anything was wrong. I guess she hadn't seen me because I startled her. Then she said the blender was on the blink and Eleanor wasn't answering her phone and people were going to be there soon. So I told her that I'd run get Eleanor and for her to go back to hosting."

"You'd 'run'?" Ida Belle asked.

Gertie gave her the finger.

"Anyway, when I got to her cabin, no one answered the door. There's only one entrance and it was locked. I yelled and banged some more and looked in the windows, but I couldn't see anything. I figured she'd already left so I called Kim, but that's when I saw a red light in the back window. It was the light on the sauna door—the one that indicates it's occupied."

"Is the sauna soundproof?"

"No. And most people don't bring electronics in there because they can be damaged. Eleanor always said the sauna should be used for cleansing the body and the mind, so it was essential for there to be no noise."

"So she would have heard you banging and yelling."

"Probably. I mean, it's down a hallway toward the back of the cabin, but it's not like the place is huge. Which is why I started to worry and told Kim something wasn't right. She said she'd turn around and head back as she had the key."

"How long did it take her?"

"At least five minutes or better."

"How long is the walk to the cabin?"

"From the office, about ten. From where I left Kim, I made it in probably three at a reasonable walk. But Kim does *not* work out. She trudges everywhere. It's been sort of a joke among the attendees that someone who is clearly averse to exercise is working at a yoga retreat."

I made a note. "Okay, so we're roughly thirteen minutes out from when you heard the shot. What happened then?"

"Kim showed up with the key, but it didn't do any good as the door was dead-bolted from the inside. By this time, Kim was freaking out and I was certain there was a problem, so I shot the dead bolt off the door."

"Of course you did," Ida Belle mumbled.

Ronald stared. "You've been walking around with a gun on you the entire retreat?"

"No. Just to eat and meditation. You can't do yoga when you're strapped. The weight throws your balance off."

"Why do you need a gun to meditate?"

"I feel safe with my gun. Can't relax if you don't feel safe."

He pursed his lips. "But where do you keep it?"

"Don't ask!"

Ida Belle and I both spoke at once.

Gertie rolled her eyes. "Anyway, Kim and I ran down the hall to the sauna room and saw Eleanor through the window on the door, slumped against the wall in the corner. I figured she'd passed out from the heat at best or had a stroke at worst, but then I realized her red leotard was leaking onto the floor."

"She was bleeding."

Gertie nodded. "I hurried over but I could tell she was

already gone before I even lifted her head and saw the hole in her chest. Kim started screaming at me to do CPR, but no one could have saved her. She was already gone."

I nodded. If I assumed a range of fifteen to twenty minutes from the time Gertie heard the shot until she got to Eleanor, a shot through the heart would have long since done its work.

"Anyway," Gertie continued, "I slapped Kim across the face to get her to calm down and told her to call 911 and tell them we had a gunshot victim. Then darn if she didn't pass out right there in the middle of the sauna. Took me down with her when she dropped. I was still trying to dig myself out from under that fool when Dorothy arrived. She jumped straight into bossy mode and ordered me and Kim out. I said I'd be happy to leave if she would drag Kim off me.

"That heifer goes to tugging on Kim, and when she got off-balance, I gave Kim a good shove and Dorothy fell out into the hallway. So I took the opportunity to pull out my phone and take a picture."

I perked up. "You took a picture of the body?"

Gertie gave me a smug nod. "And the gun. I hadn't seen it at first because I was too busy concentrating on Eleanor, but it was there on the bench right next to her. Unfortunately, I only had time for one before Dorothy got up and started yelling again."

She accessed the picture and passed me her phone. Ronald covered his entire head with a dish towel, apparently wanting no part of the viewing.

Eleanor was slumped over in a corner just as Gertie had described and even though her leotard was red, the giant stain in the middle of her chest and running down onto the bench and dripping onto the floor was darker. Her right arm was extended out on the bench, trapped between her body and the wall, and I could see the pistol underneath her hand. To her left sat a sweating plastic water bottle with a hand towel beside it.

I texted the picture to my phone and Ida Belle's and yanked the towel off Ronald's head.

"You're safe," I said and turned back to Gertie. "So Dorothy started yelling again and then what?"

"By then, Kim was starting to stir, so we got her outside and closed up the cabin—best we could anyway. I said I'd wait there for the police, but Dorothy was having none of it. Then Silvia, Lucy, and Ronald came running up as they'd heard Kim screaming when they were on the walking path. We told them what happened and we all headed back to the main building."

"Where was Mildred?" Ida Belle asked.

"In her office doing paperwork," Gertie said. "She came out to see what all the fuss was about, and poor Kim almost passed out again trying to tell her. I finally had to explain. I've never seen a woman go from flushed to pale that quickly, and for a minute, I thought she was going to hit the floor like Kim had. But Silvia shoved a chair behind her and she dropped onto it. She was shaking all over."

"Poor thing has lost her entire family," Ronald said. "I think there's some extended family of sorts off in other states, but that's not the same."

"No, it's not," Ida Belle agreed. "I wonder, does she have someone to stay with her for a while?"

"Kim lives in Mudbug and said she'd stay with her," Gertie said. "Mildred has serious mobility issues because of her spine. Can't bend or lift all that well either. She was strictly office staff."

I nodded, processing the scene in my mind. "So the cabin only has one entrance. What about the windows?"

"None were open," Gertie said. "And I tried every one of

them when I was waiting on Kim to get there with the key, but they were all locked."

"And the door was dead-bolted from the inside. So why do you think this looks suspicious?"

Gertie frowned. "I'm not sure exactly. I mean, Eleanor was always pretty impressed with herself, and that's usually not the sort of people who lend themselves to this kind of thing. I know none of us knows what goes on in another person's mind, but it doesn't fit what I know about her. Quite frankly, the whole retreat felt off."

Ida Belle put her hands in the air. "It was yoga and Zen... not exactly your day-to-day."

"I know that but..." She sighed. "I just can't explain it."

"She's right," Ronald said. "I've been to a bunch of these venues, and there was something off about the whole thing. But it's hard to put a finger on."

"Try," I said. "Just tell me what you felt."

"I felt undercurrents," he said. "Like all the meditation and exercise were just masking some very real problems."

"I thought you went to these things *because* you had problems and were looking for solutions," I said. "So wouldn't that make sense?"

He shook his head. "The undercurrents weren't from the attendees. They were from Eleanor. Something was just off about all of it. I ignored it because the fees weren't exactly small or refundable, but Gertie's right. I felt it too."

I leaned back in my chair and blew out a breath. "Well, unless there's another way in that cabin that you didn't know about, I don't see how this is anything other than what it looks like."

"But you'll look into it," Gertie said.

I had no idea what I could possibly do about it or what

there even was for me to investigate, but Gertie and Ronald were clearly troubled so I couldn't really refuse.

"Of course."

———

RONALD LEFT AFTER OUR DEBRIEFING, THEN GERTIE decided she was going to head home as well. And even though I offered to run her home, she opted to walk instead, claiming she needed to clear her head. I told her I'd drop her stuff off later when I took Ida Belle home.

Ida Belle waited until the front door closed behind her before turning to me and raising one eyebrow. "So?"

I shook my head. "I got nothing. I didn't want to say to them that maybe they've gotten this one wrong, but the evidence is going to settle it one way or another. I guess I'm wondering why this seems to bother Gertie so much, especially given everything we've seen."

"Suicide is different than murder. Homicide victims don't have an option and the reality is our chances of being murdered are extremely low. But suicide is a deliberate choice, and someone's chances of some form of mental break..."

"Yeah. I guess so. Then I suppose we need to figure out what Eleanor had going on that might have driven her to this action. Maybe knowing that will be enough for them to put it to rest."

"Maybe. But digging into someone's private thoughts is never easy. Mildred had only been back for a few months and even if she knows anything, her own mental state is questionable now as well. I'm not sure how far we can push her."

I nodded. "But that's where we have to start. We do the casserole thing anyway. That will give us an opportunity to draw her into conversation. And since Gertie is the one who found Eleanor, Mildred might be drawn to talk more to her than she would to others."

"Shared tragedy. It's possible. But Calahan is an obstacle we don't need. If this gets ruled a homicide and you get caught in the middle of it, that reflects poorly on Carter. If it gets ruled a suicide and you somehow prove otherwise, that might be worse."

I blew out a breath. "I know. I'll make it work."

I just had no idea how.

———

CARTER DIDN'T GET HOME UNTIL LATE THAT NIGHT. WITH forensics and taking statements from Kim and Mildred, all with Calahan breathing down his neck, I didn't expect anything else. Nor was I surprised by the fact that he looked tired and irritated when he dropped onto the couch. I had seen him pull up and had already grabbed him a beer.

"Are you hungry?" I asked as I passed him the bottle.

He took a long swig and shook his head. "Myrtle got us some sandwiches from the café."

"Us? I take it you had to come home to shake Calahan?"

"I'm pretty sure he would have come home with me if I hadn't told him straight out I was going home for the night, and he needed to leave as well. I could tell he was itching to stay behind and have a go at Myrtle."

I snorted. "Like he would have gotten anything out of her."

"No. But he'd have gotten more worked up. She wouldn't have hesitated to tell him exactly how she felt about Celia *and* him. He's already got an axe to grind. I don't need Myrtle throwing fuel on the fire."

"Why does he have an axe to grind? Do you have some sort of past I need to know about?"

"Not at all, but I know the type. He's bucking for a big promotion."

"And he thinks taking you down can get it for him."

Carter shrugged but I could tell he was unhappy about the entire situation, and I couldn't blame him. His relationship with me had put a target on his back in ways I hadn't anticipated.

"So I guess it's useless to ask about the case?" I asked.

"Ha. I think you already know the answer to that. When forensics is back, I'll make a determination and an official statement. Until then, I need you to stay out of it."

I nodded. "Of course, but you know I'll be going with Ida Belle and Gertie over to Mildred's tomorrow. That's a Baptist thing, not a PI thing."

He sighed. "It would probably look stranger if you didn't, but don't stir up anything. My guess is this is all going to turn out like it looks."

"You know Gertie saw the body, right? And the gun?"

"Dorothy said as much. Apparently, when Gertie shot the dead bolt off the door, that was two gunshots too many for Dorothy and she went to see what was wrong."

"Ah, and then Kim started screaming and that brought her running."

"Yep. She had a lot to say about how Gertie was always causing trouble. I told her I didn't see how, this time anyway, as Gertie was the one who managed to get the door opened so she and Kim could see if Eleanor needed help. It was hardly her fault that it was too late to render aid. Hell, it would have been too late if they'd broken in a second later."

I nodded. I'd seen the picture. And even without seeing the wound, a direct shot into the heart at close range was the kind of injury there was no coming back from, especially that far from a hospital.

Carter downed the rest of his beer and rose from the couch. "I'm going to hit the shower and then bed. Tomorrow is going to be another long one and probably no less irritating than today."

I waited until he was out of the room to frown. I hated that I was the reason things were so hard on Carter. If I'd never come to Sinful, Celia would have been a problem, sure, but her grievances with me were the reason she'd made it her life's work to take him down.

Maybe Gertie and Ronald were wrong. Maybe they were just in their feelings because the woman they'd taken a yoga class from an hour before was dead.

But I had my doubts.

CHAPTER THREE

"WHAT IS SHE DOING?" IDA BELLE ASKED. "WE'RE GOING TO miss our window of opportunity."

Gertie had walked out her front door, casserole in hand, only to set it on a bench and head back inside. The window Ida Belle spoke of was because Celia's band of non-merry women had a church event this morning so we could get in to see Mildred without them present. That didn't mean it would be all clear, as I'm sure other people besides us and Celia's crew would be dropping in to pay their respects and offer up any assistance Mildred might need, but it was better odds.

The sooner I could get to Mildred and get a read on her, the better. Because if Eleanor had anything going on that was causing her that much pain, Mildred was likely the only one who knew about it. They'd lived and worked together, and even if Eleanor hadn't been forthcoming with details, Mildred should have at least noticed something was off.

Finally, Gertie came back out and headed to the car with a cardboard box that I assumed held the casserole.

"What took you so long?" Ida Belle asked. "You know we need to get over there before Celia's cult descends on her."

"I was buying us some more time," Gertie said.

"How were you doing that?" I asked.

"You know Celia and her crew are putting together gift baskets for a raffle this evening," Gertie said. "I just made sure the fire sprinklers went off. It will take them hours to recover but they won't have a choice but to address it right away."

"And just how do you know the sprinklers will go off?" Ida Belle asked.

"Because Nora's headed over there to smoke in the bathroom."

"Nora's Catholic?" I asked.

"She is today," Gertie said.

"What's she smoking?" Ida Belle inquired.

"I didn't ask."

Good. God.

I said a quick prayer that Nora smoked something legal and didn't start an actual fire, but I didn't have time to intervene. I needed to see Mildred before the shock wore off and the wisdom of keeping her mouth shut set in.

Eleanor's house was just off Main Street in downtown Mudbug. It was a pretty one-story cottage with white siding and navy-blue trim. Severely blocked hedges lined the front of the house and the sidewalk. There were no flowers at all.

"This," Gertie said, waving her hand toward the yard, "is a great reflection of Eleanor. All service, no flair. No color. Nothing pretty."

Since her house looked a sight more lived-in than my condo in DC I started to argue, but then I recalled how I was in DC and realized that my condo had indeed been a reflection of my life at that time. Now I had lovely landscaping, mostly courtesy of the previous owner, and I couldn't take credit for anything but maintaining it. Still, I hadn't replaced all the pretty things with easy and serviceable, so I was probably moving in the right direction.

"Choosing efficiency over flash isn't exactly evidence that she didn't have strong feelings about things," Ida Belle said.

Gertie stared at her for a moment. "Oh, I'm well aware."

I couldn't help smiling at the implication.

Ida Belle gave her a dirty look and climbed out. "Well, let's go find out what excited Eleanor."

"I'm pretty sure I know one thing," Gertie said as we headed up the sidewalk.

"No asking Mildred if her sister was getting frisky with the yoga guy," Ida Belle said. "We don't want to put her on the defensive straight away."

Gertie looked indignant. "Of course I'm not going to ask her. What do you take me for, a gossip amateur?"

Ida Belle knocked on the door, and we waited a good while before she knocked again.

"Maybe she's not here," I said. "There might have been arrangements or for all we know, she could be talking to Carter, or at the cabins shutting things down."

We waited a while longer and I was just about to suggest we head into Mudbug and grab an early lunch, then check back, when the door inched open and a woman peered out.

Midforties. Five foot five. A hundred forty pounds. Hip higher on the right side and leaning slightly forward. Overall soft body tone indicative of most full-time desk sitters. Zero threat. And it looked as if she'd been crying.

"Gertie," she said, her eyes misting up. "And Ida Belle."

"And this is our friend Fortune," Gertie said.

She gave me a nod. "I've heard about you. Nice to finally meet you. Come on in."

"Are you sure?" Gertie asked. "We don't want to interrupt if you're busy with things."

Mildred shook her head and motioned for us to follow her.

"I'd welcome the company," she said as we followed her down a hall to the back of the house. I noticed she had a pronounced limp and that her right foot didn't lift all the way off the ground when she walked.

"I'm not used to all this quiet. And Eleanor usually took care of everything... I mean, it's her house and all, so I don't have things to do really. The cleaning lady was just here two days ago, and we haven't been here to make a mess. I did a load of laundry this morning, but that's not exactly an all-day event."

We stepped into a pleasant kitchen with navy cabinets and white countertops. A sturdy oak table with four chairs stood on the other side of the room. No curtains, no pictures on the wall, no whimsical cookie canisters or dish towels.

Gertie lifted the tray she was carrying. "I made these for you last night."

Mildred's eyes widened. "Enchiladas?"

Gertie nodded. "You said they were your favorite. I'll put this in the fridge."

I held out a gift bag. "And this is from Ronald, who sends his condolences and regrets. He feels really bad, but he wasn't up to coming with us."

She nodded as she plucked the tissue paper out of the bag, then pulled out a bottle of liquor. "This is a four-hundred-dollar bottle of scotch."

"Like I said, he feels really bad."

She nodded and sniffed again.

"Do you want some tea?" Gertie said as she peered into the refrigerator. "Or maybe coffee? I could make up a pot if you'd like."

Mildred sat the scotch on the counter, then shuffled over to the table and leaned over to clutch the edges as she eased into a chair with a big foam cushion in it. Then she motioned for us to sit.

"Coffee would be wonderful," she said. "I kept meaning to put a pot on, then I'd think there was something else I should do. Then I'd forget the coffee *and* what I needed to do and ended up sitting here doing nothing. That load of laundry was all I managed the whole morning, and I still haven't folded it, even though I've been up since 4:00 a.m."

Gertie gave Mildred's shoulder a squeeze before she sat next to her. "I'll finish up that laundry while we're here. And if you want those enchiladas heated before we go, I'll take care of that as well. Do you have any doctor's appointments or anything you need help with getting to?"

"Nothing for a few weeks, and I can drive all right as long as it's not long distances. Got my disability tag so I never have to walk too far. And my walker folds up nicely and is light. I can manage it in and out of the car."

"Don't take any unnecessary risks," Ida Belle said. "If you need a ride anywhere or any errands run, you call. I mean it."

Mildred gave her a grateful look. "I appreciate it because I know you mean it. You and Gertie were always the nicest people in Sinful. Mother always said so."

She looked over at Gertie. "And how are you doing? Being the one who...who..."

Gertie nodded. "I'm okay. Just sorry I didn't shoot that door open sooner."

Mildred shook her head. "Carter said there was nothing you could have done, even if you'd gotten there right after. Don't you go blaming yourself for anything. You did what you could, and I know it had to be a shock seeing her like that."

I'd give Gertie an A for the effort of looking suitably distraught, but I knew better. Still, Mildred must have believed it because she leaned over to pat Gertie's hand.

"I sent poor Kim home a couple hours ago," she said. "I know she wanted to help, but the girl was beside herself and making me crazy. I heard her crying all night. And there you were up baking me my favorite food. It means a lot to me, but I need you to take care of yourself as well. It's been a big shock to everyone, but you, me, and Kim are going to have a worse time than others."

"Dorothy saw her too," Gertie said.

Mildred huffed. "That woman is made of ornery and disgruntled. I have no idea why she even wanted to go to a place like the retreat."

We all smiled and nodded at the accuracy.

Mildred noticed our smiles and her lips quivered. She looked at Gertie. "I wouldn't have picked you for it either."

Gertie shrugged. "Ronald invited me and I got to buy new clothes."

"Those are not clothes," Ida Belle said, "and you are forbidden to wear them anywhere with me."

Now Mildred's smile broke through. "One of the silver linings of all my back issues—no one asked me to put on tights and bend around on the ground."

Her smile turned bittersweet and she sighed. "Eleanor surprised the heck out of me when she told me she was turning the cabins into a yoga retreat. I thought she was joking at first. You knew my sister well enough to know she wasn't a New Age sort. Or particularly tranquil, to be honest."

Ida Belle nodded. "I admit to raising an eyebrow when Gertie told me about it. But then, she's had some big losses recently and everyone grieves differently."

"That's true enough," Eleanor said, then frowned. "But I doubt she'd have ever found her way that direction if it hadn't been for that fraud Zion Gates. I lay blame for all of this directly at his feet."

"You think he killed your sister?" I asked.

She shook her head. "I don't see how he could have done it himself, but I think he caused it. Romancing her...making promises. I tried to tell her it was all just to get a hold of her property, but she wouldn't listen. I'm sure she was missing Jasper. No way Zion could have weaseled his way in otherwise. But why she didn't see it... He was ten years younger than her for goodness' sake, and on top of everything else, the man—if you can call him that—is married."

"Wow!" Gertie said. "I did not know that. I mean, I'll admit that I picked up on the vibes between the two of them. I'm a woman, after all. But married... That's one I didn't see coming."

Mildred put her hands in the air. "He gave her all the usual lines— 'It's a marriage of convenience, I'm going to divorce her, have to work out the business end of things so I don't lose everything I've built.' All a bunch of bunk if you ask me."

"How long had she been seeing him?" Ida Belle asked.

"I'm not sure when the actual *relationship* began, but she said they met at some charity thing at the church a month or so after Jasper died. I was still in Colorado, so I couldn't tell you when things actually took hold. Truth is, she never came out and admitted to me that she was seeing him in a romantic way. Just kept insisting it was a business thing. But I knew better."

Gertie frowned. "Zion didn't seem like the sort to be at a church charity event."

"Probably shopping for widows with some inheritance," Mildred said. "I know it sounds cynical but I can't seem to find anyone in Mudbug who'd seen the man before then, and by all accounts he zeroed right in on Eleanor from the get-go."

"I don't think it's cynical," Ida Belle said. "I think it's an unfortunate truth of our world today."

"So you think Eleanor was twisted up over Zion and that's why she did it?" I asked. "That sucks."

Mildred nodded. "They had a fight yesterday after class. I saw them in the parking lot out the lobby window. I couldn't hear what they were saying, but the body language told me everything I needed to know. Eleanor was upset when he drove off, and her face was flushed when she came inside to grab her keys. She tried to play it off as the heat when I asked, but she hadn't looked like that a few minutes before and y'all had just finished that outdoor yoga class."

"I wonder what they fought about," Ida Belle said.

Anger flashed across Mildred's face. "My guess is since he had Eleanor locked in with a contract, it wasn't necessary to keep up the pretense of any relationship any longer. But maybe I'm off. It might have been too soon to cut ties completely. Maybe she was just pressing him on leaving his wife and didn't like the answer."

She sighed and slumped back in her chair. "Regardless, I still say the reason she did it lies squarely on that man."

"I'm really sorry," I said. "He hardly sounds worth it. Not that anyone is."

Ida Belle nodded. "What will happen to the cabins now? Are you going to continue the retreat?"

"Good Lord no! I don't have the ability, or quite frankly the interest, to keep such a place going. I can't teach classes. I can't even lead nature walks. The only thing I'm suited for is office work. I sure was grateful I'd majored in accounting when my back issues started. As for what happens to the property, I'm not sure. It's all in a trust, but I know she signed a contract with Zion. Until I talk to the lawyer, I don't know how any of that works now."

"But if the cabins are in a trust, then surely you could have prevented Eleanor from doing a business deal with Zion," Gertie said.

Mildred shook her head. "Eleanor was the executor. Father set it up that way. Even Mother couldn't touch his money or property as it was all inherited from my grandfather. Father always said that if he couldn't outlive my mother, he'd at least make her beholden to him for the rest of her life. And he did. As long as she remained in this house and never so much as held hands with another man, she could draw enough off the trust to live on. But just barely."

"Good Lord," Ida Belle said. "I knew he wasn't a good man, but I didn't know he was that spiteful."

Mildred nodded. "I caught a lot of flak from people here when I went off to school. And even more when I didn't come back after I graduated. But the truth was, I couldn't watch it any longer. Him being a tyrant and her taking it like she had no choice. He didn't scrimp on his treatment toward me either. It wasn't no life for a young girl."

"How did Eleanor manage?" Gertie asked.

"He always favored Eleanor, so she didn't have it as bad as Mother and me. She took up with Jasper right after high school and married him quickly, which I guess was her way out without leaving, so to speak. I tried to convince her to go with me, but she was never the adventuresome type. Getting married got her out of the house, and I guess it was easier to ignore what was happening if she didn't see it. I can't really say anything, or I'd be a hypocrite since I went half a country away to go blind to it. The guilt was always a problem, though, and I had a good wave of it every time I talked to Mama. Not that she ever said anything, mind you. But I knew."

"Does it bother you being back here—in your childhood home?" I asked.

Mildred frowned, considering. "If I'm being honest, it did

at first. It bothered me a lot, but Eleanor said this house was built sturdier than the one she and Jasper had and she was tired of living miles away from town. It's definitely better for me physically than their place would have been. It was a two-story with all the bedrooms upstairs, and a dirt road, so no sidewalks. My doctor wants me walking a little every day, but I need a flat surface and no fear of being accosted by wildlife. Lord knows, I couldn't outrun a tortoise."

"Is there anything that can be done for your back?" I asked.

"I've spoken with a neurosurgeon, and he'd like to try fusing it, but it's a fifty-fifty chance of improvement or making it worse. Doesn't seem to be a neutral area in their calculation."

"That's a big dice roll," I said.

She nodded. "Which is exactly why I'm still holding the dice. Of course, there was no way I was going to take the chance when I was in Colorado. I'll need 24/7 help for months. Eleanor was pushing me to think about it now that I was here and she could help, but I guess I hadn't quite worked up my nerve enough yet. Now everything's on permanent hold again."

"Well, if you decide to move forward, you know you can count on Ida Belle and me to get you covered," Gertie said. "And we've got all the Sinful Ladies who'd be more than willing to pitch in."

Mildred sniffed and grabbed a napkin to dab her eyes. "I can't tell you how much I appreciate that. I had a decent life out in Colorado but I missed this—the sense of community. I never found it out there. I met some nice people, but it wasn't the same."

"Small towns have their issues," Ida Belle said, "but all told, they're a good place to be."

The doorbell rang and Ida Belle rose. "I'll get it," she said. "Do you want more visitors?"

"We should be leaving anyway," I said as I rose. "I'm sure you'll have a day full of this, and we don't want to take up more of your time."

"Well, I appreciate your company and the enchiladas. And please give Ronald my thanks for that scotch. I'll call him myself when I'm feeling up to it."

We headed to the front door, and when Ida Belle opened it, Dorothy stood there, glaring at us.

"I should have known you troublemakers would be here before sunrise," she said.

"It's 10:00 a.m.," Gertie said. "We can't help it if good manners take priority over sleeping in."

"I was helping with a charity event until that fool Nora darn near set the church on fire!"

"Maybe you shouldn't ask her to help," I suggested.

"You know good and well we didn't. That woman is a black mark on our decent town, just like the three of you."

"I see all that Zen stuff really took hold," I said as I walked past her. "Namaste."

I heard her grumble as she pushed into the house, but I couldn't make out what she said. It was probably just as well.

"Well, that was interesting," Gertie said when we'd climbed into the SUV. "I told you there was something going on with Eleanor and Zion."

"Yes, but it sounds like maybe Zion was putting on the brakes," Ida Belle said.

"A little late for brakes given that he's married," I said.

"No doubt," Gertie said. "Do you think a tough old bird like Eleanor would take herself out over that fake?"

"Based on what we know of the woman, no," Ida Belle said. "But maybe he was the final straw. Eleanor had lost her mother and her husband in a short amount of time. I know Mildred is here now, but they haven't been close since high school. If

Eleanor put all her emotional energy and a good chunk of her inheritance into a man who made promises he had no intention of keeping, maybe it was enough to drive her over the edge. You never really know how strong someone is until they're tested. And that was a lot of testing."

"That's true enough," Gertie said. "But what about my feeling that everything was off?"

"You were right about that," I said. "Eleanor was clearly caught up with a bad guy, and maybe that's the energy you were tapping into."

"Not to mention Mildred and Kim's unease over it as I'm sure they all knew exactly what was going on," Ida Belle said.

Gertie sighed. "I guess that's true enough. But I'm still not satisfied that's all there was to it. Are we going to talk to Kim now? I figured we'd be able to hit her up at Eleanor's, but since she's already gone..."

I nodded. "I think we should feel her out over this Zion situation. Being Eleanor's assistant, surely she would have been onto it."

"It will be easier to get her to spill the beans if she's over-wrought," Ida Belle said.

"How well do you guys know her?" I asked.

"Never met her," Ida Belle said.

"I met her at the retreat but didn't spend a lot of time with her," Gertie said. "She's not an instructor. She showed us to our cabins, gave us schedules, served meals and snacks...that sort of thing. And I will say, she wasn't the most competent at any of it."

"Probably not the highest paying of jobs," Ida Belle said. "Might be hard to get good help."

"So how do we frame this drop-in?" I asked. "Are we checking on her since Mildred sent her home?"

"I have another casserole," Gertie said.

I perked up. I'd assumed that the box was because the enchiladas had some weight to them.

"You do?" I asked.

Gertie shook her head. "What do you think I am—an amateur? I brought a backup. As for our reasoning, the woman saw a dead body and passed out on me. I have a duty to check on her."

"Sounds good to me," I said. "Last name please?"

"Barnes," Gertie said.

CHAPTER FOUR

I DID A QUICK SEARCH AND LOCATED A KIM BARNES AT A duplex on the outskirts of downtown and we were off. The duplexes were in a short row on a cul-de-sac, ten of them in total, spanning both sides of the road. They were all the same but with different paint colors on the siding. The landscaping was vibrant in some but lacking in most. I wondered how many were rentals, because small bayou towns took gardening almost as seriously as religion.

Kim's unit was in the middle of the cul-de-sac and painted a cheery yellow. The landscaping was sparse, and I heard Gertie sniff as we walked up the sidewalk and saw her staring at a patch of weeds in the corner of a flower bed that contained a few skinny bushes and spanned the front of the house, framing the doorway.

Since Gertie was the only person Kim knew, we let her knock and stood back, hoping she was home. After a second knock, we were about to give up when I saw a blind lifted up at the corner inside and shortly after, the door slowly opened and a woman peered out. I wasn't sure what I'd been expecting, but this wasn't it.

Early twenties. Five foot six. A hundred thirty pounds—thin but not in shape thin. So pale she looked like she'd never seen sunlight. Limp red hair and brown eyes—bloodshot from crying—gave her a bedraggled appearance. I couldn't fathom any area where she might be a threat.

"Kim? Are you all right?" Gertie asked. "Mildred told us you'd come home, and I wanted to check on you and drop off a casserole. It's not on the retreat-approved diet plan, I'm afraid, but I know cooking probably isn't high on your priority list right now."

Kim nodded and sniffed and gave Ida Belle and I curious looks.

"These are my friends Ida Belle and Fortune," Gertie said. "We just came from Mildred's house, paying our respects. Can we come in for a minute?"

She nodded, stepped back, and waved us into a small living room with fluffy white leather furniture. "I'm sorry. I've completely forgotten my manners. My mother would be appalled if she was still around to appall. I've just been so spaced out. I went home with Mildred to help but I'm pretty sure I was more of a hindrance. I just can't get myself together."

I looked around the room, then over at Ida Belle, who raised one eyebrow. I would never claim to be an HGTV goddess of any sort, but it didn't take an interior designer to know that the contents of this one room were probably worth more than the entire duplex. It was like walking through a portal into a different universe.

"You had a horrible shock," Gertie said reassuringly. "No one expects you to be firing on all cylinders."

She gave Gertie a curious look. "But you seem fine. You even brought me a home-baked casserole."

"Honey, I'm a bit older than you."

Ida Belle coughed, and Gertie shot her a dirty look.

"I keep casseroles in my freezer for these occasions," she explained. "Then I just have to thaw them out and deliver."

Kim stared. "You have an inventory of casseroles in your freezer in case you find dead people? I should have never moved here."

"No," Gertie rushed to explain. "Although that happens more than one might think. It's just when you live in a small place you know everyone, and as you age, they start to drift off, so you have to pay respects more often. And paying respects means bringing food."

"Oh. Yeah, I guess so," Kim said, but she still didn't look convinced.

"How long have you lived here?" I asked.

"Since March. I've lived in New Orleans all my life right off the French Quarter. The house had been in the family for generations, and it was expected that I'd go on living there and pass it on to my kids, I guess. But when I first attended one of those yoga retreats, I loved the peace of the bayous and thought I'd be happier outside of the city. But I may have been mistaken. Twenty-three years in New Orleans and I've never once seen a dead body except at a funeral, much less someone who—"

Her voice cracked and she covered her mouth with her hand.

Gertie, who'd sat next to her on the couch, rubbed her shoulder. "It's okay. Most people go through life never seeing such things. I don't think we're meant to unless it's in our line of professional work, but when it happens, we just have to sort it out in our mind and move on."

She gave us a look that was slightly desperate and completely frazzled.

"How do you do that? I've tried everything already. Helping

Mildred made me feel worse...just seeing that lost look of disbelief on her face last night. I had whiskey hoping it would knock me out but all I did was cry. I looked everywhere for my sleeping pills but must have left them at the retreat—not that they were working well anyway, but my stupid doctor won't give me Ambien anymore. So I sneaked out back and smoked a joint. I prayed, and I'm not even religious!"

She shot us a guilty look. "I'd appreciate it if you didn't tell people."

"About praying?" Ida Belle asked.

"No. Well, maybe that too, but about the joint. I don't want to add getting arrested on top of everything else I've got going on."

"Did you meet Eleanor at a retreat?" I asked, because I couldn't see any other way that the two women would have come into contact.

She shook her head. "Zion put us together. Eleanor was opening her retreat, and he said she could use the help getting started. And that way I could see if I liked it and might be interested in opening my own retreat someday."

And now it all made sense.

"Zion is such a nice, attractive young man," Gertie said. "Are you two involved?"

A flash of fear crossed her face, but she quickly rushed to denial.

"Oh no! I've just been talking to him about being in business and all."

Her mouth might be saying no, but the blush and uncomfortable look gave her away. If she wasn't romantically involved with Zion, she wanted to be.

Gertie nodded. "Well, I suppose there's still time for all that, with you two being young folk. I'd swear if I didn't know any better that Eleanor was sweet on him. I don't know what to think about that given that he was a good ten years younger than her, but then with her losing her husband recently, I'm sure it was just loneliness taking hold."

I watched Kim closely as Gertie rambled on in her seemingly woolly-headed old lady way. She had forced her expression as close to blank as she could, but I saw the flex of her jaw and how her hands clenched the pillow next to her.

She was a goner, all right.

Kim twisted the hem of her shirt. "Do you think that's why Eleanor... I mean, her husband passing and all? And her mother too, right?"

"I'm afraid no one really knows but Eleanor," Gertie said. "She didn't leave a note, so we can only speculate. Did you talk to her yesterday after class?"

"No. She came in long enough to grab her keys, then hurried back out. I never saw her again after that. I mean until..."

"Right. So you stayed in the main building with Mildred."

"Yeah. I mean, Mildred was locked in her office, banging away on her keyboard. She said something about tax estimates and looked kinda peeved before she closed herself in. I guess it's hard."

"It's definitely not fun," I said. "Something you'll have to figure out when you open your own place, I suppose. So you were in your office then?"

"No. I don't have my own office. I was in the dining area dealing with the fruit. Then the blender stopped working and I called Eleanor, but she wouldn't answer so I started walking to her cabin. I really hate walking in all that humidity, especially in the middle of the day."

"It was definitely a hot one," Gertie agreed. "That class wiped me out."

"I can imagine," Kim said. "I was so grateful when you

offered to go get Eleanor for me, and I thought we'd just be behind schedule a bit but no big deal. Then everything just went upside down."

She teared up. "I still can't believe she's gone, you know? It doesn't seem real."

I nodded. But it was definitely real.

———

WE'D BARELY GOTTEN THE DOORS ON THE SUV CLOSED before Gertie exploded.

"That man is a menace! He's after that girl for her money. Her couch cost more than Ida Belle's boat."

"I'm sure money is at the top of the list," I said. "She is a lot younger than Eleanor too."

"But so plain," Gertie said. "Of course, that just makes her the perfect target for men like Zion. Young, rich, naive, and probably doesn't have men lined up to date her. She might as well be holding a neon sign over her head that says Easy Pickings."

Ida Belle nodded. "She definitely didn't strike me as having any street smarts."

"No," I agreed. "I wonder if she knew what Eleanor and Zion had going on. All of what they had going on, I mean."

"She's a woman," Gertie said. "If she didn't see it then it was only because she didn't want to."

"He could have been telling her that Eleanor had a crush on him and he was trying to be kind to her given the recent death of her husband," Ida Belle said. "They all have the same stories."

Gertie shook her head, still clearly angry. "Especially when they've got a target in their sight and that girl's furnishings practically screamed wealth."

"I agree," I said. "And reading between the lines, her mother is gone and she might have sold the family home, which was probably worth a pretty penny if it was in the French Quarter and held in the family for generations."

"Do a search," Ida Belle said.

I whipped out my phone and did a quick search on Kim Barnes. It didn't take long to find exactly what we were looking for.

"Only child of Beverly and Maynard Barnes sells landmark home for 2.5 million," I said.

Ida Belle shook her head. "He'll take that girl to the cleaners."

"Maybe Eleanor's death will put the brakes on that," I said.

"It won't for long enough," Gertie said. "I never saw Kim and Zion together, so I couldn't tell you how far it's gotten. But I don't need your CIA skills to read her body language. She's fallen for him hard and unless someone intervenes, he's going to have her inheritance sunk into a business she's not qualified to run any more than Eleanor was."

"Don't worry," I said. "I'm not giving up just yet. I want to check out this Zion anyway. If his play is taking advantage of lonely people who are grieving, I'd like to change that."

Gertie perked up. "If you could shut him down, that would be something at least."

"Unless he's doing something illegal, I wouldn't count on it," Ida Belle said. "Even if you exposed him as a fraud and a parasite, he'd just move somewhere else and pick up the same tactics. Those kinds of people never change."

"They don't," I agreed. "But at least I might be able to send him down the road. And if he took his maneuvering too far, there could be a case for police action."

"How are we going to manage a closer look?" Ida Belle said. "If he targeted Eleanor at that charity event, then he's working off a playbook. He's already met Gertie and even if you or I put ourselves in his path, he'd do his research like any good scammer does. It won't take him five on Google to know to steer clear."

"Where is Zion's retreat located?" I asked.

"South of NOLA," Gertie said. "Maybe an hour's drive from the city."

"I wonder how he targeted Eleanor then," I said. "Because I agree that whole charity-event thing reeks of a setup. Why would someone who lives two hours away be at a church in Mudbug for a charity gig?"

"It's easy enough to read the obits and cross-reference them with property records," Ida Belle said. "If he's a pro, he'd make it a full-time job. These days, AI can eliminate a lot of the research time, but that also makes it harder for us to take a run on him as he can research us just as easily."

"What's the name of his property?" I asked Gertie.

She told me and I did a quick search. "He's got a two-day retreat starting tomorrow and there's still openings."

"Even if that man walked into my house and shot Walter, I still wouldn't wear a leotard to catch him," Ida Belle said.

"What if he scratched your SUV with a screwdriver?" Gertie asked. "Or detuned your boat engine?"

Ida Belle frowned but finally shook her head. "Nope. Not even then. Besides, I've already told you it wouldn't work anyway. He'd see us coming a mile away."

"What if he didn't?" I asked, an idea starting to form.

"Are you planning on gouging his eyes out?" Ida Belle asked.

"Nothing that dramatic, but I'll keep the suggestion in reserve. I was thinking of an undercover operation."

"There's no way different hair and a change of wardrobe would fool him with Gertie," Ida Belle argued. "He's spent too much time with her already. And all it would take is a quick picture of either of us and a reverse image search and he'd know exactly who we are as well."

"What if he didn't research us at all because we went as people who were above suspicion?"

"No one is above suspicion."

"To us, no. But to the rest of the world…"

I looked back at Gertie. "You think we can get two more nun costumes by tomorrow?"

———

IT TOOK SOME CONVINCING, BUT FINALLY WE TALKED IDA Belle into playing Catholic for a couple days. She still refused to let spandex touch her body, but since we were going full habit for maximum concealment, she could keep her regular uniform of flannel and jeans underneath and no one would be the wiser.

My plan was simple—I was a young nun whose parents had recently died. I had inherited a significant amount of land, including a small collection of cabins. Ida Belle and Gertie, my senior sisters, were worried about me and felt that some time away to reflect and mourn would be helpful. They overheard a parishioner talking about Zion's retreat at mass and, taking his name as a sign, they'd booked the three of us for the two-day event.

While we were there, I'd spread my story and see if Zion took the bait. If he was really a scammer, then a young, innocent, grieving woman with property should be right up his alley. On the way back to Sinful, Gertie called up the shop in NOLA where she'd bought her nun costume, and they had put two aside for pickup the next morning on our way to the retreat.

"I still don't see why we have to be nuns," Ida Belle said. "Can't we just get some wigs and different clothes and leave Gertie at home?"

"No way!" Gertie said. "And good luck doing yoga and keeping a wig on."

I shook my head. "Zion will be on high alert after Eleanor's death. By default, nuns won't be subject to the same sort of scrutiny as regular people."

"Yes, but part of Zion's tactics includes romancing his targets," Ida Belle said. "He can't romance a nun, so he might decide to pass completely on the opportunity."

"That's possible," I agreed. "But if I went as a regular woman and he tried to put the moves on me, how long do you think I'd be able to maintain cover?"

Gertie snorted.

Ida Belle sighed.

"Besides, a nun will have the whole innocence thing going for her," I said. "So he'll be able to play on that end of things. I'm young and lost my family and have no worldly tendencies or knowledge, especially since I was homeschooled and entered the convent at eighteen."

"Good Lord, talk about having no life," Gertie said. "This is the worst undercover gig ever."

"Nuns can drink," I said.

"So can Baptists," Gertie argued.

"But we're supposed to hide it," Ida Belle countered.

"We don't check in until noon, so it's really only a day and a half," I said in an effort to make Ida Belle feel better.

"Thirty-six hours too long is what it is," she said. "And what do you plan on telling Carter? Because we've got to get our stories straight."

"We're going to NOLA and staying overnight as we intend to gamble, drink, eat, and shop, not necessarily in that order."

"Carter will never buy that you're going to shop, especially if we go without Ronald."

"It's a girls' trip."

"And that excludes Ronald, how exactly?"

"Point taken. I'll let Ronald in on it and tell him he has to fake an illness or bursitis. Whatever. Even if Carter suspects us of doing something, he won't ask. He knows better."

"That's true," she allowed. "Good God, I can't believe I'm going to have to wear a dress and be a Catholic."

"It's easier than being Baptist," Gertie said. "You just do whatever, then go to confession and it's like you didn't do it. And Father Michael isn't even allowed to tell anyone what you said."

"Father Michael wouldn't remember what you said or that he even talked to you," Ida Belle pointed out.

"Like I said, seems like a better deal."

Ida Belle dropped me off and I headed next door to put Ronald in the loop. He was disappointed that he couldn't tag along but understood that he didn't exactly meet the criteria for the mission. And he had a therapy session the next day and said he really needed it, so it was just as well.

Since I figured Carter's day would be long and frustrating, I threw a slab of beef on the grill to cut up for fajitas. I was just taking it off when Carter walked out the back door.

"What did you do?" he asked.

"Huh?"

"You're cooking. You never cook."

"Grilling is not cooking and I cook."

"Scrambled eggs are not cooking. A five-year-old can make them."

"Then find a five-year-old to start cooking yours."

He raised one eyebrow. "We could always make one of our own."

I froze as all witty comebacks fled my body.

After several uncomfortable, silent seconds, I saw his lips quivering and then he started laughing.

"I think that's the first time I've ever seen you afraid," he said.

"I should shoot you for even joking about it."

"It would probably be easier to ask me to move out."

"If you keep talking about making five-year-olds, I will."

He took the tray of beef from me. "Looks good. I appreciate you throwing this on. I didn't feel like eating a sandwich but didn't have the energy to cook either, and since that idiot Calahan was headed to the café, I refused to get takeout. If I spent one more second in his presence, I was going to be the lead suspect in the next Sinful homicide investigation."

"That bad, huh?"

"I'm surprised he didn't drug test me when I went to the bathroom."

"How long does he plan on sticking to you?"

Carter took out a huge knife and started hacking the meat in strips as if he were using a machete on the enemy. "He hasn't said. Unless he gets called back by his boss, my guess is until he finds something to use against me."

"I could probably persuade him to move on."

"Your methods of persuasion aren't legal and are often permanent."

I waved a hand in dismissal. "Details. Are you going to make a statement about the case anytime soon?"

"Still waiting on forensics and the ME. I should have reports tomorrow."

"Okay, well, I'm going to make the next couple days easier on you. Ida Belle, Gertie, and I are clearing out tomorrow. Going to hit NOLA, do some gambling and drinking. I'm going to get us a room at the casino so no worries on the whole drinking and driving thing.”

He narrowed his eyes at me. “You’re voluntarily going to NOLA overnight? You don’t even gamble.”

“I was CIA. Of course I gamble.”

“Okay. I’m sure I don’t want to know. Did you call Detective Casey and let her know you’re headed her way?”

“One, I don’t need to because Casey’s a homicide detective. And two, she’s on extended vacation with her daughter. They’re hitting half of the islands in the Caribbean.”

“Good. They deserve a vacation.”

I nodded. “Maybe Calahan will loosen his grip if he knows I’m out of the way.”

“I wouldn’t bet on it, but it can’t hurt. Please don’t get into any trouble.”

“I’m taking Gertie.”

CHAPTER FIVE

WE HEADED OUT FIRST THING THE NEXT MORNING, figuring we'd have breakfast in NOLA while waiting for the costume shop to open. The drive to the retreat would only take an hour from the city, so we had some wiggle room. Not that I wanted to wiggle around NOLA for too long. There were far too many things Gertie could get into there. It was like taking a toddler into a glass shop.

"I wonder if Carter will issue a statement today," Gertie said as she took a bite of a beignet, sending powdered sugar all over the table and her shirt.

"I guess so," I said. "I know he has to wait on the ME and forensics, but it seems like overkill. I'm pretty sure we know how she died."

"They'll do toxicology," Ida Belle said. "Even suicides are investigated, which is good. We need to know why people do these things, both to give the family information and to hopefully prevent them in the future."

I nodded. "I suppose you're right. God knows, Carter was by-the-book anyway but with Calahan standing over him, he won't even fart if it's not a hundred percent within the guidelines."

Ida Belle shook her head. "I hate that he's dealing with this. That Calahan is clearly looking for a reason to wind both of you up."

"Carter says he's bucking for a promotion and getting something on him would be a feather in his cap, especially given Carter's and my reputations."

"This is all that cow Celia's fault," Gertie said. "She'll never accept that Carter is doing a great job."

I nodded. "Why can't the woman get a hobby? Or I suppose a *different* hobby, would be more accurate."

"It would have to be a hobby because it wouldn't be a man," Gertie said. "There isn't a man alive foolish and brave enough to take that on."

"Celia never struck me as the sort that was looking for a man," Ida Belle said. "Not after her disaster of a marriage."

"She never struck me as the sort to be a parent, either," Gertie said, "but she went ahead anyway, and look how that turned out."

"You know better than most how small-town mentality works," Ida Belle said. "Women are supposed to get married, have kids, and bake casseroles, and women like Celia just went along with the status quo."

"Well, you each ticked one off the list," I said. "I'm batting zero."

Gertie grinned. "You'll be checking off marriage soon, unless you put Carter on hold until he's drawing Social Security, like Ida Belle did Walter."

"Things are shifting," Ida Belle said. "Don't get me wrong, people are still as judgmental as ever, but their narrow-minded beliefs don't tend to have as much effect on women's decisions as they used to."

"I disagree," I said. "Social media is full of toxicity and a ton of it is directed at women, mostly young women. What to wear, who to date, how much he needs to make, is he doing 'the me work'—whatever the heck that's supposed to mean. They are pushing so many qualifiers on each other that it's no wonder half of them remain single."

"Don't forget the body count question," Gertie said.

I stared. "Even I don't tell my body count."

Ida Belle grinned. "You don't *know* your body count it's so high, but that's not the kind of body count they're referring to."

"Sexy-time body count," Gertie explained.

I stared at her in dismay. "They're keeping score?"

Gertie nodded. "*And* lying about it *and* deciding if they're going to go out based on the lies. It's like one big reality show —*The Real Daters of Social Media*. All performative, no substance."

I shook my head. "Well, at least social media gives us some info on the people we're investigating. Most people say too much and once it's out there, it's usually forever."

"Did you work up the details on our cover story?" Ida Belle asked. "If Zion takes the bait, he's going to want to know more about the property."

I pulled my laptop out of my backpack and cued up some photos. "Not only do I have backstory, I have property."

I turned the laptop around for them to see. "A lovely collection of cabins, right on a Florida island peninsula of white sand and turquoise waters. Deed registered to the Sandy Days Corporation, which is part of the Ford Family Estate."

"Beautiful, but I don't get it," Gertie said.

I smiled. "The Sandy Days Corporation is one of Big and Little Hebert's interests, but it's so buried, no one would be able to suss it out. They had their attorney write up some fake estate documents and that corporation is one of the assets. I am the only heir."

I pulled IDs out of my backpack and passed them over. "I figured I would go as close as I could manage to real so we hopefully don't completely ignore people calling us by our fake names. So you're Sister Eileen and Sister Gerianne. I'm Sister Britney. Britney Ford."

"Britney doesn't sound anything like Fortune," Gertie said.

"It was one of my undercover aliases, so I'm used to responding to it."

"I can't believe you allowed the CIA to call you Britney," Ida Belle said.

"It was a Harrison and a haircut thing…long story."

"Given how your hair was cut when we met, I doubt it's all that long," Gertie said.

"Anyway, if Zion wants information about the property, all I have to do is contact the Heberts' attorney and he'll be happy to provide information as he's in on our play."

Gertie smiled as Ida Belle parked in front of the costume shop. "Then let's go get us some nun suits and catch a scammer."

I was paying for the outfits when I heard a voice behind me.

"I hope you're not about to pull an art heist in the St. Louis Cathedral."

I spun around and smiled. "Detective Casey! I thought you were still island-hopping."

She shrugged. "All that relaxation was starting to make me antsy. And Audrey got a call for another interview. She flew to DC this morning."

"You still can't tell me who?"

She couldn't control the grin. "CIA. But you can't repeat it. I figure you of all people can manage that."

She looked over at Ida Belle and Gertie. "That goes for you two as well, as you're Fortune-adjacent."

"That's great," I said as I grabbed the packages and we headed out of the store. "She's sure she wants to go that direction?"

"She's twenty-one. Does anyone know what they want at that age? I mean, you know what you want at that moment, but long term is never really clear."

"Where were you when you were twenty-one?"

"Finishing police academy and juggling a baby."

I nodded. "And I was already in the CIA. Ida Belle and Gertie were in Vietnam. And while there's things I didn't like about the agency, I honestly don't think I'd change anything."

"Me either," Gertie said, and Ida Belle nodded.

Casey sighed. "Hell, neither would I. But I can't help it if my mother gene takes over sometimes. Just don't tell anyone. They'd razz me about it down at the precinct."

"Don't worry," I said. "We'll keep it a secret that you love your daughter and want her to be safe. I'm sure they suspect nothing."

"I missed sarcasm while I was on my extended vacation. Adult sarcasm, I mean. Audrey has her own brand. Half the time I'm not sure whether we're having a conversation or she's insulting me. So should I even ask about the nun thing?"

"Probably not. But you'll be happy to know we won't be donning these until we're well out of your beat."

"Might be less interesting, but probably not a bad thing overall. Give me a call next time you're coming through. We'll grab food or drinks or both."

She gave us a wave and headed down the street.

"Let's get this show on the road," I said. "I found a motel about ten miles from our turnoff for the retreat. I booked us a room for two nights so we'll have a place to change without being noticed. It's the 'pay cash when you get there' kind of place."

"Good call," Ida Belle said. "No paper trail and having a place to change in private is even better. Three regular women walking into a bathroom and three nuns walking out sounds like the start of a great sitcom, but it would definitely get lips flapping, especially in these tiny bayou towns. And I have no interest in pulling on that gear until the very last minute."

"What about NOLA?" Gertie asked. "Where are we staying here? I mean, for the story?"

"The casino," I said. "Makes the most sense since we're supposed to be gambling."

Ida Belle laughed. "Who says we're not?"

———

WE MADE THE DRIVE TO THE MOTEL IN FORTY-FIVE minutes. I stuffed my hair up in a ball cap and donned a pair of huge sunglasses when I checked into the motel, and of course, I paid cash. If for some odd reason Calahan decided to try to track us down, it wouldn't be to here. It wouldn't be to the casino hotel either, but we could always claim we went on a bender and gambled all night. Wouldn't be the first time someone had done so and short of having a warrant for the casino security cameras—which he had zero probable cause for —he had no way of proving otherwise.

The motel room was dingy and dark and reminded me of the Bayou Inn before the Heberts had bought it and started renovating. I tossed my overnight bag on the bed and the springs squeaked. Gertie sat on the other bed and almost slid off onto the floor when the side collapsed.

"I'm glad we're not really staying here," she said. "This place is a pit."

"Don't sit on anything," Ida Belle said. "We don't have time for a hip replacement or a staph infection. Let's just get changed and get out of here."

"Are you in a hurry to wear a habit and pretend to Zen?" I asked.

"I'm in a hurry to get this over with and get home. Redfish are running and I've got empty space in my freezer."

Ida Belle and I had opted to wear our usual casual wear and only had to pull the habits on over it. The headdress took some work as we weren't exactly pros, but we finally managed to get them on and our hair stuffed underneath. Gertie had headed for the bathroom and came out wearing a pink glittery bodysuit.

"Seriously?" Ida Belle asked.

"No one will see it," Gertie said.

"That's probably what Sister Mary Catherine thought both times you defrocked her," I said.

"It's a yoga retreat. It's not like anyone is going to be disturbed by someone wearing a bodysuit."

"I'm pretty sure seeing an old nun in a bodysuit would disturb most people," Ida Belle said.

"Well, then it's a good thing there's no old people around."

Ida Belle sighed. "I've got some more stuff in the SUV. I'll be back."

I grabbed my cosmetic bag before heading into the bathroom, which was the only room that held a mirror. I wasn't applying makeup, of course, but I had decided that the additional step of colored contacts was advisable. Calahan had seen me up close and my particular shade of turquoise eyes wasn't all that common. Basic brown wasn't interesting or memorable.

Ida Belle walked back in when I came out, and she gave me an approving nod. "Good call on the contacts."

Fortunately, Gertie had finally donned her habit, so we no longer had to squint in the presence of the pink glitter nightmare. Ida Belle hefted a plastic bag on the desk and pulled out crucifixes and rosary beads.

"I figured if anyone dug through our stuff for any reason, we should probably have these," she said. "I also swapped the plate on the SUV to one registered to a rental car company."

"Nice," I said.

"Where did you get it?" Gertie asked.

"Does that matter?" Ida Belle asked. "Fortune didn't ask where I got it."

"Because Sister Britney Ford would never question her elders," I said. "How are you at voices?"

"Huh?" Gertie asked.

"Zion was one of the last people to see Eleanor alive. On the off chance that Carter shows up at the retreat to talk to him and we can't duck out, I think it's best if we slightly alter our voices—at least Gertie and me. Calahan has heard both of us talk. I have no problem with it, obviously. I'm trained to be most anyone. What about you, Gertie?"

"I hadn't thought about it, but it sounds like fun. I'm going to go with the grouchy nun from *Sister Act*."

"Less grouchy, more Southern," Ida Belle said.

"We'll see."

"Okay, let's lock up our personal stuff and electronics in the secret compartment in the SUV," I said before an argument could start. "Keep your phones but put them on vibrate. I really want us to appear to be out of the loop on modern society."

"I have to admit," Ida Belle said, "the one advantage of these outfits is so many places to conceal a weapon."

Gertie nodded. "You could have a machine gun under here and no one would know."

Ida Belle and I both gave her a nervous look as she skipped happily out the door.

"Surely she couldn't skip..." Ida Belle said. "You know what? I don't want to know."

―――――

THE RETREAT WAS BURIED DEEP IN BAYOU COUNTRY, BUT IF I was being honest, the property was pretty. Huge cypress trees dominated the grounds and aside from a small area around a building labeled Office and paths extending out from it, the land had been left uncleared. A white Mercedes SUV was parked in front of the building with a sign indicating this was where we would sign in.

The lobby contained a small counter, reminiscent of the motel I'd just checked us into but a lot cleaner and with ten times the amount of light. The inside was painted a soothing pale green and there were beautiful flowers and plants on the counter. I'd already told Ida Belle to take the lead on everything as it would make more sense for the senior nuns to be handling things, so she strode up to the counter and rang the bell.

A couple seconds later, a man stepped out from an office. He managed to lose his what-the-heck expression quickly, but clearly, he'd been surprised to see three nuns standing there. However, his serene smile was plastered in place as he stepped forward

Midthirties. Five foot eleven. A hundred sixty pounds. Lanky with decent muscle tone but not nearly enough muscle mass. It was a body that would have looked great on a woman, but on a man, didn't quite get the job done. Threat level low unless you were a lonely, naive woman with a recent inheritance.

Despite all the negatives, I had to admit, he was very good-looking. Not at all my type, clearly, as I didn't find men I could beat in an arm wrestling match attractive, but with his blue eyes, surfer-messy blond hair, and chiseled features, I could see the draw for normal women.

"Welcome to Synergy Wellness," he said. "I'm Zion. Are you here for the flash retreat?"

Gertie put a hand to her chest. "We're not required to flash people, are we?"

His eyes widened. "No! I'm sorry. I just call it that because it's quick. You are welcome to wear whatever you're comfortable in or whatever your beliefs require. We welcome all."

"Good," Gertie said, putting on a proper look that must have served her well as a teacher. "I'm still not sold on this whole spiritual enlightenment stuff, but Sister Eileen insisted. Some people believe in everything."

The look of dismay on Ida Belle's face was so profound, I struggled not to laugh. Gertie's grouchy nun voice and demeanor were perfection.

"You're a nun," Ida Belle said. "Your entire existence is spiritual enlightenment."

"There's no yoga in the Scripture," Gertie said.

Ida Belle sighed. "I'd think you could hold your tongue for once. We are here for Sister Britney's benefit in her time of sorrow and despair."

"We could have been spiritual and enlightened back at the convent," Gertie said. "We're nuns, for Christ's sake."

Zion sucked in a breath and glanced up, apparently afraid God was going to send lightning down from the heavens.

"The Holy Spirit is everywhere," Ida Belle said. "And we needed to get Sister Britney away to clear her head. You're welcome to Uber back if you'd like. They're bleaching all the school bathrooms this week."

Gertie pursed her lips. "Hmmmm. Maybe you're not as foolish as I thought."

Zion stared back and forth between Ida Belle and Gertie, clearly confused and uncertain how to take this conversation. Finally, I jabbed Ida Belle in the side.

"I'm Sister Eileen," she said. "The one who talks too much is Sister Gerianne and this is Sister Britney. We have a reservation for the large cabin."

"Of course," he said, slipping back into business mode. "If I could just get a copy of your IDs. Are you wanting to pay by card?"

"Don't believe in cards or interest," Ida Belle said. "I'll be paying in cash."

"That's fine," he said as he took our IDs and made a copy of them. "If you'll just sign here. That will be seven fifty."

I wondered if I'd have to jab Ida Belle again for her to turn over the money. I'd already given her the cash and told her the cost, but her outrage at paying two hundred fifty bucks apiece for a day and a half of what she dubbed 'New Age BS' was epic. I had to agree with her. Two fifty bought a lot of ammunition, and the shooting range had never let me down when it came to decompressing.

She dug the money out of the purse Gertie had lent her for our adventure and counted it out on the counter. Zion stuck it in an envelope and placed it in a drawer from which he withdrew three keys.

"If you follow the path behind the office and take a right when it branches, your cabin is at the end of that branch."

"How far is the walk?" Gertie asked.

"About a hundred yards," he said. "I can bring your bags for you. It's a pleasant walk and you've got plenty of time before our first session. I suggest you use the walk to relax and center yourself. It's a very beautiful place and one that's easy to escape into."

"No one said anything about all this walking," Gertie grumbled.

"I'll help you with the bags," I said softly with a bit of a drawl and averting my eyes when he looked over at me. "You shouldn't have to carry all three."

Ida Belle gave me an approving nod. "You're always looking for acts of service, Sister Britney. The Lord will reward you."

"Your corns should be rewarding her," Gertie said. "Let's get going. I want to get there before all that coffee I drank on the way runs through me."

I showed Zion to the SUV and pulled out my overnight bag, leaving him Ida Belle's backpack and Gertie's massive suitcase. He looked at both of them as I slung my tote over my shoulder, clearly confused.

"Sister Eileen is old school and minimalist," I said. "Sister Gerianne is always saying she should have been born hundreds of years ago. Sister Gerianne, on the other hand, has a bit of bling and modern to her. She likes street clothes, even though no one sees them but her."

He extended the handle on the suitcase, and we set off down the path. "Are nuns allowed bling?"

I gave him a shy smile, then looked away. "We're allowed to wear whatever we'd like under our habit. Most of us are very boring and discreet, but Sister Gerianne insists that's one of the only areas where she's allowed individuality, so she's taking it."

"She sounds like a bit of a character."

"She is, but they are both so nice. I don't know how I could have handled everything without them."

"Sister Eileen mentioned they were here for you. May I ask why?"

"My aunt passed away. She was the only living relative I had left."

"You're so young—what about your parents?"

"They were killed in a car accident when I was eight. She raised me—even homeschooled me—until I was eighteen and could join the sisters. I've never wanted any other life."

"I'm very sorry about your aunt and your parents. That's a lot of loss to deal with at such a young age."

I nodded. "If it were just the loss, I'd probably be okay, but it's all the other stuff that comes with it that has me so stressed. I don't know anything about trusts and legal stuff, but I have to go to Florida and deal with it all next week. Sister Eileen thought this retreat might help me to stay relaxed, but I don't see how. No offense to you."

"None taken. It's definitely a challenge to introduce life-changing skills in such a short amount of time, and I would never lay claim to being a miracle worker. I believe you already know that guy."

I forced a small laugh, hoping it sounded legitimate and clueless.

"I introduced these short retreats more as a way to show people the value of such a program in their lives," he continued. "And the occasional retreat to re-center, to learn new things, and to fellowship with others seeking a path to better living are highly beneficial. Most of my clients are repeats and come several times a year."

I nodded. "If it brings people comfort, then you're offering an excellent service for people."

"If you don't mind my intrusiveness, what is burdening you about the legalities of the situation? Surely your aunt had everything arranged if she went to the trouble of establishing a trust."

"She left me everything, which is fine when it comes to the

bank accounts and all of that. It's her resort that I don't know what to do with."

I watched him closely and saw the slight change in his expression as soon as I said the word *resort*.

"What kind of resort did she have?" he asked.

"Not anything big. Just some cabins on an island in Florida. It's where I was raised. My aunt and uncle bought the place right after they got married. He'd had a small inheritance and back then, the property was a lot cheaper, so they decided to make a go of it. He passed before I was born, but she told me it was practically falling down when they took it on."

"It sounds lovely now. I don't understand what the problem is. Assuming you have no interest in running it, surely you could sell it for a fair price."

I frowned and shook my head. "No. Well, I mean, I could. Legally. But that place meant the world to my aunt, and she made me promise that I wouldn't ever sell it. I know it probably wasn't fair of her to do so, especially as I'll never have children myself to keep it in the family. And that's why I'm so stressed. I can't run the property myself, I can't let it just sit there and deteriorate, and I don't know that I could find someone I trusted to do it for me. Right after my parents died, my aunt tried briefly to live inland to raise me, but the people she hired stole money and let things get run-down. She said she'd never let strangers oversee something she loved again. But I can't focus on *my* purpose if I'm worried about her legacy."

"I understand your dilemma. You have some very hard decisions ahead of you. Hopefully your time here can help with your clarity and then the decisions won't be as difficult to make."

"If you could help lessen the burden of this load, I would be forever grateful," I said as we stepped up to the cabin.

"Don't tell the sisters, but I brought some of the paperwork and pictures with me to pray over. They wanted me to leave it all back at the convent, but I need answers."

The door to the cabin flung open and Gertie stood there, glaring. "Took you long enough. I need my biking shorts. These leggings are hot as heck. The humidity is just rolling off that bayou. I sweated so much on the walk down here, I didn't even have to pee."

Zion stared for a moment, then finally found his voice. "I hope you settle in well. Introductions and our first meditation start in thirty minutes down by the bayou. Just take the path to the right and follow it all the way to the water."

"Thanks," I said as I grabbed the remaining bags and headed inside.

Ida Belle peered out between the blinds, then let them drop. "He's headed back to the office."

Gertie lifted the blinds. "No butt at all. Such a disappointment. Still, he's kind of hot in a tree-hugger sort of way. Which means there is zero chance that guy was having a romantic fling with Eleanor because of unrelenting passion."

"He's not my taste at all," Ida Belle said, "But I'd have to agree with that. He's way out of Eleanor's league, even when she was twenty years younger." She looked over at me. "So did you get anything out of him?"

"Despite the outfit, I can't perform miracles," I said. "But I did lay the groundwork."

I filled them in on our conversation.

Ida Belle gave me an approving nod. "You managed to get a lot into a short conversation. Did he take the bait?"

"He wants to," I said. "He was straining to control his excitement. I've got the fake paperwork along with some pictures of the cabin in my backpack. I'm just going to leave it on the bed when we head out. He knows which pack is mine."

"After talking to you, he'll sneak in here to check them out," Gertie said confidently.

"How's he going to do that if he's the one leading the classes?" Ida Belle asked.

"There's always meals and for all we know, there are other instructors...maybe his wife even," I said.

Ida Belle held up crossed fingers. "So now that the setup is in place, what do we do otherwise?"

"I say we break into his cabin and put a bug in there," Gertie said. "We don't have much time to make this work. And since we couldn't risk bringing the parabolic because of size, a bug is the best way to go."

Ida Belle raised one eyebrow. "And I suppose you're carrying all that tech equipment in your giant, unnecessary suitcase?"

"Don't be foolish. I have snacks in the suitcase. I've been this route before, remember? They think people can live off smoothies, cucumbers, and water. Not doing that again. I put the tech stuff in the secret compartment in the SUV along with my spare guns."

"How many spare guns do you need?" Ida Belle asked. "How many do you have under that habit?"

"The only way you'll ever know is if you pull it off me," Gertie said. "But I'm warning you, Ronald helped me pick out new exercise clothes and they're all butt floss. Most have sequins."

"Then where the heck are you keeping your guns? Don't tell me they're all in a sports bra."

"Of course not. I'm wearing a waist holster. Real Old Western sort of stuff, except no revolvers."

Ida Belle stared at her in dismay, and I cringed at the mental picture of butt floss leotards and a gun holster.

"Thought so," Gertie said. "And to answer your first question you can never have too many guns—backup or otherwise."

Ida Belle frowned but since neither of us could exactly argue the point, she remained silent.

"So what about bugging the cabin?" Gertie asked.

I shrugged. "If an opportunity presents itself, it's not the worst idea. Even if he found the device, who would suspect nuns?"

"Exactly," Gertie said. "If he's a scammer, he'd probably attribute it to someone he took money from before. Not a new target."

Ida Belle nodded. "We better set up that paperwork and head out. We have to do that fake slow walk everywhere or we blow our cover."

"Who's faking?" Gertie asked. "My legs are killing me. Jeb and I are trying this new workout. It's a pre-sexy time workout and it's supposed to make everything more intense. So far, it's just intensified the arthritis in my knees and aggravated Jeb's back, but we committed to trying it for a month. If we call it quits after that, there's this massage chair with—"

"No!" Ida Belle interrupted. "I let that go on three sentences longer than I should have."

I grinned. "Then I guess we best get to hobbling down to the lake for our hour of enlightenment."

"I have to change first," Gertie said. "I put on my exercise outfit. Meditation is different."

Ida Belle sighed as Gertie pulled a smaller bag out of her huge suitcase and headed into the bathroom. "The things we do for this job."

"You went to the Middle East to assist with a rescue mission that even our military couldn't have pulled off."

"And you think that was more dangerous than me doing yoga?"

CHAPTER SIX

WE TOOK OUR TIME ON THE WALK…NOT AS THOUGH THERE was any choice in the matter. Between maintaining our cover and Gertie's shot knees, it was necessary. We were the last to arrive with only a couple minutes to spare. Three other women stood in a row looking at Zion, who stood at the edge of a wide bayou. He smiled when he caught sight of us and the other ladies turned around.

To say they were surprised to see three approaching nuns was an understatement.

Midtwenties. Five foot five to five foot seven. A hundred twenty pounds give or take, ten of it hair extensions and boobs. All bottle blondes. All wearing matching skimpy yoga outfits in different colors. All looking at Zion with adoring looks. Zero threat unless they figured out Zion was into me. Women like this were worse than the CIA in disabling their competition.

We made our way over and Zion made introductions, but I promptly forgot their names as they were now embedded in my mind as the three Barbies. They were obviously confused by our presence but since we were no competition, they quickly lost interest and turned their attention back to Zion, who I could tell basked in the admiration but was careful not to give any indication of interest. Maybe none of them had cabins he wanted to get a hold of.

I struggled not to shake my head. What had the world come to when a man was more interested in getting his hands on a woman's cabins than her big fake boobs? But then I guessed business really was business.

"Now that we're all family," Zion began, "let's get into the reason we're all here. Centering your mind with your body is the best gift you can give yourself."

"The Lord is the best gift you can give yourself," Gertie said. "Or maybe an Aleve."

One of the Barbies giggled, then covered her mouth with her hand when she saw the disapproving look on Zion's face.

"This is a physical centering," Zion said. "Our spiritual center is a very individual journey and not one I'm qualified to take you on."

"Individual my foot," Gertie said. "There's God and then there's phonies."

Ida Belle jabbed her in the ribs. "This is not helping Sister Britney in her time of need. I suggest you start centering your body by closing your mouth."

"Let's start by relaxing the body so that we can relax the mind," Zion said, and sank gracefully onto the ground in a cross-legged sit.

Ida Belle and I followed suit, Ida Belle not as gracefully, but without mishap. Gertie, on the other hand, squatted a bit, then dropped onto the ground and fell over onto her side. A grape rolled out of her habit, and she picked it up and popped it into her mouth. The three Barbies were all struggling not to laugh, and I'll admit to scratching my face to hide my grin. Zion had no idea what he was in for.

"Okay," he said. "Now everyone, relax as much as possible

while remaining in a seated position but maintain an erect torso."

"Erect is not relaxing," Gertie grumbled, but she pulled herself up straight.

"Now," he continued, "we will learn to breathe."

"Oh for Heaven's sake," Gertie said. "If we didn't know how to breathe, none of us would even be here."

"You need to know how to breathe properly."

Zion's expression remained serene, but I could tell he was struggling to maintain it. I had to give him points for patience. And if the average attendee was anything like the character Gertie was playing, I had a little bit of sympathy for his thieving ways. The man was probably looking for enough money to get away from people forever.

We spent several minutes learning how to breathe properly, which was a bunch of hooey. If people really wanted some useful breathing lessons, I could have trained them on holding their breath for several minutes, which saved lives if you were in an underwater scuffle or a chemical or smoke grenade had been launched at you. But since I was supposed to be a naive, innocent nun, I had to pretend to find all of this incredibly interesting and worth trying.

It was so much easier when I could just shoot people and go home for dinner.

Once we were all breathing properly, Zion explained the meditation exercise to us. We were to focus on the sound of the water, lapping at the bank, and attempt to screen out all other noise, including the noise of our own thoughts. The only other sound allowed was if we could hear the beating of our hearts.

I closed my eyes, mostly so he wouldn't see my eye roll, forced a serene look on my face, and mentally started running down my firearms inventory so that I wouldn't doze off. If I had been home, this would have been prime naptime weather. The sun was shining bright but there was a gentle breeze coming off the water. It was hot but not blistering, and the humidity was probably only 80 percent, which was a sight lower than the normal two thousand.

I had just finished inventory and decided I was deficient in a couple areas when Zion said it was time to return our now-melded bodies and minds to the present. I have no idea where he thought we'd all gone because even wearing yoga pants and a habit, I could still feel sand digging into my rear. There was no escaping the present when it was offering up a sand wedgie.

I heard giggling as I opened my eyes and then snoring to my right. I looked over and saw Gertie, slumped over on the ground, out for the count. Ida Belle was staring up, her hands pressed together, and I wondered briefly if she was praying for deliverance or rain.

I leaned over and gave Gertie a shake and she jolted up, her glasses dangling from one ear.

"What?" she asked, looking around. "Did Christ return? Because that's the only reason to wake a sleeping nun."

"If Christ had returned, you wouldn't be here," Ida Belle said.

"Who says I am? Maybe we all ascended."

"Your snoring says otherwise. You're supposed to get a new body in the afterlife, not limp in there with old goods."

"What kind of nuns are you?" one of the Barbies asked.

Gertie stared at her as if she was stupid. "Catholic."

"Let's all stand and stretch our bodies before we head to bar," Zion said.

"Whoo-hoo!" Gertie cheered. "I love a bar almost as much as forgiveness."

Zion gave her a tight smile. "We'll be serving cucumber

smoothies with additives to help cleanse your body of toxins. It's all part of your journey to mind-body connection."

"The only connection my body is going to make with cucumbers is gas," Gertie grumbled.

The three Barbies giggled again, their heads down, trying to hide their amusement from the obviously disapproving Zion, who rose from his seated position exactly as he'd sat. One fluid movement as if he didn't have bones.

Everyone else did a normal knee-to-butt thing except me, who chose to show off my skills and rise as fluidly as Zion had. He gave me an appreciative nod.

"You have very good muscle control and balance, Sister Britney," he said. "Perhaps you'll seek to further your education in this form of enlightenment after the retreat."

"Maybe I will," I said, pasting on a fake cheery smile. "I really enjoyed the meditation. We pray a lot, of course, but I've never really sat in reflection for that long on anything but Scripture. I can see where it would really help to clarify thought."

Zion practically beamed, and the three Barbies looked confused. I wondered if they were trying to figure out if being jealous of a nun would send them to hell.

"I'm going to need some help here," Gertie said. "Darn knees have locked up completely being down on the ground this long. Next time, you need to get me a chair or something."

She was leaned to one side, trying to push herself up, but it wasn't happening.

"Let me assist you," Zion said as I leaned over to help her up.

We each took an arm and Zion said, "On three...one, two, three."

We both pulled upward and Gertie gave it everything her knees had, which turned out to be much more than either of us had reckoned on. And Zion must have been stronger than he looked. Gertie had still been leaning slightly toward Zion, so when we pulled, she flew up, her head cracking Zion directly under his chin.

But her knees weren't yet warmed up and buckled as soon as she tried to stand. She fell to the right, grabbing on to Zion to try to maintain her balance, but all she managed was to pull his yoga pants down to his knees, exposing the very tiny bright red bikini underwear he had on.

And very skinny legs. Why did yoga guys always skip leg day?

With his pants wrapped around his knees and Gertie wrapped around his thighs, and both of them right on the slope of the bayou, there was no preventing the fall. They crashed onto the ground, then rolled toward the water, picking up momentum as the slope got steeper.

It was a bundle of black with flashes of red moving like a tumbleweed for the bayou. And someone was screaming. Given the high pitch, I would have said it was Gertie, but knowing Gertie and given the situation, it was more likely Zion. I probably should have tried to stop them but to be honest, I was afraid I'd end up grabbing something I didn't want to touch.

Instead, Ida Belle, the Barbies, and I all stood and watched as they hit the bottom of the slope and splashed into the edge of the bayou. Now that they'd stopped rolling, we all rushed down to help, and then a strange woman ran up from the side.

"What the heck is going on, Zion?" the woman asked, hands on her hips, staring down at the fray below her.

Midtwenties. Five foot four. A hundred five pounds. Low muscle tone. Zero threat to me, but the wedding band on her left hand probably represented a big threat to her husband, especially in his current state.

I shot a glance at Ida Belle, who had also caught a glimpse of the ring and raised her eyebrows. Gertie's habit had rolled around her body during the fall, binding her like the Michelin Man around the waist. Thankfully, her holster was covered, but her underclothes were on full display. She wore biking shorts in lime green and on top of them was the dreaded butt floss in fuchsia. Lettering down the front of the shorts read It's Party Time.

Zion was draped across Gertie's legs, and his hand was currently resting in an awkward-to-explain location on Gertie's chest. At first, he didn't respond to the woman's demands, and I wondered if he'd knocked himself unconscious, then he finally stirred and glanced around, confused. When the situation all clicked, he sprang up like a cat.

Unfortunately, his pants were still wrapped around his knees, so he went right back down. At least this time, he wasn't draped across Gertie in some weird R-rated movie scenario. He landed face-first in about a foot of water, and I waded in to right him before he drowned, while the woman on the bank just stood there, arms crossed, and clearly disapproving of whatever all this was.

"Your pants," I said as he sputtered, sending water everywhere.

He looked down and then clearly panicked, yanked the pants up so hard and fast that he gave himself a wedgie, which elicited a yelp. He bolted up again, this time managing to stay upright, and pulled at the legs of his pants to get them out of his nethers, then leaned over and peered at Gertie.

"Are you all right, Sister?" he asked. "I'm so sorry. I couldn't maintain balance for both of us on the slope."

Gertie, who'd sat up to watch the whole pants debacle, said, "I don't recall seeing 'baptism' on the itinerary. You really need to brush up on your religion."

Zion looked so perturbed that I struggled not to smile.

"I'm so sorry," I said, my voice low. "Let's get you up, Sister Gerianne."

"Let me handle it this time," Ida Belle said, wading in. "I think you've got bigger fish to fry," she said to Zion.

The angry woman on the bank glanced at the three Barbies then back at Gertie as she tapped her fingers on her arm. Zion hurried over to explain.

"The sister has bad knees. I was trying to assist her with rising when she lost her balance and fell into me. We were just on the edge of the bank and took a tumble down into the bayou."

"And you just happened to lose your pants as you went?" she asked.

"Yes."

When the woman gave him a disbelieving look, he threw his hands in the air. "She's a nun, for Christ's sake!"

Ida Belle and Gertie both automatically made the sign of the cross, and he gave them an apologetic look as the woman spun around and stomped off toward the office, shooting the three Barbies an angry glare as she went.

"I apologize," Zion said. "My wife has clearly gotten the wrong impression, although how she could...never mind. Let's push smoothies back half an hour. Some of us need to shower and change."

"And apparently pick pants with a tighter waistband," Ida Belle said and looked over at Gertie. "Let's go before you flash any more of God's children with those completely inappropriate underclothes."

"They're not inappropriate if no one sees them," Gertie argued.

"God sees everything," Ida Belle said and gave Zion another withering glance.

I looked over at the Barbies, who still stood there not uttering a word. "I'm so sorry we've disrupted your peace," I said.

One of them laughed. "This is the most entertainment we've had on a mini-vacation since that time we got on a boat with randos in Florida and ended up in Cuba. Thought they weren't going to let us out—the Cuban government I mean, not the randos."

The other two perked up at the memory and nodded.

I gave them a smile and a half wave and we set off for our cabin.

"Are you trying to blow this?" Ida Belle asked. "Zion might have to cut this whole thing short if he can't sort out his wife."

Gertie laughed. "I would say it's clear who wears the pants in the family, but that setup was just too easy."

"She didn't look pleased at the other guests either," Ida Belle said.

"Probably because they were staring at Zion like he's a prime cut of beef and he was flashing his sexy underwear around," Gertie said.

"The flashing was all your fault," Ida Belle said, "but I have a feeling she's still not going to like it."

I nodded. "I wonder if she knows about Eleanor. Obviously she knows about her if Zion was in business with her, but does she *know* about her?"

"Women always know," Gertie said. "They might not admit it if they're not wanting to subject themselves to pressure from others to bail, but they know. Probably why she jumped straight to mad instead of concern for him physically."

"She looked young," I said. "Midtwenties maybe?"

Ida Belle nodded. "A good ten younger than him or better and at that age, it's a huge difference."

"And Eleanor was ten plus years older than him," Gertie

said. "I mean, does he really think people don't see what's going on?"

"I guess as long as his targets are willing to stick their heads in the sand, he can still work the situation," Ida Belle said.

We headed into the cabin and Gertie went to hop in the shower. I was hanging our habits out the window to dry when Ida Belle's phone rang. She pulled it out of her pocket and frowned at the display.

"It's Mildred," she said before answering.

"Oh, Ida Belle," Mildred wailed. "It's just too awful."

"What's happened?" Ida Belle asked and put her on speaker.

The bathroom door flew open and Gertie stood there, towel wrapped around her and dripping on the wood floor.

"Carter was just here. He was asking me all these questions about Eleanor and drug use. I told him my sister didn't use drugs. She rarely even had a drink. And if she was going to use something, why on earth would she take barbiturates? Eleanor was pessimistic enough as it was. She didn't need chemicals to bring her down even further."

"Drugs showed in her tox screen?" Ida Belle asked.

"That's what Carter said. And she'd taken them recently, probably right before she went into the sauna. There's just no way she'd do something that foolish."

"Mildred, this is Fortune. Did Eleanor have anything to eat or drink before she went into the sauna?"

"Not at the office. When she grabbed her keys after that fight with Zion, she headed straight for her cabin. If she had anything when she got there, the ME would know that too, right?"

"Anything she consumed would be in her stomach, yes, but

they might not have finished the autopsy yet. The drugs would show in her bloodstream."

"I just don't believe it. I don't care what that test says. My sister was not some junkie."

"No one is saying that," Ida Belle said. "Are you sure there wasn't anything bothering Eleanor? Something she might have self-medicated over? If she wasn't really familiar with drugs, she could have made a bad choice."

"And then gone into a sauna and killed herself?" Mildred started to cry. "That doesn't make sense. None of this makes sense."

"I don't want to upset you any more than you already are," I said, "but did Eleanor own a gun?"

"Of course. Doesn't everyone in these parts?"

"Did she have a .357 Sig?"

"I don't know. She carried a nine, like me. I never knew her or Father to own one and Mother never would touch one, but who knows what either of them acquired while I was gone, and then Jasper would have had his own preferences... Is that...?"

"Yes. Carter didn't ask you about it?"

"No. I guess maybe he didn't think it mattered since it had to be her that...you know. And surely it would have been registered to her, Father, or Jasper."

"I'm sure you're right. Did Carter give you any more information?"

"No. And I was too flustered to ask anything. He did his best not to upset me, but I couldn't help it with what he was asking."

"Of course you were upset," Ida Belle said. "No one is expecting you not to be."

"And then that parasite Zion called me this morning, asking about the bookings for the retreat and if I'd run the credit cards. Like I'm going to charge people who were staying at a crime scene."

"I'm so sorry," Ida Belle said. "Is there anything we can do to help?"

She sniffed. "I know what you girls get up to...what Fortune does for a living. I need you to figure out what happened to my sister. Find out who gave her those drugs, because none of this was like her. Doing drugs, making deals with that snake Zion. I know I haven't been around for a long time, but I still say she wasn't herself. Something was off."

"I agree it all sounds strange," Ida Belle said. "We're out of town overnight but will be back later tomorrow."

"Do you think Carter will tell you guys something? Because I get the feeling he's not leveling with me."

"Carter would tell you before he told me," I said. "He can't talk about an ongoing investigation, especially now as he's being audited by the state police. Not like he would have talked before, but he's not going to give an inch on anything. The investigation will be strictly by the book. He can't afford to deviate, even a little, if he wants to win the election."

"Is that who that fool with him was? I was afraid he was a new deputy. Strolled in my house like he owned the place and never introduced himself. Rude is what he was. I'm sorry Carter's dealing with that but glad that guy won't be sticking around to police in these parts. We don't need any of that."

"Mildred, I hate to ask," I began, "but do you know what Eleanor's agreement with Zion was? I assume you signed the contract, right?"

"Ha! I didn't even see the contract. Mildred was the executor of the trust. She didn't have to get my permission for anything."

"But surely, as a beneficiary, you had some input into how your inheritance was being used," I said.

"Wasn't my inheritance. I get a small monthly draw and that's it. The bottom line is Father rewarded Eleanor for sticking around and punished me for leaving. Not that I'm complaining, mind you. I wouldn't have stuck around for Rockefeller's money."

"So what happens to the assets in the trust now?" I asked.

"To be honest, I'm not sure. I never saw all the paperwork. The lawyer explained to me what my part was, and that was that. I didn't ask to see anything. Wouldn't be able to decipher that legalese even if I did."

"I think you should call the lawyer and ask him these questions," I said. "And see if you can find the contract between Zion and Eleanor. You need to know what the legal obligations are now."

"Do you think he did something to her—you know, got his hands on the cabins but didn't want what came with it?"

"I'm not saying that. I just think you need to get your lawyer on this right away. Let us work on what happened to Eleanor."

She sniffed again. "Okay. I can do that. At least I'll feel like I'm doing something. Just sitting here stewing has my back in spasms."

"Put your heating pad on it and try to relax," Ida Belle said. "Maybe a shot of that expensive scotch will take the edge off."

"I'll try it. I'm so sorry to burden you with this, but I didn't know who else to call. I don't have much, but I can pay you."

"We'll worry about that later," I said. "I'll bring over some client paperwork so that you have confidentiality, but let's not worry about the money right now. You've got enough going on."

"Thank you."

She choked on the last words, then disconnected.

Ida Belle shook her head. "I have to agree with Mildred on

this one. I just don't see Eleanor taking downers. She'd already lost her mother and her husband and not only held everything together but took Mildred in and started her own business. None of that spells weak to me."

"But if Zion dumped her after inking a deal, that changes things," Gertie asked. "Maybe it was the final straw of loss that sent her over the edge."

"We've seen stranger things," I said.

"He's supposed to be the expert on all that mind-body stuff, right?" Gertie asked. "Shouldn't he have been able to see if she was at risk and tried to help her?"

I nodded. "Unless he was the one putting her there deliberately."

"Which moves beyond scamming and into downright evil."

"Get back in the shower and stop dripping on the floor," Ida Belle said. "What reason would Zion have to want her dead? The retreat just opened, and if he's asking about running credit cards, then he clearly needs the money. Why kill the golden goose when you've barely gotten the doors open?"

Gertie shrugged. "Maybe that goose was going to start honking to his wife."

She disappeared back into the bathroom and Ida Belle looked over at me, her expression grim.

"It looks like Gertie might have been right about this after all."

CHAPTER SEVEN

With Gertie 'laundered' and all of us back in the habit, so to speak, we headed to the dining area at the main building for what was certain to be horrible smoothies. Fortunately, we'd tapped into Gertie's snack stash and had some pretzels and beef jerky before we left. At least we wouldn't starve.

Given what we'd learned from Mildred, I had to find a way to accelerate my play, which meant either making time for Zion to snoop through my paperwork or cornering him for more private conversation about my situation. I'd have to wait and see his demeanor and how the smoothie snack time played out before I decided which route was going to work best. The number one factor being whether or not his wife was there. I had a feeling that as long as the Barbies were in residence, she would be hovering, which complicated everything given our short time frame in which to work.

The Barbies were already sitting at one of the round tables when we walked in and they looked over and smiled. They'd all changed into coordinating yoga outfits, each in a different color, all of which flattered the group as a whole. I had a feeling it was an intentional move as they made a striking picture, sitting there like a pastel sunset.

Blue Barbie waved.

"Are you okay?" she asked Gertie.

"Oh heck, I'm fine," Gertie said. "Been down on my knees plenty of times in the church. Getting wet along with it wasn't that big a deal."

"You were laid flat out," Ida Belle said, "after rolling down the bank with a man on top of you. You're going to be saying rosaries for the next fifty years to get past that one."

Gertie waved a hand in dismissal. "Ain't got fifty years, and if God didn't want that man landing on me then he should have gifted him with more strength."

Pink Barbie giggled and I gave her a warm smile. They appeared to be into Zion, which meant if I could gain their confidence, I might get some information out of them. And if people didn't trust a nun, then they weren't going to trust anyone.

I took the lead and headed toward their table, bypassing the other, and asked politely, "Is it all right if we sit with you?"

The Barbies looked pleased and all nodded and gave me genuine smiles. I wondered if I hadn't been a little harsh with my initial judgment. Despite their looks, arguably shallow pursuits, and somewhat questionable ethics, given the pursuit was married, they seemed nice enough. And not remotely suspicious, which was ideal.

"Have you ladies done one of these retreats before?" I asked.

They all nodded, earnest expressions on their faces.

"Oh yes," Purple Barbie said. "We try to do at least one of these a month. We're all in sales, and it's horribly stressful. The only good thing is our schedules are somewhat flexible as long as we're meeting numbers, so we can do these mini-retreats during the week when the rates are so much better. Most all of the places offer some kind of a deal at least every couple months. So we've been trying different places for about a year now."

"And do you find that they help with stress?"

"Definitely," Pink Barbie said. "We were all ready to either take permanently to the bottle or start selling something entirely different on Bourbon Street. Oh my God! I'm so sorry! Oh no! Now I'm swearing on God. I'm definitely going to hell."

"It's okay," I said. "Believe it or not, nuns have a sense of humor too."

"Sister Eileen doesn't," Gertie said, giving Ida Belle a disgruntled look.

"That's because I've been living with you for forty years," Ida Belle said. "I would think the Lord would be done testing my patience, but apparently not."

I raised one hand as if to say 'see' and they all laughed.

"So is this your first time doing a retreat with Zion?" I asked.

They all shook their heads.

"We did one here two months ago," Blue Barbie said. "The location is lovely as far as being serene goes and the cabins have good beds."

"The smoothies aren't great though," Purple Barbie said. "Fair warning."

"Sister Gerianne brought snacks," I said. "We might have imbibed before heading down here."

"Smart," Blue said, and they all nodded.

"So is all of this normal?" I asked. "I mean, I've never been to one of these before. Zion seems nice enough, but that woman who stomped down to the lake didn't seem very peaceful."

Pink Barbie rolled her eyes. "That was his wife, Sapphire. She doesn't like women around her husband."

I blinked and stared. "But it's a yoga retreat. I'm making an assumption, but isn't it usually women who attend these things?"

"Pretty much," Blue said. "You get the occasional guy whose girl dragged him along or some sad boy who is desperate for a solution to all his problems, but mostly, it's women. And let's face it, if you're straight and have a pulse, you're going to notice Zion, even if that's not your play."

The other two nodded.

"She was so rude last time we were here that we were going to take this place out of rotation," Pink said, "but then Zion contacted us and offered us a big discount if we'd try this flash yoga thing he was wanting to test."

"So we chucked the one we had in mind and booked here again," Purple said. "But now I'm almost wishing we hadn't. I mean, I like his classes, and Zion's friendly and definitely not hard to look at, but it's hard to get all Zen with Sapphire glaring at you the entire time. If you're really worried about your husband cheating, then maybe don't marry men like Zion. He's clearly a player."

"What does he play?" I asked innocently, and they all giggled.

"A player is a man who likes to have a lot of women on the line at one time," Blue explained.

"He's a man-hoochie," Gertie said.

"Oh!" I said, widening my eyes. "I didn't mean to imply..."

They all laughed.

"You didn't imply anything," Pink said. "You probably assumed we were after him too, right? I know that's what Sapphire thinks."

"Well, you did say you found him attractive and you're

always dressed and made up so pretty, so I guess I thought—but that was before I knew he was married."

"Trust me, that doesn't change things for a lot of men," Blue said.

"Or the kind of women who chase them," Purple added.

Pink nodded. "But we're in sales, remember? Our biggest clients are married men. You show a little cleavage, smile a lot, and laugh at their inane jokes, and you can sell them anything."

"Exactly," Blue agreed. "But in this case, it's not the sale we're after but the discount. And trust me, it was a good one. Although I would have paid full price just to see Sister Geri-anne tackle him into the lake."

"I did no such thing," Gertie said. "The man needs to stop all that pondering and pick up some weights. Can't handle a hundred and ten pounds."

Ida Belle snorted. "You haven't weighed a hundred and ten pounds since you were twelve. But he could probably do with some squats."

"Like the priests are any better," Gertie said. "Can't even lift a communion chalice unless they're using both hands."

"It's a ceremony," Ida Belle said. "They're supposed to use two hands. What do you want them to do—put the wine in a funnel and pass it around like a fraternity party?"

"It would speed up mass, which would be fine by me," Gertie said. "Those benches are hard and my sciatica is kicking before they get through the opening announcements."

The Barbies all giggled again, and I couldn't help but smile. Ida Belle and Gertie were really playing the grouchy-old-nuns role to the hilt. The door to the dining area opened, and Zion walked in carrying two pitchers of brown liquid. Sapphire walked behind him with a tray of glasses. She shot a dirty look at the Barbies before setting the tray on the bar and then stomping to a two-top in the corner and flopping down, arms crossed as she glared at all of us.

Gertie leaned over toward the Barbies. "She doesn't act old enough to be wearing a training bra, much less be married."

They all covered their mouths as it was clear by his stiffening that Zion had heard her not-so-low comment. He looked over at Gertie as he poured the brown liquid into the glasses.

"I hope you're doing okay after our tumble."

"Why is everyone treating me like I'm some relic that will break at the first mishap? I'm not asking *you* if you're okay."

He forced a smile. "Great. Then you'll be able to complete the retreat with us. First, we're going to hydrate and replenish nutrients with a smoothie."

He passed the glasses of brown stuff around the table. The Barbies all took small sips, so I followed suit. I'd drunk and eaten strange things from all over the world, so how bad could it be? I got my answer quickly. Bad. Really bad. It was so bitter it tasted as though someone had picked weeds from the woods and put them through a juicer.

Ida Belle lifted her glass and downed the entire thing without stopping, and I was forced to admit she might just be tougher than I was. Gertie eyed the glass suspiciously.

"What's in it?" she asked.

"Cucumber, kelp, kale, apples, carrots, and some spices that help with cleansing your body."

Gertie took a whiff of it and pushed the glass back. "I'll just remain toxic. Unless you want me to be in my cabin 'cleansing' for the rest of the retreat."

"I told you no one likes those smoothies," Sapphire said. "People aren't cows. They don't want to drink grass. Why don't you throw some ice cream and root beer in a mug? You'd get more takers that way."

"Now you're talking!" Gertie agreed.

Zion was clearly annoyed with her comment. "You may be fine poisoning your body with such things, but that is not what I'm teaching people to do." He gave us an apologetic look. "If you'll excuse me for just a moment. Please enjoy your drinks. We will meet at five by the bayou for yoga."

He headed straight for the door but flashed a look over at Sapphire on his way out. She gave us all a triumphant smile and followed him. Pink and Blue jumped up with their glasses, one of them grabbing Purple's and the other grabbing mine, and rushed over to the sink behind the bar and dumped them out.

"You didn't want that, right?" Pink said as she set my empty glass in front of me. "I thought I read your face right, although you are excellent at hiding things."

"It was horrible," I agreed. "Thank you."

"Why didn't you take mine?" Gertie asked. "Now it's just sitting here, smelling like someone plowed a field."

"If we dumped yours out, he'd know that's what we did," Blue said. "Because he knows you're not drinking yours."

Gertie grabbed the edges of the table and pushed herself up. "What ever happened to common sense?"

She walked over to the sink, dumped the entire glass out, and left it in the sink.

"Problem solved," she said as she sat back down. "Maybe that smell will clear out before Christ returns."

The three Barbies looked a bit sheepish and Pink gave Ida Belle a curious look. "Did you actually like that?"

"Don't know," Ida Belle said. "Burned my taste buds off twenty years or so ago. Makes keeping a diet easy enough."

"What do you think that was about?" I asked, inclining my head toward the door.

"Maybe he's going to remind his wife who the head of the household is," Ida Belle said.

Purple frowned. "I don't know. Last time we were here, I overheard her complaining to him about having to live among strangers all the time. I got the impression she wasn't keen on the whole retreat thing."

"That's probably true," Ida Belle said. "Especially when the guest list includes women who look like you and the dress code is tight and clingy."

"Man's gotta make a living," Gertie said. "You young folk might find him nice to look at, but that's not going to pay the bills. It'd be a waste of space to keep all of this for just the two of them, although I can see why they might have the need for separate spaces with those personalities."

I nodded. "I suppose teaching classes at a gym or rec center wouldn't be nearly as profitable as doing your own thing, especially if you already own the facility and can rent it out like they do the cabins."

"That's true enough," Pink said, "but if he really wanted to make bank, he'd have started a cult. The real money is in religion. Oh my God! I'm so sorry."

"Ha!" Gertie said. "Got expensive art hanging like postage stamps in the Vatican. You ain't wrong. Guess that's what they call an 'investment' though."

"It's not really an investment unless it's income-producing or you're holding it to sell," Purple said. "But 'sell' is the key word in that. It is, however, a common misconception."

Ida Belle raised one eyebrow.

"I'm in commercial real estate sales," she explained. "My father ran one of the biggest hedge funds in Atlanta before he passed. I could read a set of financials by first grade."

Interesting, I thought. The Barbies were turning out to be so much different from my original assessment.

"You didn't want to follow in his footsteps?" I asked.

"Absolutely not! That man worked himself into a heart

attack by fifty-five. There's too much life to live to go out that soon. I enjoy commercial real estate sales, and it satisfies my right and left brain requirements."

Blue snorted. "She's leaving out the part where she's not a Realtor—which is how she makes it sound. She buys the buildings, remodels them, then leases them out to businesses or turns them into condos. She is fabulous with design, so she gets to indulge the artsy side of her personality while still making money."

Pink nodded. "Work you do because you want to is completely different than work you do because you have to. I love my job but not like she does."

Purple blushed a bit. "I don't like to tell people all that. I don't want people to label me by my father's accomplishments. The whole 'trust fund' thing really gets on my nerves. I make my own way."

Ida Belle put her hand on Purple's and gave it a squeeze. "That's perfectly okay. You're doing something you're passionate about, and we'd all be better human beings if our life pursuits were our passions."

"If they're legal, sure," Gertie said, and everyone laughed.

I smiled but the wheels were turning. Did Zion know about Purple's portfolio? Likely, she started her business with inheritance and if her father was that wealthy, then there would have been press surrounding his death. Zion had our driver's licenses. It wouldn't be all that difficult to figure out that Purple was a high-net-worth individual with a lot of commercial real estate at her disposal.

Which put a completely different spin on the big discount Zion had offered the Barbies for this retreat. Maybe he was hoping to set up something with Purple. I wasn't sure how that would work with Sapphire hanging around, but it let me know that Zion was probably still on the prowl.

There was no doubt in my mind that he'd take a look at my documents at first opportunity. Maybe, if he'd managed to shed his wife, he was perusing them now. I was really glad I'd struck up a conversation with the Barbies because I had a feeling we were definitely on the right track. Now I just needed to figure out a way to have another conversation with Zion without Sapphire supervising.

———

AFTER SMOOTHIES, WE HEADED BACK TO THE CABIN. I'D already burned off the beef jerky and chips I'd had earlier and needed to hit Gertie's stash before we all had to go stand by the lake and bend like rubber. Plus, the habit was stifling hot and I was itching—quite literally—to rid myself of it for a bit.

The first thing I did when we went inside was check my backpack. Sure enough, the string I'd pulled through the clip was gone.

"He's been here," I said.

"Seriously!"

"Wow! He's not wasting any time!"

Ida Belle and Gertie both spoke at once.

I yanked the habit over my head and sat down at the table to dig through the pile of snacks. "Did one of you eat the Oreos?"

They both shook their heads.

"Ha," I said. "Then I guess Mr. Clean Eating took them because they're gone."

"He's a con artist," Ida Belle said. "But I still haven't completely figured out his play. This whole yoga retreat thing can't be a huge moneymaker. So why keep pushing that angle?"

"I don't know," I said, "but if the Barbies overheard things properly, then he married Sapphire to get a hold of this place."

"The Barbies?" Ida Belle asked.

I shrugged. "It seemed to fit. At first, anyway, but they're definitely smarter than they want people to think."

"They're smarter than they want *men* to think," Ida Belle said. "Shrewd saleswomen. I wonder just how much of a discount they got for this farce."

"Enough to make Sapphire angry about letting out her family's place to women I'm sure she considers skanks," I said.

Gertie nodded. "If I were her, I'd be on my way out before Zion figures out how to finagle her out of her property."

"It's probably all in a trust," Ida Belle said. "Lots of times it's set up so that a person is the beneficiary of the trust, but they have no ability to transfer assets to other people, even on death. Rich people don't like the idea of someone marrying their kids for the money and then divorcing them, and their assets leaving the family. A trust also keeps potential murders down among the wealthy as the assets rarely shift to someone who isn't blood."

"That's grim," I said.

"But an unfortunate reality," Ida Belle said. "How did the Heberts have their attorney write up your fake trust?"

"I think it's basically all within my control."

"Good," Ida Belle said. "I mean, not good if that was actually the case and you were really a naive nun, but good for getting Zion to bite."

"You think he'd actually attempt to get me to make him my beneficiary and then kill a nun?" I asked.

I had a pretty low opinion of most people, but that was really scraping the bottom of the barrel.

"He wouldn't be the first," Ida Belle said. "Well, maybe the first to kill a nun but only because most don't have assets. And not that he'd be successful in this case, but you know what I mean. We still don't know yet if he benefits from Eleanor's death so all of this is speculation at this point."

"Even if he benefits in some way, he didn't kill her," I said. "Not unless he can walk through walls."

"He could have given her the drugs, though," Gertie said. "He was there that day."

"I thought you said he'd left earlier," Ida Belle said.

"He did, but we didn't follow him to the parking lot and watch him drive off, and even if we had, that wouldn't have stopped him from returning, parking somewhere along the road in, and walking to Eleanor's cabin."

"We need to find out when Zion got back here," I said.

"How the heck do we do that?" Gertie asked.

"Sapphire."

Ida Belle and I answered at once.

"Oh, yeah. Let me handle that one," Gertie said. "If there's one thing I know it's a high school setup for gossip."

"Go for it. If you can keep Sapphire away long enough for me to plant more seeds with Zion, that would be great."

"We don't have much time to get information," Gertie said. "And I'm still afraid Carter might show up with that goon in tow, especially if Mildred throws around those accusations to the cops."

"Yeah, that thought has already crossed my mind," I said. "But as long as he doesn't see us, we're good."

"You think he'd recognize us?" Gertie asked.

I laughed. "In one second flat. But that idiot Calahan probably wouldn't. I get the impression he's not much of a critical thinker. Still, if they show up before this is over, we should definitely disappear."

Gertie nodded. "And my plan for bugging Zion's cabin?"

"It's too risky," Ida Belle said. "If we get caught then all this setup that Fortune has done is for nothing."

I tapped my fingers on the table. "I know it's risky, but I think I should. We're running against the clock here and we can't make this play a second time."

"Agreed," Gertie said. "Besides, there's no way someone like Zion is going to catch Fortune. She could run circles around him in her sleep."

"I'll need a distraction," I said. "When we're not in a group, we're at our cabins. So I have to have a way to get Zion and Sapphire out of their cabin, but not for an event I'm supposed to attend because it would look odd if I'm not there."

"Leave it to me," Gertie said. "I'll just need my other bag from the secret compartment in the SUV."

"Your *other* bag?" Ida Belle asked.

Gertie grinned. "That one doesn't have food."

CHAPTER EIGHT

Since Zion had already riffled through my paperwork and apparently stolen some contraband calories, I didn't figure he'd make a return visit to our cabin to snoop, so I headed to the SUV and retrieved Gertie's second handbag. This one weighed considerably more than her entire suitcase, which gave me pause, but I refused to open it. If I knew what she had in there, then I became responsible for what she might do with it. As long as I could plead ignorance, I was solid, which meant Carter was solid.

Gertie poked around in the bag for a bit, nodding and smiling, and snapped it shut when Ida Belle leaned over to take a peek.

"This is my mission," she said. "You just worry about playing lookout for Fortune."

"Stuff that under the mattress just in case anyone comes looking," I said. "We have to hurry or we're going to be late for yoga class. I can't believe those words just came out of my mouth."

We headed for the lake, Gertie still going at a slower pace, this time claiming it wasn't an act.

"I talked a good game, but that tumble with Zion tweaked my knee all over again," she said. "And just when Nora's latest brew was kicking in."

Ida Belle flinched but neither one of us asked any questions. Nora's concoctions were often potent and rarely legal. It was better not to know. We were the last ones at the lake—no surprise there—but Sapphire was nowhere in sight, which *was* surprising. Zion was standing in the midst of the Barbies, smiling and chatting as if his angry wife wasn't lurking behind a bush with a sniper rifle, and I wondered if he'd managed to calm her down or she'd decided that leaving was the best option. Either worked for me. Angry wives were not in my playbook, and we were at the two-minute warning.

"Ladies," Zion said as we approached. "I hope you enjoyed the smoothies."

"You know I didn't," Gertie said. "But I don't go anywhere without my own groceries. People eat too many odd things these days. All that health stuff when it doesn't make a bit of difference. When your number's up, it's up."

"I think the goal is to have a better quality of life before your bingo card expires," Zion said. "But we all have our own ideas about what that looks like."

"Mine looks like refined sugar, Cheetos, and cheap wine," Gertie said.

"Then let's start with some gentle stretching that's good for digestion," Zion said. "It will help process all that sugar and that will lead to better sleep."

"I sleep eight hours a night and take two hour-long naps a day," Gertie said.

"That's prayer time," Ida Belle said.

"So I prayed for more sleep and God answered."

"Everyone start with your feet shoulder-width apart," Zion said, trying to get control of his class.

We all turned our attention to him, and he took us through some very basic yoga positions, offering modifications for Ida Belle and Gertie. I didn't have problems with any of it, of course, and Zion gave me an appreciative nod.

"You're doing very well, Sister Britney," he said. "You have excellent balance."

"That's because she hasn't been hauling double-Ds around for thirty years," Gertie said.

"Those Ds have been sitting in your lap for thirty years," Ida Belle said. "You've been hauling 'em for at least sixty."

"Thank you," I said to Zion. "I'm really enjoying this, which I'll admit, surprises me. I think I will continue some of these exercises and stretches when I return to the convent."

Zion looked pleased. "I can print out some of the poses we've done so that you'll have a reference if you'd like."

"That would be wonderful. I know they say everything is online these days, but we only have one computer and time is limited. Mostly the nuns just use it to email family."

The Barbies all stared.

"You don't have smartphones?" Pink asked.

"The Mother Superior has some that she lends out when sisters are going to be away from the convent for errands or events," I said. "But they're only to be used in case of emergency. We don't have our own personal devices."

"We're *in* the world not *of* the world," Ida Belle said. "And the internet is all about the 'of' part. It's better if we don't dwell there."

Zion nodded. "Probably better if all of us didn't dwell there, but this is where the rest of us are today, I'm afraid. I'll print those out and then you'll have copies so you don't have to try to remember everything."

"Thank you, that's very kind," I said.

Zion looked around the group. "Dinner is in an hour."

"I hope it's not one of those smoothies again," Gertie grumbled.

"I'll be serving grilled red snapper and asparagus with fresh fruit for dessert."

"I could probably make do with that," Gertie said. "Is there booze?"

"We want to cleanse our bodies," Zion said. "Alcohol is problematic for the body and the spirit."

"Bull crap," Gertie said. "We drink wine in church. If it's so bad for us, why are we doing it there?"

"We'll have mineral water," Zion said, not even trying to argue a completely valid point.

"I'm hitting the shower," Purple said. "This humidity is killer. I don't know how you ladies are handling it in those long robes and with your head covered so it can't even breathe."

Ida Belle nodded. "It is a bit like being in a sauna all day."

"It's torture is what it is," Gertie said. "If the church wasn't run by men, we might get a fair shake."

"No one's holding you hostage," Ida Belle said. "Shed your robes and launch into society."

Gertie stared at her as if she was crazy. "That crowd is on a bullet train to hell. I sometimes wonder where you get your ideas. We took vows before all these modern ideas invaded the church."

She shook her head and went limping off. Ida Belle sighed and followed suit. I gave the Barbies a wave and set off after them. The Barbies headed toward their cabins in the other direction.

"Sister Britney," Zion called, and I turned around.

He held up my hand towel. "You forgot your towel."

"Oh! Thank you."

I went back to retrieve the towel I'd deliberately left behind and he met me halfway.

"I'll walk back with you until the path branches if you don't mind," he said.

"That would be fine. I really do appreciate your offer to print those yoga positions. I know Sister Gerianne is a bit of a trial at times, but I think they did a good thing by bringing me here. I'm not as stressed as I was when I got here."

"That's good to hear. So have you made a decision on what to do with your aunt's property?"

I sighed. "No. Not completely. I know I can't sell it, and I can't run it. I really don't want to hire a management company because then it still all comes back to me, but one of the other ladies at the retreat was talking about her job in real estate, and she mentioned something about leasing. I don't know that it's the kind of property I could lease out in its entirety, but it's something to explore, right? Maybe someone retired would want to live there and run it, although I suppose corporations are more likely to have the funds."

He nodded, barely able to control his excitement. "You might consider splitting profit with someone instead of a fixed lease. They'd be responsible for the maintenance, taxes, and insurance and the like, and they'd do all the on-site work of getting and servicing clientele and work out an equitable split of the profit."

"Do you think someone would be interested in such an arrangement?"

"I think the right person would. And such a setup would allow for someone without a ton of resources to take on a passion project if they didn't have a set amount of lease fees to make every month. That way you've got someone with a vested interest in making a profit and maintaining the property as it affects their bottom line as well."

"That makes a lot of sense. I'd much rather have an arrangement with an individual or a couple than a corporation.

My aunt made sure guests were treated like family. It never felt impersonal. I'd like that to remain the same."

"I think the personal touch is invaluable. Obviously, my entire business is about catering to individual needs. In a group setting, of course, but by keeping groups small, I have the ability to modify things as needed to assist with any guest's special requirement."

I laughed. "Like Sister Gerianne and her knees."

He smiled. "Sister Gerianne presents a few challenges, but I can tell she cares deeply about you if she's willing to go this far out of her comfort zone."

I nodded. "The sisters are like mothers to me. Well, grandmothers might be more appropriate, but don't tell them I said so."

"Your secret is safe with me." He was silent for a bit. "I wonder...no, never mind."

"Tell me."

"It's too much to ask."

"I can't imagine what I could do for you, but if there's some way for me to repay your kindness, I'd gladly offer it."

"I guess I was just thinking that your aunt's property would make a lovely retreat. The ocean has healing power, you know. And a warm setting would provide an escape for people with many ailments, arthritis especially. It's much harder to fill slots locally during the winter. I offer indoor classes as well, of course, but it's not the same as being one with nature."

"I can see that. I never really thought about a retreat. I just figured it would continue as vacation cottages as before, but after seeing what you do here, I can picture it. It would be nice to have a yoga class right there on the beach or meditate at sunrise."

"I think it would be very healing."

I pursed my lips and scrunched my brow as if in thought.

"So how would that work? Would we just do a contract, and you'd run the retreat for a percentage of the profit? What would happen to this place?"

"I'd keep this running, of course, but I could hire a manager to oversee the day-to-day and I could lead special retreats at both locations. Now that I've dialed in my programs and menus, I've been considering expansion. I hope you don't take offense to my saying so but it's almost as if you coming to this retreat was prophetic."

I smiled. "Yes. I guess it was."

———

"WHAT A SNAKE," GERTIE SAID WHEN I FINISHED TELLING them about our conversation.

"He definitely didn't waste any time," Ida Belle said.

I nodded. "Makes me wonder if he's just taking advantage of an opportunity presenting itself or looking for the quickest way out of Dodge."

"Between his wife and his dead business partner, my guess is both," Gertie said. "I wonder if that's the kind of deal he made with Eleanor?"

"It must be something along those lines, or he wouldn't have been interested in the accounts receivable," Ida Belle said.

"How would something like that work?" I asked. "Because in theory, it doesn't sound horrible, so why did I feel the need to shower after our conversation?"

"Ha!" Ida Belle said. "Because a place with that kind of deal will never show a profit, that's why. The scammer knows every trick in the book to take in the money but never show anything left to split with his partner. If you're not on-site to monitor everything, you'll never see a dime."

"So cash off books for rentals, fake invoices for expenses," I said.

"The masters of the craft even set up other businesses and pay them," Ida Belle said. "Caterers, cleaning services, plumbers, and other contractors. You can run thousands of dollars every month away from the property and it would all look completely legit."

I sighed. "Why don't people work that hard on something legal? It seems like a lot of effort to risk going to jail over."

"Stupidity and an overwhelming sense of entitlement mostly," Ida Belle said. "But the pros pick their targets well, so they get away with it a lot."

Gertie nodded. "Look at Eleanor—an older woman, recently widowed, and whose mother just passed. Someone who isn't that attractive and then this young, good-looking man comes along, building her up. If you were really a young nun with no street smarts, you'd be easy pickings to a pro."

I frowned. "Do we really think Zion is a pro? He just seems more opportunistic than deliberate."

Ida Belle's phone rang and she checked the display. "Maybe we'll find out. It's Mildred."

"Oh, Ida Belle, I don't know what to do!" Mildred cried out. "It's just horrible."

"Calm down. I've got you on speaker. Tell us what happened."

"That murdering Zion Gates is what happened. I talked to the estate attorney and his agreement with Eleanor gives him the cabins on her death."

"What?"

"No way!"

"You've got to be kidding me!"

We all responded at the same time.

"How could she do that?" Ida Belle asked.

"Because she was the executor and the main heir, and because my father didn't have any provisions to prevent something like that from happening. The agreement she had with him was a royalty split on profit for the yoga retreat, which still wasn't a good contract in my opinion since she owned it all and put up the money for the improvements, but at least it wasn't straight up immoral."

"Will the contract hold up?" I asked.

"I don't know. I mean, the attorney said the documents she signed appear to be legit. They were drafted by an attorney in NOLA—probably working for Zion—but the estate attorney is going to contact him and make sure everything was aboveboard. He killed her. He might not have pulled the trigger, but he had to have caused it somehow. Got her to sign off on the biggest asset she had and then killed her."

"I'm so sorry," Gertie said. "But don't you worry. We're already on the case. If anyone can get the goods on Zion, it's Fortune."

"Please, whatever you can do. I still have the house, but the bank accounts for the retreat are low. She spent so much on getting it ready for that nonsense. And I don't know when I'll get access to Eleanor's personal accounts or if there's even anything left in them. There aren't high-paying accounting jobs in Mudbug and with my back problems, I couldn't handle a commute to New Orleans every day. But this place wouldn't sell for all that much and even if I did sell it, I'd be paying more in rent somewhere else. I should have stayed in Colorado."

"Let's deal with one thing at a time or you'll get overwhelmed," Ida Belle said. "You've got the estate attorney checking on things. We're looking into Zion. Have you told Carter all this?"

"Yes. I called him right after I talked to the attorney."

"Great," I said. "I know it's impossible to do so, but please try not to stress. The last thing we need is for you to work yourself into a heart attack."

"But I need to do something. What can I do? Give me an assignment. I can't just sit here, or it will drive me up the wall. And it's not like I can go out jogging or something to burn off the energy."

"Look for any correspondence between Eleanor and Zion. If you have access to Eleanor's email or text messages, go through them and see if you can find anything that might help your attorney build a case for fraud."

"Carter took her phone, but I can probably get her text messages off her laptop."

"Good. And go through her paperwork as well. I know most everything is digital these days, but you never know what might be important. Send me anything you question even a tiny bit. Let me be the judge on whether or not it's important."

She blew out a breath. "Thank you. I feel better knowing you believe me. Carter is a nice man, but I don't think he's jumped to the same conclusion as me."

"Carter has to have evidence in order to do his job, and his hands are tied in regard to how he can obtain it. Mine aren't. Start digging and let me know if you come up with anything."

"Hang in there, Mildred," Gertie said before I disconnected.

"Well, now we know why Zion would want to kill Eleanor even though the retreat just opened," Ida Belle said.

"It's a heck of a motive," I agreed. "But even if we can prove he gave her the drugs, it's a hard task to prove the psychological pressure caused her to kill herself."

"Maybe she didn't kill herself," Gertie said.

"Then how did he manage to pull the dead bolt after leaving the cabin?" Ida Belle said.

Gertie frowned. "Yeah, I keep forgetting that part. But if all Carter gets on him is a drug charge, that probably isn't enough to keep him from getting the cabins. Not if the documents Eleanor signed are legitimate."

I shook my head. The further into this investigation we got, the muddier it became. And the higher the difficulty level rose. We went from trying to find out if Eleanor was being scammed to trying to find out if someone had contributed to her suicide by providing her with drugs. Now we had to figure out a way to save Mildred's inheritance from the very person who likely set it all in motion, even if he didn't actually pull the trigger.

————

THE BARBIES WERE ALREADY IN THE DINING AREA WHEN WE arrived, showing off their third wardrobe change of the day. They went for bolder colors for dinner, all wearing matching sets of yoga pants and tanks, each in their signature color—Pink, Purple, and Blue—but this time, they were more jewel-toned than light and serene. They still, of course, looked stunning as a group, which I assumed was the point.

I gave them all a big smile when we sat.

"I just love your clothes," I said. "They're so bright and cheery and with you all together, it's like a painting."

They looked pleased with the compliment.

"We take an afternoon off to shop for these retreats," Pink said. "It's part of the decompression before the Zen."

"Remember that time we went snow skiing?" Blue said. "That one was tough, finding the right colors, especially for outside sports, fancy dinner, and hot tub."

Purple nodded. "I thought we'd never find snow boots that came in all three colors."

Gertie frowned. "I don't see how all that shopping is decompressing. Sounds stressful to me. I'm glad we all have to wear the same thing and what we've got on underneath don't matter."

"It matters if you're rolling down a hill and into a lake," Ida Belle said.

"That was a fluke," Gertie said. "At least we're getting real food tonight. I'm going to run out of snacks if he doesn't cough up something besides those awful smoothies."

"We had the snapper last time we were here," Blue said. "It was really good."

"The service wasn't," Pink said drily.

"Sapphire helped Zion get the food out," Purple explained. "It was a bit like being back in the cafeteria in elementary school. Lots of frowning and shoving of plates."

"I was a bit surprised she wasn't lurking for class this afternoon," Blue said. "I wonder if she's finally had her fill and taken off?"

"Why would she take off?" Purple asked. "She owns this property. If anything, she should send him sniffing somewhere else."

I gave her an inquiring look, and she waved a hand at me. "I'm nosy. It's the real estate thing. I look up properties everywhere we go."

"She does," Pink agreed. "And then she buys things. She bought the condo we stayed at in the Virgin Islands, a chalet in Colorado, and that cute studio in New York City, which is where we go for some of our advanced shopping trips."

"I don't like a regular trip to Walmart," Ida Belle said. "I have no idea what 'advanced' shopping entails, but I'm not a fan."

"Sounds like she's acquiring more real estate than clothes," Gertie said.

Pink nodded. "There's that cabana in Cancun. Gorgeous beaches just a block away."

"And don't forget that percentage ownership she has of a ranch in Montana," Blue said. "We're definitely going back there in the fall. All those lovely mountains."

Pink giggled. "And lovely cowboys. Although ranches don't make any money. That one wasn't based on a great business decision regardless of what she tells you."

Purple laughed. "Sure it was. The property has increased in value by 40 percent since I invested."

"Doesn't matter what it's worth unless you're going to sell, remember?" Blue asked, grinning.

"Okay, maybe the cowboys influenced me a little," Purple agreed. "But it's so pretty there."

The door at the back of the room opened and Zion entered, carrying a tray of dinner rolls. I could see a kitchen in the room beyond and wondered how much of our conversation he'd overheard. Every time we talked to the Barbies, I got a clearer picture on why he was offering them discounts. Purple, with all her real estate investments and deep pockets, was like hitting the lottery to someone like Zion. Unfortunately for him, Purple already had his number and was playing the player, which suited me just fine.

"Ladies," he said. "I hope you're all refreshed and relaxed. I have an excellent meal prepared for you and will begin serving. The dinner rolls were baked fresh this afternoon, the red snapper comes off a fishing boat at a dock in New Orleans, and the fruit is organic and shipped from a Florida farm."

He placed small plates in front of us and three tubs of butter for the rolls, then headed out.

"I wonder if they churned the butter," Gertie grumbled.

Pink pulled off a corner of one of the rolls and put the

tiniest bit of butter on it. "Nope. It's Kerrygold, but the rolls are home baked."

"I suppose it wouldn't look good to serve packaged rolls with all those preservatives," I said.

"It would if all people are going to eat is a corner," Gertie said, and helped herself to a whole roll and set about buttering it up. "You girls need to eat more. I could fit all three of you in my habit and people would never know you were there."

"Fifty bucks says she has a bag of chocolate in her suitcase," Purple said.

"You're one to talk, Fritos and bean dip," Pink said.

We all looked at Blue, who held up her hands. "I'm beef jerky. I do the low carb thing."

"I like all those," Gertie said. "If I run out of snacks, I know where to go."

Zion served the fish, and I had to give him points there. Even Ida Belle looked mollified after the first bite, and she was very judgmental on fish preparation. The asparagus was a little too crunchy and could have used a couple minutes more on the grill, but it had a good flavor and paired well with the fish.

When we started on the fish, Sapphire flounced out with a pitcher of water to refill our glasses, her face pinched with tension as she attempted to force a pleasant expression. She would have looked less threatening if she'd just kept glaring. When she was done sloshing water, she sat at a two-top with Zion in the corner, both of them eating in complete silence.

Pink glanced at them, then looked at us and raised an eyebrow.

"Trouble in paradise," she said, her voice low. "I wonder if we should worry about aloe vera in our water."

"Well, it would fit that whole cleanse narrative they've got going," Gertie said.

I nodded and took another bite of the fish but now that I

knew Zion and Sapphire were both out of their cabin, it was the perfect opportunity for me to bounce out and get the bugs in place. I was just about to make my excuse and getaway when there was a knock on the dining room door.

Then Carter's voice called out. "Is anyone here? It's Sheriff LeBlanc."

CHAPTER NINE

GERTIE'S EYES WIDENED AND SHE LOOKED OVER AT ME, BUT I shook my head a tiny bit. I didn't know if the place had a back door and even if it did, all three of us getting up and running out would look stranger than sitting here, continuing to eat our dinner, and letting whatever was about to happen play out. With any luck, Zion would hustle them out of the dining area before Carter locked in on us.

Unfortunately for me, I always sat facing the door, so I was visible as soon as they walked in. Zion jumped up as the door eased open and Carter peered inside. When he caught sight of Zion headed his way, he stepped in the room, Calahan right on his heels. I dropped my head down instinctively but since it would look odd if I wasn't interested in the cops showing up, I forced myself to raise my head back up.

Carter picked that exact moment to swing his gaze over to our table, and I saw his jaw flex as he locked in on me. I have to give him credit for immediately shifting focus away from us, but it was too late. Calahan was already eyeing us, a confused look on his face.

"I need to speak to you about Eleanor Stout," Carter said.

"*We* need to speak to you," Calahan said.

Carter's jaw clenched. "Last time I checked, you are no part of this investigation. Nor are you qualified to be. Mr. Gates, if we could step into the other room?"

"What is this about?" Sapphire demanded as she stormed up to glare at Zion. "You told me you were going to end things with that woman."

Calahan gave Sapphire a once-over. "Oh, things have ended all right. The woman's dead."

The color drained out of Sapphire's face, and she stared at Zion for several seconds. Zion either had no pulse or was putting all that meditation to use, because he didn't so much as flinch. I think that was the first time Sapphire actually got a clear picture of the kind of man she'd married.

"I'm going to my cousin's," she said and fled the building.

Carter whipped around to face Calahan. "You will refrain from providing any details of *my* investigation. If you can't control your mouth, then I suggest you head back to New Orleans, before I file a complaint and you find yourself in the spotlight."

Calahan opened his mouth and I was certain he wanted to lay into Carter, but he gave us all a glance before wisely shutting his trap. Too many witnesses to his breaking of protocol.

Carter gestured to the door and followed Zion out, avoiding looking at us altogether. But Calahan was irritated and wanted a place to expend his energy. Since he was supposed to be an observer and therefore couldn't interject himself into questioning Zion, I guess he decided he'd head to our table so he could pretend to be a real detective. He'd already locked in on the Barbies, and his leering grin as he approached and looked down at them had my trigger finger itching.

"Good evening, ladies," he said with a smug smile. "I'm

Lieutenant Calahan. State police. I just wanted to make sure you're all okay over here."

Given the Barbies' talent for getting a quick read on people, especially men, I had no doubt they'd had Calahan's number before he'd even opened his mouth. All three of them stared at him, their expressions bored with a tiny hint of aggravated.

"Why wouldn't we be okay?" Purple asked.

"We're questioning Mr. Gates about a woman's death. A woman he was business partners with. You're staying here and I wanted to make sure you felt safe, especially being the more vulnerable sex."

Ida Belle reached under my robe and squeezed my leg with one hand and covered her mouth with her other. I wasn't sure if she was trying to prevent me or herself from shooting him.

"What kind of nonsense are you on about?" Gertie asked. "The only thing that man has threatened us with is bad smoothies. And if those three didn't have big hooters in tight tops, you wouldn't have bothered to come over here. I'll pray for you, but only if you go away."

Calahan glared at Gertie, then looked completely baffled before shaking his head and stalking off. The Barbies barely waited until his back was turned before bursting out laughing. Calahan stopped for a couple seconds and stiffened but must have had another rare moment of clarity, because he kept walking.

"We should take you barhopping with us, Sister," Blue said. "You could fend off all the guys we aren't interested in."

Gertie nodded. "No one messes with nuns. We can call in favors."

I rose from the table. "If you'll excuse me for a moment, I had so much water earlier..."

"There's a bathroom in the lobby," Pink said. "Oh, but I guess…"

"It's no problem," I said. "I'll just make a quick run back to our cabin. Don't wait on me to finish. I imagine our fish is already getting cold."

"There's no back door," Purple said. "You're going to have to walk through the lobby to exit."

"I'll hurry past them then," I said and speed-walked to the door.

Carter stood in the lobby with Zion. Calahan had flopped down on a chair and was playing a game on his phone. Carter glanced over when I walked into the room, but I just kept my head down and hurried past.

"As far as I know, Eleanor didn't use drugs," Zion said as I passed. "It goes against everything we were trying to accomplish."

"You've got a bunch of mouthy nuns here," Calahan said, glaring at me as I slipped by. "Clearly, God didn't bring them peace. I don't see how sweating in weird positions is going to do anything."

I glanced back as I exited to get a good look at Zion, who'd had his back to me when I'd entered the room. His expression was a mixture of worry, confusion, and just a hint of fear.

"What exactly was your relationship with Ms. Stout?" I heard Carter ask as I hurried away.

I would have loved to stick around and find out what Zion's answer was, but I had to get what I needed to bug Zion's cabin. This was the perfect opportunity, assuming Sapphire actually left the premises. I grabbed the equipment and hurried through the woods toward Sapphire and Zion's cabin and arrived just in time to see a sleek silver Tesla speed off, spraying gravel as it went.

I figured Ida Belle and Gertie knew exactly what I was up

to, so they'd do whatever was needed to create a distraction if it became necessary, but I still needed to move as quickly as possible. Zion would probably come looking for Sapphire as soon as Carter was done questioning him.

The door was no challenge, so I was inside in a flash, then it was a matter of locating the best place for the bug. Air vents were problematic because of the noise, and the AC would definitely be running. Plus, there was always the possibility of Carter getting a search warrant if this investigation intensified, and air vents were a classic hiding place for money, drugs, and weapons.

I finally settled on the inside of a lampshade in both the living room and the bedroom. I quickly cut a slit in the top inside seams, then slipped the bugs inside. Then I put a spot of glue on each and pressed them shut. It wasn't the best job I'd ever done, but Zion wasn't a terrorist. And even if he found one of them later, he wouldn't know how long it had been there or who'd placed it. Based on what I'd seen, it would be far more likely he'd think Sapphire had done it.

I had just stepped into the living room when my phone signaled an incoming text. I dug it out of my pocket and stared. It was from Gertie.

Don't worry. I'm on it.

Then I heard Zion's voice at the door. Holy crap!

"I don't understand why you have a warrant for my cabin," he said.

Carter must have called in a favor from a judge on this one because I had not anticipated a search warrant this early in the investigation. The cabin had no back door, so I rushed into the bedroom and lifted the only window in the room, which was so small that I'd just barely squeeze out of it. There was no way to lock it so I'd just have to hope that Zion would be too distracted to notice or would think Sapphire had left it unlocked. Surely he had bigger fish to fry than worrying about window latches.

I peered outside and saw rosebushes right below the window. Good God. There was no way to exit without sliding headfirst or feetfirst and not enough drop to push myself away from the bushes below. I had no problem with some thorn injuries, but I'd have to toss the habit out first or it would be shredded.

I yanked it off and flung it into the woods behind the cabin. I heard the front door open as I started to pull myself through the window and knew I only had seconds to get clear before they had traversed the tiny cabin. And since it was still daylight, I had to get deep enough in the woods to keep them from spotting me if they looked out the window. Given that the blinds were all the way up and there were no curtains, I would be easy to spot.

Gritting my teeth, I shoved myself through the window, covering my head with my arms as I fell into the thorny bushes. Fortunately, my training covered ignoring pain in lieu of the mission, so I rolled out of the bushes, popped up, and made a dash for the thick undergrowth behind the cabin, snatching the habit off a bush as I ran.

I just needed to find a spot to duck down until I was certain of their positioning in the cabin, then I could skirt the woods back to the office. I couldn't feel any scratches on my face, and the habit would cover everything else but my hands, which were definitely scratched, but I could come up with a good lie for that one. I had just tucked in behind a thick clump of foliage when a huge boom blasted through the sky and the ground shook.

I peered through the bush and saw the bedroom window fly up, and Carter looked out. "What the hell?"

Calahan ran around the corner and pointed in my direction. "I saw someone run into the woods!"

"That blast wasn't nearby!"

But the accuracy of Carter's statement didn't deter that fool Calahan, who took off straight for me. I clutched the habit and dashed off toward the lake. Carter was right—that explosion wasn't nearby, but I recognized the sound. I would bet my life only one person at the retreat had dynamite, and I knew exactly where she'd use it.

There was no way Calahan could catch me in a footrace, but the dense forest and lack of path slowed me down. I was certain it slowed him down as well, but he had the luxury of chasing me rather than attempting to cut a path in a sea of cypress trees and brush. I could hear him pounding behind me, cursing the entire time, which was just fine with me. Maybe he'd use up what little cardio fitness he had on swearing and I'd make a clean break.

Because I couldn't just get away. I had to put enough distance between us to don my habit again and get back with the rest of the group or at least show up when everyone else did. Because no way I could claim I'd decided to stay in my cabin after that blast, and any normal person would go looking for the source immediately. If I didn't make an appearance with the others soon, Calahan might take a much closer look at me and that was something I couldn't afford.

I saw a break in the tree line just ahead and hoped that I'd calculated correctly and would come out close to the bank where we'd had class earlier. I slowed a tiny bit and glanced back. I couldn't see Calahan, but I could still hear him and knew he wasn't far behind. I flicked the habit out to unravel it so it was ready to pull on as soon as I cleared the woods, but as I ran past a set of brush, it caught on a branch that ripped it out of my hand. The branch whipped back and sent the habit flying past the tree line and into the open.

I bolted out of the woods and reached down for the habit just as a huge gust of wind got under it and sent it flying across the clearing. I sprinted after it, aware that Ida Belle, Gertie, and the three Barbies were all standing at the edge of the bayou staring at me, eyes wide, and the Barbies' jaws dropped.

Then I saw a flash of movement on the path behind them that led to the main building and realized that Carter and Zion were about to burst into sight. A second gust of wind blew the habit right across the shocked faces of the three Barbies.

It was only twenty yards away, but I was out of time.

I sprinted to the group and dove under Gertie's habit, trying to flatten myself against her legs.

CHAPTER TEN

"Hide it," I heard Blue Barbie say.

"Is everyone all right?" Carter asked.

I heard footsteps pounding toward us and Calahan yelled, "Where is he? He came this way."

"What are you talking about?" Ida Belle asked.

"The man I was chasing," Calahan said. "He would have come out of the woods right over there. You had to see him."

"You must be mistaken," Purple said. "The only people here are the three of us and the two sisters."

"I am *not* mistaken," Calahan ranted.

"Then you're hallucinating," Ida Belle said. "Because there's no one else here. Maybe he turned off somewhere and lost you. I can't imagine you'd be hard to outrun. I could probably do it."

"I've about had enough—" Calahan started but Carter interrupted him.

"There was no one else here when we arrived," Carter said. "And I didn't see anyone come out of the woods."

"Neither did I," Zion agreed.

"This is bull—"

"Ah, ah, ah," Ida Belle said. "I know you're not about to curse in the presence of the Lord's representatives."

"I'm done with this crap," Calahan said. "I'm going back to the main building. I've got a million scratches on me and they're starting to itch."

"You probably ran through poison ivy," Ida Belle said.

"One can only hope," Pink mumbled.

I heard Calahan stalk off and Carter sighed.

"What happened here?" he asked.

"Sister Gerianne said she was going for a walk to digest her dinner," Blue said. "We were just getting up to leave with Sister Eileen when we heard the explosion and then Sister Gerianne yelled."

"Are you okay, Ger—uh, Sister?" Carter asked.

"What?" she yelled. "Why are the church bells ringing? They're so loud."

"It blasted her eardrums," Carter said.

"But what *was* it?" Purple asked.

Fortunately for me, Carter knew exactly what it was and who had caused it, but he had as much of a vested interest in keeping things a secret as we did.

"Probably someone fishing," he said.

"You're joking," Pink said.

"I wish I was. Some people fish with dynamite. It's illegal but that doesn't stop them."

"I've never—" Zion said. "There's never been anything like that happen here."

"First time for everything," Carter said. "Do you want me to call the medic, Sister?"

"What the heck for?" Gertie answered, her hearing apparently returning. "I had indigestion. I came down here to clear it out without offending the rest of you. Don't see any point in steaming up an ambulance."

I struggled not to laugh at her obvious implication, then figured why not take advantage of the setup. I made a huge farting sound and everything went silent for a moment.

"This is what happens when you serve greens to old digestive systems," Gertie said. "I feel another doozy of a round coming on, so if you gentlemen would be so kind as to leave me to it, I'm sure the ladies will see that I make it back in one piece and significantly less bloated."

I struggled not to laugh because I knew if I started to shake, Gertie's weak knees wouldn't last and the jig would be up. Fortunately, Carter took the cue.

"We'll leave you to it," Carter said. "Zion...if we could head back to your cabin so I can finish up."

I heard them hurrying away, but I needed to stay put until they were out of sight.

"Everyone hold position," Ida Belle said. "I'll be right back."

At this point, I gave up my squat and shifted to all fours. Gertie, whose knees were clearly over it, sat promptly on my back.

"Are you okay down there?" Purple asked.

"Peachy," I said. "As long as the good sister doesn't really develop a problem with the greens."

I heard them all giggling and then approaching footsteps.

"You're clear," Ida Belle said. "Get out and get back in the habit."

"Can you guys help me up?" Gertie said.

A couple seconds later, I was relieved of my passenger and popped out from under Gertie's habit. Purple, Pink, and Blue all stared at me as if I was a magician performing in Vegas.

"Do you have my habit?" I asked.

"Oh yeah!" Blue reached into a tote bag and pulled out the habit and passed it to me.

Gertie stared down. "You heard an explosion and you grabbed your tote before running to look?"

"It's Gucci," Blue explained and Gertie nodded.

"Oh my God, what happened to your hands?" Pink asked. "It looks like you've been crucified. Is this one of those horror movie things?"

I looked down at my hands and saw the dried streaks of blood across them and shook my head. "I fell in a patch of thorns and used my hands to protect my face."

"Good call," Blue said. "Makeup does not cover that sort of thing."

Pink stared at me, her absolute confusion clear. "Did you fall because that idiot cop was chasing you? And why were you running from him? And naked? I mean, not naked, but you know, naked for a nun?"

Purple crossed her arms and narrowed her eyes at me. "You're not really a nun."

I shook my head, having already decided on my course of action while I was playing barstool. "I'm a private detective. The two good sisters are my assistants."

Pink's eyes widened. "You have nuns as assistants?"

Purple rolled her eyes. "They're not nuns either. They're undercover."

"Oh!" Pink said, then frowned. "But why? Who are you investigating?"

"Since the cops are here asking about the death of his business partner, my guess is Zion," Purple said. "Is there anything we need to know?"

"Probably nothing you haven't already caught on to," I said. "We have reason to suspect that Zion takes advantage of women with his business practices. I came here posing as an innocent young woman who'd just inherited some real estate and needed to figure out what to do with it. I went with cabins on an island in Florida."

Purple nodded. "You think he's scamming vulnerable women into business deals that only benefit him. After I realized that Sapphire was actually the owner of this place, I figured his interest in me went beyond just collecting the fees for retreats."

"I'd bet on it. With all of your properties, you'd be a winning lottery ticket to someone like Zion."

She blew out a breath. "And we've played right into his hands with our whole discount-getting routine. He probably thinks I'm just a trust fund baby ripe for the taking."

Blue bit her lower lip. "That cop—the idiot, not the cute one—said a woman died. Did Zion kill her?"

"It looks like a suicide," I said, "but there are extenuating circumstances, and I'm attempting to get answers for her sister. But I'd appreciate it if you ladies kept this all quiet. If Zion even gets an inkling of who we are, we'll be tossed out and get nothing."

They all gave me earnest nods.

"Our lips are sealed," Pink said. "If that man had anything to do with a woman's death, even indirectly, I want him to go down."

"Me too," Blue said. "But I'm confused... Who caused the explosion?"

"Oh, that was me," Gertie said. "I was creating a diversion for Sister Britney, who was off on a mission, so to speak."

"Holy crap, you walk around with dynamite in your robe?" Pink asked.

"I usually carry a stick under my boobs, unless I've got my gun there."

They all stared and then Purple gave me a curious look.

"That cute sheriff seemed in a hurry to get away," she said.

"I would have figured he'd at least ask where you were when he saw us all standing here."

"Yeah, about that," I said. "I might be engaged to the sheriff."

Pink raised her hand and gave me a high five. Blue hooted and Purple smiled.

"It's an election year," I explained. "And with that idiot Calahan following him around, hoping to catch him doing something wrong, I can't afford to get caught interfering with his investigation."

"All your secrets are safe with us," Purple said. "Just tell us how you want us to play the rest of the retreat and we've got you covered."

"We're all back to playing our roles," I said. "The three of us are nuns and the three of you are playing dumb for discounts."

Pink shook her head. "If women are getting killed, we might have to stop the shenanigans and pay full price. I can't believe we're caught up in a murder investigation, even if indirectly."

We started back up the path, and I looked over at Purple. "Is there any way to find out how this property is held?"

"It's probably in a trust if it was inherited," she said, "and the trust documents wouldn't be public, but I know a guy. Let me make a call. I buy so much stuff and ask that question so often, he won't even bat an eye at it, and he definitely won't tell anyone I asked."

"I appreciate it," I said. "Well, looks like this is our fork in the road. I assume we're done for tonight?"

"We usually have a short meditation session after dinner to relax us for sleep," Pink said, "but I think Zion is a little busy for all of that."

"And not very relaxed," Blue said. "I'm going to dead-bolt myself in my cabin and have a long hot shower."

Pink nodded. "We're going to need a spa day to recover from our yoga retreat."

I pulled cards out of my wallet and passed one to each of the Barbies. "If you hear or see anything tonight that bothers you, call me."

"I thought you didn't have phones," Pink said, then slapped her own forehead. "I keep forgetting you're not really nuns. I need a drink. Thank God I packed that box of wine in my suitcase."

"We're only here overnight," Blue said.

Pink raised one eyebrow. "Are you really going to question my judgment on that one given everything that's happened today? I can offer up your share to the fake sisters."

Blue clamped her lips shut and drew her fingers across them in a zipping motion.

We all smiled and I gave them a wave as we took the left fork in the trail and headed to our cabin.

"If I didn't have some of Nora's brew in my suitcase, I'd be following her for some of that wine," Gertie said.

Ida Belle shook her head, then looked at me. "Well, that was something else. What the heck happened?"

I told them about my headfirst plunge out the cabin window and my dash through the woods to get away from Calahan.

"Why didn't you let me know they were on their way to the cabin?" I asked.

"Because we didn't know," Ida Belle said. "We heard the door when you left and figured they were still in the lobby, but since we were holding cover at the time, I didn't figure I could go put my ear on the door to listen or the Barbies might think that was a little odd. Then we heard the door slam again and figured they'd left, so Gertie claimed a bathroom break and headed up to check."

Gertie nodded. "But it was that idiot Calahan. Carter and Zion must have left quietly sometime before because Calahan was the only one I saw on the path to Zion's cabin. So I sent you that text but was afraid it would be too late for you to get clear. So I yelled back to the others that I was going for a walk and ran for the bayou, figuring an explosion would send them running my way and give you a chance to get out if you were trapped inside."

"Yeah, your message came through seconds before Carter and Zion appeared at the door. It's a good thing you had that stick on you."

Ida Belle sighed. "Now she'll be carrying dynamite everywhere."

"You act like I wasn't already," Gertie said. "So is the bug going to work?"

"I hope so," I said. "But we're going to have to get closer to hear anything."

"Then what are we waiting for?" Gertie asked. "I want to know what Carter is looking for."

I shook my head. "Calahan will be patrolling the woods around the cabin like a game warden. We can't get close enough without him spotting us. I had one narrow escape already. If Calahan gets it in his head that someone else is interested in that cabin, he'll push until Carter has to do a sweep."

Gertie sighed. "And Carter will definitely find the bug because he's good at his job. Oh well. If Sapphire doesn't come back, we're not going to get anything unless Zion calls someone or talks to himself. Hey, maybe he talks in his sleep."

Ida Belle stared. "Are you going to sit in the woods all night, sweating and itching, in case he might say something?"

She sighed. "This whole proximity thing is for the birds. We need some better equipment."

"I'll get some better equipment," I said, "but the high-grade stuff doesn't come cheap. And you end up losing pieces along the way."

Ida Belle nodded. "It's not like you can just stroll back into a private residence and ask people to let you remove it."

"Exactly," I said. "And once the police have locked onto someone, they're hyper protective and aware. Anyway, it's beside the point. Even if I'd had better equipment, I probably wouldn't have brought it. This whole thing looked like a suicide, remember? And when it comes down to it, I still can't see how it's anything else."

"But we need to prove that Zion is shady or he'll take the cabins from Mildred," Gertie said.

"Oh, he's shady," Ida Belle said. "But if he's not criminally shady, it won't matter."

"We could shoot him," Gertie said.

"Tempting," I said, "but for all we know, that might just send the cabins even further down the line to Sapphire."

Gertie frowned. "So what *do* you think Carter is looking for?"

"Drugs probably," Ida Belle said. "If Mildred is standing firm on Eleanor never taking downers and there's no prescription on the books, then she got them somewhere. Given that Zion is the clear beneficiary in Eleanor's death and shady as all get-out to boot, it makes sense to start looking there."

I nodded. "I wonder about the gun as well. Obviously, it's possible that it was Eleanor's as most people with any common sense have more than one, but verifying ownership will also be a priority."

"That might not be as easy as one would hope," Ida Belle said. "Too many guns around here are passed around to family and friends or sold at gun shows and pawnshops. Heck, I bought a thirty-year-old cast-iron skillet and a .38 special at a garage sale last week."

"Only in the South do both of those make perfect sense," I said.

"Well, what do we do now?" Gertie asked. "I assume we'll try to hear something after Carter leaves, but what about tomorrow? Do you think Zion's going to clear us out early since the cops showed up and basically called him a suspect right there in front of us all?"

"A normal person would," I said. "But Zion is anything but normal. And besides, he's interested in my cabins. The smart thing would be for him to tuck tail and run but thank God for us, most criminals aren't all that smart."

Ida Belle nodded. "Not only is he too interested in what Fortune has to offer, if he can scam her into a deal, it would allow him to get out of Louisiana. And that's probably sounding like a really good idea about now."

"So we listen tonight and hope Sapphire comes back or he makes a juicy phone call," Gertie said, "and then tomorrow you do some more pushing on the inheritance thing, but what about after that? Even if Carter got proof that Zion gave Eleanor the drugs, can he charge him with anything? Ultimately, it's still a suicide."

"There's laws for criminal assistance of suicide, and it's a felony," I said. "I did some googling earlier. It wouldn't be a picnic to prove, but if Zion supplied the drugs or the gun, then a case could possibly be made."

Ida Belle raised one eyebrow. "But?"

I huffed. "Something isn't right. Or I guess I should say something else isn't right. Don't get me wrong, I think Zion is sketchy as heck, and I have no doubt he preys on women, but there's an undercurrent to all of this...like there's something even bigger moving below the surface."

"Like what?" Gertie asked.

"I have no idea. I just don't feel like this is as straightforward as we think it is."

"So what do we do to raise the kraken?" Ida Belle asked.

I considered this for a bit. "I think we need to dig deeper into all the major players. Not just what happened in the last couple days or even months, but altogether. Who is Zion? Where did he come from? And I need a bigger picture of Eleanor. If we move forward on the premise that Eleanor was prompted into her action, then the question is how and by whom. Was Zion the only one with something to gain? What about Sapphire? For that matter, Kim isn't exactly on the perfectly innocent list as she clearly had a thing for Zion as well. We've seen women do more for less."

"That's true enough," Ida Belle said. "And as much as I hate digging up dirt on a dead woman when we're working for her grieving sister, it needs to happen. I agree with you that something bigger is going on than what is currently on display."

But what?

CHAPTER ELEVEN

"I don't know why I have to stay behind while you two get to do all the fun stuff," Gertie groused.

Ida Belle stared. "Trekking through the woods, on a hot humid night, wearing long sleeves and a mask is fun? The mosquitoes alone are the stuff horror movies are made of."

Gertie waved a hand in dismissal. "You traipse around in long sleeves all the time, masks are cool, and mosquitoes never killed anybody."

"Said no one with malaria ever," Ida Belle said.

"Mosquitoes here don't have malaria."

"They also don't have shoddy knees or dynamite," I said, cutting in. "If we have to run, you'd be at a huge disadvantage. Besides, I need you back here in case another diversion is necessary."

Gertie huffed but ceased arguing. I figured either her knees were bothering her more than she wanted to admit or she didn't want anyone else potentially getting to play with her dynamite. Probably both.

"Ida Belle will text periodic updates once we're in place," I said. "But if we have to run, all bets are off. If she goes more than fifteen minutes without sending an update, assume something is going down and figure out what kind of diversion we might need."

I pushed open the small window on the back wall of the bathroom, and the warm breeze wafted inside along with bugs.

"Leave that window open in case we need an alternative entrance," I said as I pulled the bathroom door shut.

"Great," Gertie groused. "Might as well be peeing outside in a bush with all the bugs and humidity coming in there."

I pulled a spare ski mask from my backpack and tossed it to her. "You can still wear a mask if you'd like, although I advise taking it off if Zion shows up."

Gertie tossed the mask on the bed. "I have a cucumber mask. I'm going to put it on as soon as you leave."

Ida Belle stared. "Why on earth would someone make a mask out of cucumbers?"

"It's a face mask. Like a peel? It's good for the skin—you know what, never mind. It's something Ronald gave me."

"Well, why didn't you just say that to begin with?"

"Let get going," I said. "I'm hoping Zion didn't make a phone call as soon as Carter left."

I'd heard Carter's truck leaving thirty minutes earlier but since it wasn't dark, I hadn't wanted to risk trying to sneak out just yet. Plus, I'd been afraid that Zion might decide to play good host and check up on the guests given our disruptive dinner, but so far, all had been quiet. Maybe he hadn't worked up a good explanation for what had occurred and would avoid us until tomorrow morning.

We skirted the edge of the woods along the trail, then hurried across the road before we got to the main building and continued in the woods paralleling the trail to Zion's cabin. We were almost there when I heard the crunch of something heavy on gravel and the light whine of an electric car.

"That's Sapphire," I whispered. "Hurry."

I set off through the woods at as fast a pace as I could manage, watching Sapphire's taillights fade around the corner in front of me. When we reached the outskirts of the cabin, I dropped down in a squat and pulled out my laptop.

"It looks like she's still in her car."

"Probably on the phone."

"Or deciding whether or not to shoot him."

"Valid. This will only take a couple seconds to connect."

"Good, because she just climbed out and the way she's stomping up to the door. I don't want to miss what happens when she gets inside."

I pulled out the earbuds and passed one to Ida Belle, then set everything to record.

"Did you text Gertie?"

She nodded. "And set a timer."

Sapphire yanked open the door and walked inside the cabin, slamming the door shut behind her. Ida Belle and I winced as the sensitive microphone blasted her disapproval.

"What are you doing back?" Zion asked, not sounding remotely repentant. In fact, he sounded put out that she'd returned.

"It's my property," Sapphire said. "Why should I be the one to leave?"

"Well, if you think I'm going anywhere you can think again. As I've said before, if you want me out of here, it will cost you."

"I've already paid enough! You're a liar and a cheater. And now the cops show up here insinuating that you had something to do with that old hoochie's death. I didn't sign up for any of this, and I'm not giving you another dime."

"Maybe before you put on your high and mighty tone, you'd

like to discuss what the cops found when they searched our cabin."

"What do you mean the cops searched my cabin? They can't do that!"

"They had a warrant."

"What did you do, Zion?"

"I didn't do anything."

"That's what you always say, but I know you're lying. Did you have something to do with that woman's death?"

"As far as I know, her death was a suicide, but there were drugs in her bloodstream, which is problematic because she didn't have a prescription for them."

"You gave her drugs?" Sapphire's voice shot up several octaves.

"I didn't give her anything, you stupid cow. The drugs were in *your* nightstand."

"I don't take drugs!"

"You know that's a lie."

"I don't take stuff that will kill you, and I could hardly roll up to her place and pass her a bottle of stuff to take, now could I?"

"No. But you could slip it into a bottle of water. You weren't here when I got back on Monday."

"So? You think I should sit here pining away for you while you're off with one of your women?"

"Where were you?"

"It's none of your business where I was then or where I'm about to be as soon as I grab my things."

There was more slamming around and then Zion stalked out the front door. Ida Belle and I were already low but we ducked down even lower. He yanked open the door to the Tesla and climbed inside.

"Is he going to steal her car too?" Ida Belle whispered.

I shrugged. I had no idea where this Jerry Springer show was going.

A couple minutes later, Sapphire stomped back out with a tote bag and Zion jumped out of the car.

"I knew it!" he said. "You were at Eleanor's retreat on Monday. Don't try to deny it because your car says as much."

"Of course I was at Eleanor's retreat Monday. I was following you, you moron! I knew you had something going on with that woman, and I was going to catch you."

"I was *not* sleeping with her!"

"Only because she was old and gross and you didn't want to do it, but I have zero doubt that's what you led her to believe was going to happen. What happened, Zion? Was she putting the screw to you? Literally? So you had to kill her? I'm out. You'll hear from my attorney and if you're smart, you won't make this difficult."

"Or what?"

"Maybe there will be two funerals for yoga instructors."

She jumped in the car and took off. Zion glared at the retreating taillights, then cursed and spun around but instead of heading back inside, he set off down the path to our cabin.

Crap!

I grabbed the laptop and jumped up, then hustled through the woods as quickly as possible without making a ton of noise, which wasn't easy given that there was no path. Fortunately, there was a bit of wind so the trees rustling masked some of our passage. I heard Ida Belle behind me as I skirted the edge of the woods, keeping an eye on Zion's retreating figure.

When we reached the point where the path veered left but the gap to the woods tripled in size, I started jogging. No way we could make it inside the cabin before Zion had it in sight. And we hadn't had time to warn Gertie either, so I could only hope she was ready for some improv. As we edged around the woods toward the back of the cabin, I could see Zion just twenty yards from the front door. There was no way we could both get inside before Gertie had to answer the door.

"Stay here," I told Ida Belle as I rushed out of the woods and sprinted for the back of the cabin. Two of us in the bathroom wouldn't make any sense. I'd just have to hope that Zion wouldn't insist on doing bed roll call on all three of us. Since I was the one he was currently fixated on, it made more sense for him to want to ensure I knew he'd checked in.

I pulled myself in through the small window and eased down headfirst into the bathtub, trying to avoid any crashes. The last thing I needed was Zion thinking one of us had fallen in the shower and rushing in to help. I heard Gertie opening the door as I yanked off my mask and black clothes and shoved them in the vanity cabinet. Then I turned on the water in the sink, splashed it on my head and wrapped a towel around it. Zion had never seen my hair, and I didn't want to risk him getting a more complete look at my appearance.

"What the heck?" Gertie said. "Is there a fire?"

"Oh!"

I could hear the shock and dismay in his voice and didn't even want to know what Gertie had on. I had a feeling it was something from her shopping trip with Ronald, which included all manner of things that the general public was never supposed to see a person wearing unless they lived with them. Especially when they thought that person was a nun.

"I'm so sorry," Zion said. "I didn't know you were undressed."

"What the hell do you think I wear to sleep? My habit? That would be all kinds of hot and uncomfortable. You basically knock on my bedroom door at nine thirty at night and you're surprised I'm not in full nun mode? Nuns deserve me time too, you know."

"Of course. I didn't mean to interrupt your personal time. I just wanted to apologize for the interruption at dinner and to make sure you are okay."

"Why the heck wouldn't we be? We ate, we relaxed, and now we're getting ready for bed. Well, technically Sister Eileen has been asleep for an hour already and if this racket wakes her up, there will be hell to pay tomorrow for all of us."

Since I needed Zion to think we were all intact, I eased the bathroom door open and stuck my head out.

"Is everything okay?" I asked as I got my first look at Gertie.

She wore a bright pink swimmer's cap, and her entire face was covered in some sort of green gel-looking stuff. Her G-string bodysuit was bright pink like her cap. The lettering across the bust read Too Hot to Handle.

That and a disgruntled look was all she was wearing.

Good. God.

Zion's eyes widened as he caught sight of me and he stammered, probably because he was now picturing a naked nun standing behind the bathroom door and he wasn't sure what to do with that mental image.

"Everything is fine, Sister Britney," he said. "I was...um, I was just checking on you after the disturbance tonight."

"We should probably be asking if you're okay," I said. "Did a woman really pass? Should we pray for her?"

"That won't be necessary," he said, clearly ten different kinds of uncomfortable. "I mean, it's a nice thought and maybe we could revisit it tomorrow after meditation. I'll just leave you ladies to it. Have a good night."

He slammed the door and Gertie went immediately to the window and peered between the blinds. I stepped out of the bathroom and realized that she'd stuffed pillows under the covers of Ida Belle's bed.

"Nice," I said, pointing at the pillow-stuffed bed.

"I was hoping you'd turn up in the bathroom," Gertie said. "I didn't figure he'd make a stink over not seeing Ida Belle in person, but you're his target audience, so to speak."

I nodded. We'd definitely been on the same wavelength on that one.

"Where is he now?" I asked.

"Just turning the corner headed toward the Barbies' cabin."

I sent Ida Belle a text telling her it was safe to head inside, then grabbed some clothes and hurried back into the bathroom to dress.

Ida Belle was sitting at the little table when I came back out, staring at Gertie with a mixture of fear and admiration.

"Did she really answer the door like that?" she asked and waved at Gertie.

"Oh yeah. Between the very real visual in front of him and him imagining me naked behind the bathroom door, he couldn't get out of here fast enough."

Gertie frowned. "I have no idea what you're getting at. I look good."

"You look like a Komodo dragon stuffed in pink spandex," Ida Belle said.

"Oh crap!" Gertie said. "I completely forgot I had on the face mask. This thing really is like a second skin."

Ida Belle stared at her in dismay. "You weren't dressed like that to scare Zion off?"

"Why would I be? I didn't know he was going to come here. When you didn't check in at the fifteen-minute mark, I looked outside and saw him coming up the walk. I stuffed the pillows in the bed to account for you sleeping and figured I could pass Fortune off as in the bathroom, which played out perfectly, but I didn't have time for a wardrobe change."

"So this is all intentional? Good God. We might really have to start praying hours every day for you."

Gertie waved her hand in dismissal. "Wait until you feel the skin on my face when I get this peel off."

"I'm more concerned about the overexposure of the skin on your butt. If you'd like to put on some pants and wash your face, Fortune and I have important business to discuss."

"Didn't know there was a dress code for talking in my own room," Gertie grumbled as she headed into the bathroom.

A couple minutes later she came back out, her face clean, and pulled on a pair of white shorts with hot pink firehoses on them and plopped down in a chair next to Ida Belle. I queued up the recorded conversation and let Gertie listen while I listened closely again. When it was over, we told Gertie what happened with Zion and Sapphire's car, which led to his subsequent journey to our cabin, leaving us no time to give her a heads-up.

"Good Lord," Gertie said when we were done. "That's a lot gained in a short amount of time."

Ida Belle nodded. "And I have the mosquito bites to prove it, but where does that information leave us?"

"Well, we know Carter found drugs in their cabin," I said. "Neither is claiming ownership, which I find interesting."

"Of course they're both denying it," Ida Belle said. "Especially to each other. They both have good reason to want the other one on the hook. If Zion is on the hook, then Sapphire gets her quiet, pain-free divorce. If Sapphire is on the hook, then Zion probably leaves with some of her money in his pockets."

"Well, someone's fingerprints should be on them," Gertie said.

"Not if they're trying to hide their involvement," Ida Belle said.

"True," I agreed, "but if neither one's fingerprints are on the bottle then that would be interesting. I wonder what the prescription was for."

"Well, we're not going to find out from Carter," Gertie said. "We better hope he tells Mildred. Otherwise, we're playing with only half a deck."

Ida Belle snorted. "You've been playing with half a deck for years. Hasn't held you up any."

I smiled. "We're not going to solve this tonight, so let's try to get some sleep. It will be interesting to see how Zion acts tomorrow."

Gertie sighed. "With Sapphire gone, our chances of being served those awful smoothies again goes way up."

I nodded. "I think that might be the only thing in this investigation I'd bet on."

CHAPTER TWELVE

We took a walk the next morning before meditation, which meant setting out at 6:00 a.m. since meditation was at seven. Gertie groused a bit, but when we suggested that Ida Belle and I could go take a peek without her to see if Sapphire had returned, she hurried to get dressed. We figured we could play off being on Zion's side of the property with the whole long walk to relax narrative but neither his vehicle nor Sapphire's was at the cabin.

"We ought to go in and poke around," Gertie said.

"To what end?" Ida Belle said. "Unless you think Carter is incompetent, anything worth finding is currently sitting in an evidence bag."

"Carter's not necessarily looking for the same things we are," Gertie argued. "We're on the real estate fraud thing. He's on the potential contribution to a death thing. And if he's looking for drugs or any indication that the gun belonged to Zion, he wouldn't have taken a hard look at other things that might be what we're looking for. He didn't find the bugs."

"That's true enough," I said, "but after that search, my guess is that anything left that is remotely personal or incriminating has been removed and stashed. Sapphire probably took stuff with her when she left last night, and who knows where Zion is. Not like there's a shortage of places to hide things around here either, and Carter would have a hard time getting a search warrant for the entire place, not to mention rounding up enough staff to do a good sweep of the facilities alone, much less the forest."

"You know that idiot Calahan would never let him get away with that request," Ida Belle said.

Gertie shook her head. "It's like that man doesn't even care about the actual crime or the victims."

"My guess is he doesn't," I said. "None of us are real people to him. We're just pawns he can use to forward his own agenda."

"Maybe we should get rid of him," Gertie said.

"They'd just send someone else," Ida Belle said.

Gertie shrugged. "But the gap in replacing him would buy us some time and besides, it would be fun."

I grinned. "Let's keep that thought in reserve for now."

Gertie perked up. "But you're not ruling it out."

"I would never do that. Now, let's go see how Zion plans on leading us in meditation when the world is crumbling around him."

"If he doesn't have high blood pressure by now, he's either a sociopath or he needs to use all this as a marketing tool," Gertie said.

The Barbies were already at the bayou when we arrived but so was Zion, so I didn't have an opportunity to talk to them about anything that had happened the night before. I could tell Purple gave me a slight head lift as we approached, and I knew she had something she wanted to talk about. I figured we'd get an opportunity while Zion was preparing breakfast as it seemed he was on his own.

Zion smiled as we approached but I could tell it was forced. The dark circles under his eyes let me know he hadn't seen much sleep the night before, and I could see the tension in his body.

"Good morning, ladies," he said. "I trust you slept okay?"

"Like a log," Ida Belle said. "Had a pack of M&M's after dinner and chased them with a couple shots of whiskey. That got me a solid eight."

"A couple shots?" Gertie asked. "There was barely enough left for me to fill a mouth-rinse cup."

Ida Belle waved a hand in dismissal. "The bottle I brought wasn't full."

"The heck it wasn't."

Zion looked aggrieved. "Sister, you're supposed to be cleansing your body. The meditation and yoga will allow you to transcend to a different plane of relaxation. Deep sleep is a natural effect of that."

Ida Belle gave him an indignant look. "I'm not looking to transcend anywhere but the Pearly Gates, and preferably not today. I've prayed hours every day for forty years and still can't sleep right. I figure if the Lord saw fit to provide us with Kentucky and the best bourbon in the world, who am I to question him?"

Pink giggled. "I feel the same way about designer purses."

"And cheesecake," Blue said. "I really love a great slice of cheesecake. I bought a rowing machine because of it."

Zion stared for a moment but apparently realized he'd lost us before he ever had us.

"Okay, let's do some meditation and light stretching then," he said. "It will allow our bodies to wake up from our rest and center us for the rest of the day's events."

"Are we still on for everything today?" Purple asked. "We weren't sure given that whole cop thing last night."

Zion managed a somewhat blank expression, but I could tell it was forced.

"They merely had some questions for me because of my partnership with the lady and because I'd given a class that day at her retreat."

"Did she really die?" Pink asked.

"I'm afraid so," he said, and I could tell he desperately wanted this conversation to end. "If everyone will take a seat. Sister Gerianne, I brought a lawn chair for you today."

He gestured to the chair set up behind him.

"More things to be thankful for," Gertie said as she headed over and plopped down. "Might make up for Sister Selfish shorting me on the whiskey."

Zion led us through the meditation and stretching but I could tell his mind wasn't on what he was doing. He kept glancing up the path to the main building, probably afraid he would see Sapphire or the cops or both. I wondered why he hadn't just issued refunds and cut his losses, but given the occasional nervous glances he sent my way, I assumed he was still hoping to work the Florida angle for his business.

The stakes had probably been upped about a hundred notches given that he appeared to be barreling toward homeless. And even inheriting Eleanor's cabins wouldn't immediately help that situation, as Mildred could tie her cabins up in the legal system for years if she wanted to. And I had a feeling that's exactly what she would do. I would.

When class was over, he lingered for a bit, and I figured he was hoping to have a walk with me again and discuss my real estate. But the Barbies stuck around and since none of us showed any signs of separating, he finally said breakfast would be ready in twenty minutes and headed off.

"I thought he'd never clear out," Purple said.

"Probably hoping to get Sister Britney alone and get his hands on her property," Pink said.

Blue shook her head. "That sounds so much dirtier than it actually is."

"Oh, it's dirty all right," Gertie said. "Just not the good kind."

Purple nodded. "I talked to my guy last night. He called back right before we headed out this morning. It's like I thought—this property is in a trust. It's been in Sapphire's family for decades."

"So Zion can't get his grubby hands on it if Sapphire divorces him," Gertie said.

"No," Purple said. "But he has a contract with the trust to lease the property for the retreat. According to my guy, her attorney tried to talk her out of it, but she was in love and believed in her man and all that emotional nonsense that gets you into trouble."

"I like the way you think," Ida Belle said.

"It was drilled into me by my father," she said. "And it's also self-defense. I've seen too many people lose family assets over bad relationships. I'm not about to let it happen to me."

"So Zion can't force her to sell," I said, "and I assume he can't get his hands on any of her other inheritance either, but as long as he has a contract for the yoga retreat, he doesn't have to vacate the property."

"Nope. And I'm going to hazard a guess that the rent is probably way below market." Purple shook her head. "I've known men like this before, and I'd bet that place in Montana with the really hot cowboys that Sapphire will have to pay to get rid of him."

I nodded. We already knew as much from what Ida Belle and I overheard the night before, but it helped that Purple had provided confirmation and filled in some details on exactly what Sapphire's legal position was.

"I appreciate the information," I said.

"I can't believe I'm saying this, but I actually feel sorry for Sapphire," Pink said. "Being married to a cheater is bad enough, but a cheater who used you for your inheritance and who might have contributed to another woman's death is next level."

"I'm going to give you one of my cards before we leave," Purple said. "If you need any more real estate information, give me a call. If I don't know, I usually know someone who does."

Blue nodded. "She's literally like Yoda. She can find out anything."

"And if you wouldn't mind, I'd like to hear how this all turns out," Purple said and shook her head. "That poor woman..."

THE REST OF THE RETREAT WAS UNEVENTFUL. THE FOOD WAS less than stellar although the grilled chicken we had for lunch was decent. Zion took us through all the scheduled classes, but I could tell his heart wasn't in it. There was no opportunity for him to corner me about my beach property the rest of the day, so when it was time to check out, I told Ida Belle and Gertie to hang back and let me start loading up alone. I figured if he was watching, he'd take the opportunity to give his pitch again.

I figured right.

I had just opened the back of the SUV when he came out of the main building.

"Sister Britney," he said. "I'm glad I caught you before you left. Oh—are you all right? Your hands. I didn't notice the scratches at class this morning. I suppose I was distracted."

I put on what I hoped was a polite smile. "It's nothing. I picked some berries this morning on our walk. Got a few scratches, but it was worth it. The blackberries behind our cabin are wonderful."

He matched my smile and nodded. "Yes. They are indeed. I often pick some for meals."

He pulled a card out of his pocket and handed it to me. "I wanted to give you my contact information. I know the retreat wasn't as relaxing as you'd probably hoped given the unfortunate interruption, but I wanted to let you know that I'm very interested in pursuing a lease for your property in Florida. I think a retreat would be the perfect compromise between maintaining your aunt's property and not having to be involved with the day-to-day work yourself. I'd love to talk to you about it more. I'm happy to meet you in New Orleans to discuss matters."

I took the card with his information and nodded. "I enjoyed the retreat and I agree that it would be a good use for the property. And I'd feel like I was offering something beneficial. I need to talk to the estate attorney and get more details and then I'll be in a better position to discuss my options. As you know, we don't have cell phones, but I can give you my email. I check it daily, so if you have more questions, that would be the quickest way to reach me."

He looked pleased and a tiny bit surprised. "That would be great."

I gave him the Gmail address I'd set up that morning, and he made a note in his phone, then reached for Gertie's suitcase.

"Let me help you with that," he said.

"Be careful that you don't jostle it." Gertie's voice sounded from the walkway. "I don't want my pretzel sticks to look like flour by the time we get home. Darned things are wheat and expensive."

Zion gently placed the suitcase in the SUV and gave Ida Belle and Gertie a pleasant smile.

"Ladies, it was a pleasure having you here," he said. "I hope you will return."

Gertie snorted. "God's going to send lightning down on you if you keep telling lies. This whole shindig is not for me and the only thing you're going to feel when we pull away is relieved. Next time a sister is troubled, we're going to work it out on the slots in Vegas."

She gave him a disgruntled look and climbed into the SUV. Ida Belle shrugged and climbed in after her.

"Thank you for everything," I said. "I'll be in touch."

"I look forward to it," he said and headed back inside as we pulled away.

"Did you get a pitch?" Gertie asked.

I nodded. "And contact information. And I gave him that email I set up. Now, as long as he doesn't go looking for us with the Catholic diocese in New Orleans, we'll be in good shape."

"He probably won't," Ida Belle said. "That would just be more people with eyes on him and he wants you by yourself making these decisions. It was a good call to go with being a nun. People usually don't look past the outfit. That being said, I can't wait to get this off."

"I've already ditched mine," Gertie said.

I turned around and there she was in all her glory. Bright purple biking shorts and sports bra with a gun stuck in the center.

"Do not look in your rearview," I said to Ida Belle.

I pulled my habit over my head but since I was wearing

yoga pants and tee, I was good. Ida Belle just sighed. There was no way she could disrobe while driving.

We made our pit stop at the motel for Ida Belle to change and since she got a good look at Gertie, I had to haul out her suitcase so she could find something more appropriate for sitting in Ida Belle's vehicle. If Gertie didn't change clothes, Ida Belle said she'd be forced not to use the rearview mirror the entire drive home. Since Ida Belle treated every driving experience as if she were Jason Statham, Gertie gave in.

"Have you heard from Carter?" Ida Belle asked as she drove.

I shook my head. "He knows what we were up to, so he wouldn't risk blowing either of our covers by contacting me."

"So what's next?" Gertie asked.

"We need to get an update from Mildred," I said.

"Do you want to call her now?" Ida Belle asked.

"No. I prefer to see her in person."

Gertie gave me a curious look. "You don't suspect Mildred of having something to do with Eleanor's death, do you?"

"I was CIA. I suspect everyone. And the reality is they're always hiding something. You know that. But we're bucking up against a time clock here and Calahan holds the stopwatch. I need everyone to level with me about everything so I can sort this out. Because you were right—this whole situation is off. But that starts with Eleanor. Things about her just aren't lining up."

"You think Mildred is hiding something about Eleanor?"

"It wouldn't surprise me if she was," Ida Belle said. "You know how we were all raised—no speaking ill of the dead and all that. She could be trying to protect her sister's image. And after all, she has to live here with it when all the dust has cleared."

"It's only three o'clock now," Gertie said. "We told Mildred we'd be in touch when we got back, so maybe we should run over and see her before we head home. Carter might have given her more information about the drugs and the gun."

I nodded. "Sounds like a plan."

––––––––––

WE LUCKED OUT, AND NOT ONLY WAS MILDRED HOME WHEN we got there but she was alone. I was afraid she'd have well-meaning visitors or Kim hovering around, but there were no cars in the drive and she looked relieved when she opened the door and saw us standing there.

"Please come in," she said, waving us inside. "I just took a jug of fresh brewed tea out of the fridge. It's good and cold. And Lord knows, I have something to eat, if you're hungry. Seems like people have been dropping off food every thirty minutes."

I walked into the kitchen and stared. She wasn't lying. Every flat surface was covered with casserole dishes, bowls, trays, and plates.

"I don't mean to sound ungrateful," she said, "but I ran out of refrigerator space half a day in. If I didn't have back problems, I'd start hauling it around to some of the families here that I know could use it."

"We can do that," Ida Belle said. "Just give me a list and we'll make the rounds when we leave."

"Oh, that would be wonderful! I just hate seeing it go to waste but I'm only one person. If I started eating right now and didn't stop until Sunday, I still couldn't put a dent in it."

"Well, I'm happy to kick things off," Gertie said. "We've been at a yoga retreat and the snacks I packed were the best food there."

Mildred stared. "You went on another yoga retreat...after

all that?" Her eyes widened. "Oh my God. You went to Zion's retreat, didn't you?"

She sank into a kitchen chair and her eyes teared up. "I know you said you'd look into things, but I never imagined you were already doing it. I don't even know what to say."

"No words necessary," I said. "But I will need you to sign a contract so you have confidentiality. I'll email one to you and pick it up next time I see you."

"Of course. Whatever you need. But what about the fee?"

"I'll take a dollar and an early dinner."

She smiled and teared up. "Please help yourself to anything you want. I know what Zion's retreat menu calls for, and you're probably starving."

I had to admit that the smells coming from all those containers had my stomach rumbling. Mildred grabbed some plates and we checked out the offerings, then set some aside to keep whole for delivery when we left and dug into several others. Gertie even convinced Mildred to join in, after she questioned her on the last time she'd eaten, and Mildred had to admit she couldn't remember.

"So did you find anything out?" she asked as we all sat with full plates. "I can't believe he'd be loose-lipped with a detective."

"We were undercover," I said. "He thinks I just inherited a bunch of cabins on a beach in Florida. I wanted to see if he'd make a pitch."

Mildred looked confused. "But he's seen Gertie."

"Not dressed as a nun."

Mildred's eyes widened and then she started laughing. "You all went as nuns? Even Ida Belle? Oh my God. I would have drunk one of his awful brown shakes to have seen that."

"Anything to catch the bad guy," Ida Belle said.

"You wouldn't let me ride in your vehicle wearing a G-string leotard," Gertie said.

"Almost anything."

"Why were you wearing a G-string as a nun?" Mildred asked.

"It's a long story and one you probably don't want the details on," I said. "Suffice it to say that Zion is definitely interested in my cabins, and we're pretty sure his wife—who he also scammed into this whole yoga thing—is filing for divorce. Carter and Calahan showed up while we were there."

"Oh no!" Mildred said. "Did they recognize you?"

"Carter did, but he stayed quiet. Calahan probably wouldn't recognize his own mother if she changed the part in her hair. He'd make a horrible detective. Anyway, they questioned Zion, which we couldn't overhear, unfortunately, but Carter also had a search warrant for his cabin. Has he given you any more information since we last talked?"

She shook her head. "Not anything important. He's just said he's investigating and asked me some questions about the contract for the retreat and the estate and some stuff about Eleanor's health. I guess I figured he'd question Zion, but I didn't know anything about a search warrant. I wonder if he found anything."

"He found drugs," I said. "I just don't know if they match what Eleanor had in her bloodstream. Since he knows we were there and we are aware of the search warrant, you should ask him if he found anything."

"Do you think he'll tell me?"

"Probably not, but he's still more likely to give you information than me."

She nodded. "I'll call him and ask."

"Just be certain you don't say where you got the information—he'll know but we're all pretending he doesn't for his own good. And if Calahan is around, he probably won't say much at all. But it's worth a shot."

"Then I'll take it. You said Zion's wife is leaving him?"

"She stormed out of there after a yelling match where she accused him of having an affair with Eleanor. I think the police searching her property—and the retreat is *her* inherited property—might have been the last straw."

Mildred shook her head. "I can't say that I blame her. It seems that he's got his whole scam down—finding women who are grieving and have real estate he can use for his silly retreats. He definitely knows how to spot them."

"You said he met Eleanor at a church charity event in Mudbug?" I asked.

Mildred glanced down at the table, then sighed. "I said that *Eleanor* said they met at a church charity event."

"So that's not true?"

"I don't think so. I know I shouldn't have lied. Or I guess in this case, I shouldn't have omitted the truth, but I believe they met months before Eleanor claimed they did."

"Why lie about it?" I asked.

"Because Jasper was still alive," Gertie said.

"Oh!" Now Mildred's disapproving and somewhat embarrassed expression made sense.

"What makes you think they met before Eleanor said they did?" Ida Belle asked. "Did you find anything in her email or texts?"

"No. She scrubbed it clean. The only thing in any of her accounts was recent spam, and folders she saved for receipts and stuff. But nothing between her and Zion."

"He might be smarter than we think and doesn't leave a paper trail," I said. "Except for contracts in his favor, of course. So how did you figure out Eleanor lied about when they met?"

"A couple of times she mentioned things in passing that involved him, but the timeline didn't work. Like a festival he spoke at or an event he did a demonstration at... I just had a feeling she was hiding something from me about him. Every time I asked about how they met and, you know, the normal things you ask about a new relationship, I always felt that she was hedging."

"So you went and looked up some dates of things she mentioned," Ida Belle said.

Mildred nodded. "I'm not saying there was anything going on back then..."

"But it looks shady and the fact that she was lying about it only confirms the shadiness," Gertie said.

"I'm afraid so," Mildred said. "I don't want to believe she was cheating on Jasper, but it doesn't look good."

I nodded, not wanting to say what I was thinking, but the sketchy behavior was starting to spread like a cancer.

"You have that look," Ida Belle said as we drove away from Mildred's house.

"What look?"

"That look where you're thinking a bunch of things you didn't say."

"Well, I wasn't exactly going to call the woman's sister a hoochie when she just died under suspicious circumstances."

"Uh-huh. But...?"

"Well, there's a problem with our original theory of how Zion targeted Eleanor if they hooked up before Jasper died."

Ida Belle nodded. "The sad widow thing doesn't work anymore. But he still could have come across the cabins and found out she had control of the estate."

"True, but his approach appears to be mostly romantic. Not with Sister Britney for the obvious reasons, but if Eleanor was happily married, then that's a barrier to entry for someone like Zion. And a longtime husband is a big hurdle to get over."

"Sometimes a longtime husband is an easier hurdle than a recent one," Ida Belle said. "And she was caring for her mother, who'd been sick for a long time, so she was probably wrung out emotionally with the stress of it all."

Gertie nodded. "And let's face it, a lot of middle-aged women who are completely average in looks and somewhat unhappy with their current circumstances could easily be taken in by a younger, attractive man showing them attention and saying all the things they want to hear."

"True," Ida Belle said. "Losing Jasper might have just been the icing on the cake for something Zion had already set into motion."

I frowned.

"You've got that look again," Ida Belle said.

I nodded. "I think we need to find out more about Jasper's death."

Gertie sucked in a breath. "You don't think Zion killed Jasper just to open a yoga retreat, do you?"

"Honestly, no. But I've seen infatuated *women* do worse."

They both stared at me for a moment, then Gertie shook her head.

"I wish I could argue with that," she said. "No wonder you didn't say anything in front of Mildred."

"Remember back at the retreat when I said we needed to take a closer look at Eleanor? I just doubled down on that. And I think we need to start with Jasper. Who can tell us more about how he died?"

Ida Belle nodded. "Walter."

CHAPTER THIRTEEN

WALTER HAD ALREADY CLOSED THE STORE FOR THE DAY, SO we headed straight to Ida Belle's house, where we found him sitting barefoot on the back porch in shorts and a T-shirt. He gave us a guilty look as we walked out, lowering the bag of potato chips he'd been enjoying with his second beer, given there was an empty bottle already on the table.

"You just closed up fifteen minutes ago," Ida Belle said. "You had to drive home, feed the dog, and change clothes, and you're already on your second beer?"

"What do you take me for, a lush?" Walter asked. "That empty is from last night."

"So not a lush, just a slob," Ida Belle said.

"You were supposed to call on your way home," he said.

"So your mess is my fault?" Ida Belle asked and rolled her eyes. "And all those years, people wondered why I didn't get married."

Walter chuckled. "I've been leaving empty beer bottles on your tables for way longer than from when we said vows. That just made it official."

Ida Belle shook her head. "We need to talk to you about this case we're on."

"What case would that be?"

"Eleanor Stout's death."

Walter frowned. "I thought that was a suicide."

"I think that's going to be the official manner of death," I said, "but there's some wiggle room as to the actual cause."

"I don't understand."

"Eleanor had a shady business partner," Gertie said, "and we're trying to figure out if it was a taking-advantage situation or a birds-of-a-feather one."

Walter still looked confused. "You think Eleanor was shady?"

"Maybe," I said. "What can you tell me about Jasper's death?"

Walter stared at me for a moment, then looked over at Ida Belle. Then his eyes widened and he looked back at me. "You don't think Eleanor had something to do with that, do you?"

I shrugged. "He died in a boating accident, right? Do you know any of the details surrounding it?"

He nodded. "Some, but there's not much to know. The boat engine exploded and the whole thing sank, so there wasn't really any evidence to speak of that could explain exactly what happened."

"And Jasper—I hate to ask..."

"They found embedded tissue, hair, and blood up on an old piling where he was probably tied off."

"They didn't recover any more of the body?"

Walter looked pained. "That boat was torn up, so they didn't find anything but a few pieces, and that's metal, so..."

I nodded, not needing him to explain the rest. If the boat had been ripped to shreds by the blast, Jasper would have fared far worse.

"They sent divers down to try to locate the hull, but they couldn't find anything but scrap. Where he anchored was at the mouth of a bayou and the tide had started going out. It was a full moon that week, so the tide was running fast."

"How much time between the explosion and people showing up at the scene?"

"A couple hours. Weather was poor that day so not a lot of people were out. And he was pretty deep into the bayous. I know sound carries, but the truth is most around here don't even flinch at the sound of gunfire or explosions out in them bayous. To be honest, if the top of his cooler hadn't been launched onto the bank by the blast, we might have never known what happened. Had his name engraved on it."

"So any evidence that might have indicated exactly what happened either sank or was swept away by the outgoing tide."

He nodded. "But the game warden found a bit of gas in the gravel at the launch where he kept his boat parked. Best anyone could figure, he had a fuel leak and a loose wire maybe, or frayed, and a spark set the whole thing up."

"Why wouldn't it have happened when he launched?"

"Could be the leak got worse while he was driving out and kept going while he was anchored, building up a good amount of fuel just sitting and waiting. If a wire loosened more on the ride out or frayed more, it would be a bad combination."

He stared at the ground for a second and shook his head.

"You don't like that explanation, do you?" I asked softly because I could see how troubled he was.

He was silent for several seconds then said, "No. I guess I don't."

"Why is that?"

"I didn't know Jasper all that well on a personal level, but we talked boats and fishing more times than I can count when we ran into each other at local stuff. And there are two things

I'm certain he was an expert at, and those were knowing where the biggest red snapper was biting and boat engines."

"What did Jasper do for a living?"

"Ran the family shrimp house with his father until he passed. His mother had gone the year before. He sold off and went to work as a machinist in a big outfit just up the highway. I asked him one time how he went from managing a pretty big outfit to just being another guy taking orders and punching the clock, but he said the decrease to his stress level would probably give him twenty more years."

"Some people aren't cut out to run a business," Ida Belle said. "You know that. But even if Jasper knew boat engines, he still could have slipped up. People do. So that doesn't explain why it bothers you so much."

He shrugged. "I can't really say. I guess it never sat well with me that someone with that much knowledge could have missed a fuel leak, especially when it was already leaking enough to leave traces on the ground. I know most folk wouldn't even take heed to something so minor, but this is fishing country and the serious ones are darn near marine mechanics. I don't know. The whole thing just felt wrong."

"Do you think someone could have sabotaged his boat?" I asked.

Walter gave me a pained look. "I suppose they could have but Jasper was a nice guy. Why would someone want to hurt him?"

"Maybe the nice guy was in the way of his wife's affair."

Walter stared. "You're telling me Eleanor was stepping out on him?"

"I think so. With that shady yoga guy she partnered up with after he died."

"I don't like the way any of this sounds. Is that why she killed herself? You think the guilt caught up to her?"

"Something did."

———

I took some time to decompress when I got home, then took a long, hot shower, mulling over everything I knew and trying to frame it all with what I'd learned from Walter. So many possibilities but there was no way around the obvious one, which was that someone had tampered with Jasper's boat. And there were only two people that I could think of who would have a reason to do so—Eleanor and Zion.

I had just stuck some fish in the fridge to marinate, when I heard a light knock on my back door. Since anyone who walked around to the back door usually just strolled right in without knocking, I pulled out my nine and inched around the wall to peek between the blinds. I wasn't sure whether to put it back up or grab a spare magazine when I saw Dorothy standing there.

Figuring a visit from Dorothy called more for a bottle of whiskey than more rounds, I opened the door and gave her a curious look.

"This is a surprise," I said.

"Will you just let me in before someone sees me out here?"

I stepped back and waved her in. "Would you like some iced tea? Just finished brewing."

She eyed me suspiciously. "You brewed tea? Sweet tea?"

"Is there any other kind?"

She sniffed. "I might have a glass. Just to make sure you've gotten your mix right. Gertie always has too much sugar in hers and Ida Belle not enough."

I poured two glasses over ice and brought them to the table. "That's why I split the difference," I said.

She sat down, took a sip, then sniffed again. "Not bad for a Yankee."

I smiled. "So do you want to tell me what's got you sneaking over to my house? Because I know it's not to pass judgment on my tea-brewing skills."

She huffed, and I could tell she was wrestling with whether to say what she'd come to say or scrap the whole thing and bail. Finally, she nodded.

"This whole thing with Eleanor... I don't like it. Don't like any of it."

"You mean her suicide?"

"I'm going to be honest and say I mean her entire life—her youth, her marriage, this yoga retreat nonsense, her poor and erratic choices—any of it."

I sat back in my chair, surprised at her words. "I don't understand. I figured you were at the retreat because Eleanor was a friend."

"I was friends with *Dora*, not Eleanor. Dora was a nice lady and a good Catholic. Horrible taste in men, but we can't all be perfect like Jesus."

I nodded. "I'm sorry for your loss. I understand she passed several months back after a prolonged illness. Cancer?"

Dorothy's mouth clenched and she shook her head. "Doctors never could figure out exactly what was wrong. A useless lot, all of 'em. The problems seemed to move from one thing to another. They'd get her liver stabilized and her breathing would be bad. They'd get her breathing fixed and she'd start passing out and wouldn't have the energy to lift a cup. And her mind was like someone had scrubbed it with bleach. Some days I'd go to visit and she'd stare at me, even after we'd been visiting a while, and I knew she was still trying to figure out who I was. Then other days she'd be lucid as could be. Probably some of it was the different drugs they tried, but none of them helped. Fact is, they seemed to make things worse."

"That's hard. But surely they did an autopsy after she died to determine what was wrong."

"No. She had an arrythmia and high blood pressure and the doctor said it was a heart attack. Given the strain on her body, not to mention the mental stress, he didn't see the need to look into it any further. And since she'd been under doctor's care for months, it wasn't required."

"And Eleanor was okay with that?"

"Eleanor did the whole 'thankful she's no longer suffering' and washed her hands of it. Mildred told me after she moved here that she'd wanted an autopsy—said it was best for her and Eleanor if they knew what Dora had died from. For their own health history."

"Of course. If my mother had some mysterious illness that ultimately led to her death, I'd want to know what it was."

"Apparently Eleanor didn't feel the same. Told Mildred she wasn't subjecting their mother to an autopsy when it wasn't necessary. To just be thankful she'd passed peacefully in her sleep and was no longer suffering." Dorothy pursed her lips. "She had her cremated before Mildred could even get down here to view the body."

"Well, that's horrible. And isn't that against Catholic rules?"

"No. The Church changed their stance on cremation back in the '60s, I believe, but I know for a fact that Dora was dead set against it. She was an old-school Catholic and believed your body was supposed to be put wholly into the ground in preparation for the resurrection. But Eleanor took the disrespect a step further and scattered her ashes in the bayou. That definitely isn't allowed."

"And Eleanor was aware of her mother's feelings?"

"Of course she was. Given how sick Dora was for so long, before she slipped into memory lapses, Dora told Eleanor time and again what her wishes were. I heard her say it all to Eleanor one day and Dora talked to me about it several times. She wanted to be buried next to her parents in the Mudbug cemetery. Eleanor tried to claim Dora had changed her mind, but I don't buy that for a second."

I sat back in my chair and stared silently at Dorothy, understanding completely what she was trying to convey and didn't want to say out loud.

"You think Eleanor killed her mother."

Dorothy's eyes widened and her eyes flickered nervously to the wall, then the cabinets, then the floor, before finally looking back at me.

"I don't know," she said finally. "But I'm afraid. And it's been weighing on me so much I can't sleep right. I told myself I was going to tell Mildred my worries when she came to stay with Eleanor, but I'll admit to being a coward. I just couldn't work myself up to it. Kept arguing that there would be no point. Too late for an autopsy."

"What about Mildred's safety? If Eleanor was willing to get rid of her mother—for her inheritance I assume—then wouldn't Mildred be a target as well?"

"I thought about that, but that nasty, so-called man Dora was married to had everything drawn up so that Eleanor had control. Dora had to ask her own daughter for more money just to keep the house repaired. I imagine if she wanted to screw Mildred out of her share, then she could easily manage it given that far as I know Mildred doesn't have any rights except a small monthly payment."

I nodded. "And another death in the immediate family might finally raise some eyebrows."

"There is that too. Anyway, I finally figured no good could

be accomplished by saying anything to Mildred besides shifting my burdened conscience onto her. And Lord knows, she's already suffered through enough."

"I know she is in a lot of pain with her back and that it limits her in a lot of ways."

"Mildred's suffering started long before her back problems."

I nodded. "Ida Belle and Gertie told me their father was a piece of work."

"That's putting it mildly. He was an angry, bitter, small man who delighted in taking out his many frustrations in life with a bottle and then turning them on his wife. I remember being so confused about it all and talking to my own mother. Dora was ten years my senior and I couldn't understand why she was choosing to stay in that situation. I thought older meant wiser. But mama said that some women had decided that was their lot in life and wasn't nothing we could do to change it. That all I could do for Dora was be her friend and help if she asked."

"I take it she never did."

Dorothy shook her head, a sad expression on her face. "When that evil man died, I thought things would change but I should have known better. Oh sure, she wasn't being physically abused anymore, but he managed to beat her emotionally and financially with the will. Putting Eleanor in charge of everything and giving her an allowance like she was a child. And Mildred having no say in anything meant she was beholden to Eleanor."

"I knew Eleanor was the executor, but why didn't the sisters inherit equally?"

"Eleanor was her father's favorite. Eleanor stayed, after all. Mildred had that scholarship in her hand for all of five minutes before she was planning her exit, not that I blame her one bit."

"Mildred said she asked Eleanor to go with her."

"Mildred always was the kind one. Not full of herself like Eleanor. I never understood why in the world Jasper took up with Eleanor after being with someone like Mildred. The sisters favored each other in looks, sure, but in character, there was a big gap."

"Wait—are you saying Mildred used to date Jasper?"

"Of course. They were childhood sweethearts. Couldn't separate the two of them with a sheet of paper from middle school through high school. Until Mildred left, that is."

"Why didn't Jasper go too?"

"He didn't have the option—or didn't feel that he did. His father owned a shrimp house, but he'd had a stroke a couple years before. Never quite recovered and Jasper being an only child, he felt he had to stay and help his father."

"Couldn't he have hired someone to help?"

"Not back then. Margins were too low. Jasper's mother had no education and horrible rheumatoid arthritis, so she couldn't help out at the shrimp house or with getting a job. And his father wouldn't have made the same money doing something else, assuming he could even get hired with his limitations after the stroke. I think Jasper hoped that his father would eventually get better and he'd be able to follow Mildred off."

"But clearly it didn't work out that way."

"No. Because Eleanor got pregnant."

I whistled. "There's one I didn't see coming. But I didn't think Eleanor and Jasper had kids."

"They didn't. She miscarried, but her and Jasper had already married by then." She shook her head. "Jasper wore that same look Dora had before Bruno died. Oh, he tried to look happy and pleasant—and he treated Dora like his own mama—but I could tell he didn't like how his life had turned out."

"Then why not get divorced?"

She shrugged. "I don't know. Maybe he was like Dora and figured that was his punishment for taking up with Eleanor and causing Mildred a world of hurt. I was at Dora's house the day Mildred called Dora bawling her eyes out, telling her that Eleanor had called and told her she was pregnant with Jasper's baby and marrying him. She was begging Dora to tell her it wasn't true."

"Were Mildred and Jasper still in a relationship?"

"Not officially. Jasper called things off when Mildred left, saying it wasn't fair to tie her to Mudbug when she had a whole new set of options in front of her. But feelings don't go away based on a few words, and I think both of them always thought they'd be together again at some point."

"Good Lord. No wonder Mildred stayed gone. I knew the sisters weren't close, but I figured it was more because of her father and that Mildred had established her own life elsewhere and didn't want to be stuck in the past. I never realized that she'd been effectively booted from her old life and probably opted to stay away rather than stir up painful memories."

Dorothy nodded.

"Okay, so why are you telling me all of this?"

She frowned. "Honestly, I'm not even sure. I guess because I don't want anything else heaped on Mildred, but I'm also a coward and didn't want to tell her my suspicions. I know good and well you'll be in the fat middle of this, especially with Gertie finding the body. I guess I just want the truth of this sad, sordid mess to come out, although I will confess to not knowing what that is. But to be honest, whatever happened, I don't want the blowback on me. You don't seem to care about that."

"True," I said, surprised by her blatant honesty. "But the things you've brought up probably can't be proven and even if they could, what difference would it make with Eleanor dead? Do you not believe she committed suicide?"

"I don't know what else it could have been. I saw everything Gertie did and since both Gertie and Kim are claiming that cabin was locked up like a drum, I don't know how else to explain it."

"But?"

She sighed. "But if you'd asked me to make a list of the top five people who I never thought would kill themselves, Eleanor would have been up toward the top. Do you know she didn't even have a service for her mother or Jasper?"

"Seriously? Isn't that against all Southern rules?"

"To say the least."

"And what was her reasoning?"

"She was too overwrought to handle it. Of course, she had a ton of volunteers to take care of it for her—that's what we do here. But she said she could never make it through any kind of gathering and if she didn't attend, then people would never let her live it down. So...nothing. Both the Catholic and Baptist churches had special prayers for them but that was all we could do. Now tell me how a woman who was so selfish she wouldn't let an entire town grieve was suddenly so overwrought that she killed herself."

I nodded, considering what she'd said and wondering if I should push another theory on her, just to get her take.

Mind made up, I went forward with it. "What if Eleanor had something to do with Jasper's death as well?"

Dorothy's eyes widened. "You think that's the case?"

"I don't know. But what I do know is two people have recently died under somewhat mysterious circumstances, and both their deaths directly benefited Eleanor. You're a perceptive woman. I'm sure you noticed that her relationship with Zion was beyond that of a business partner."

Dorothy's jaw flexed, and I could tell she had not only noticed but was mad as heck about it.

"I caught on to her completely unacceptable behavior. Jasper barely gone and she's cavorting with a man that's far too young for her. It was just wrong."

"Did you know he's married?"

"What?! No. I did not. If I had, you couldn't have paid me money to go to that retreat. Here I am, still feeling like I owe Dora something because I couldn't change her life, and Eleanor was having an affair."

She shook her head. "I don't even know why it surprises me. It shouldn't, given everything else."

"I know you don't think Eleanor was a likely candidate for suicide, but given all you now know and suspect, could her conscience have finally been overburdened by it all? Or what if she did all that for Zion and he ended the relationship as soon as he inked that business deal?"

She considered this for several seconds. "I just don't know. Before I came here, I would have stuck to my guns on what I thought Eleanor was capable of, but you've given me more to consider. I guess the truth is we never really know what's going on in someone else's mind, and unless you're a sociopath, I suppose every person has that line that they shouldn't cross."

"Maybe Eleanor crossed hers."

Dorothy sighed and rose from the table. "I was hoping talking to you would make me feel better but I'm not sure that it has. To be honest, I think I feel even more confused."

"Most of my work is like this."

"So you are looking into it?"

I nodded. "I told Mildred I would. If I can find enough credible evidence against Zion and his scamming, then I can probably get Mildred out of that very, very bad contract that Eleanor agreed to. I don't know that I'll be able to do much more though. As much as I hate to admit it, there's just too little to go on at this point."

"If you can help Mildred, that would be a wonderful thing. Something I'd appreciate. I know we have our difference of opinion on how things should be in this town, but I think you have good intentions. At least most of the time. I want you to know that I didn't call the state police and sic them on Carter. But I will admit to calling Celia and telling her what happened at the retreat. I was out of sorts and looking back, I should have known where she'd take things. If that Calahan prevents Carter from doing his job, then that's going to be a big problem for the law-abiding."

"I appreciate you letting me know."

"You've done some good things for really good people here. I'm a big enough person and Christian to admit as much."

"Thank you."

"Don't go getting any ideas though. We're not going to be friends or anything ridiculous like that."

I held in a smile. "Of course not."

CHAPTER FOURTEEN

DOROTHY HAD BARELY MADE IT OUT THE DOOR WHEN MY phone rang. It was Mildred.

"I talked to Carter," Mildred said.

I could hear the excitement laced with confusion in her voice, so I assumed he'd given her some information.

"Did you ask about the drugs?"

"He said it was phenobarbital. Then he asked if our mother had been prescribed that. I said I didn't think so and pulled her medical files from Eleanor's office. She was prescribed opioids for the pain but no barbiturates at all."

"You're sure the list is complete?"

"Positive. It came from her doctor. Carter said he'd verify but I don't think he's going to find anything different."

"Probably not."

"That nasty man had to have given it to her. But I swear, I know Eleanor and she wouldn't have taken anything like that."

"Even if the thing she cared about most was potentially slipping away? And she realized it had all been a lie?"

She was silent for several seconds. "I don't know. Eleanor was always strong at best. Defiant at worst. I just can't wrap my head around..." She sighed. "I've been gone a long time. Maybe I just didn't know my sister like I thought I did."

"Don't put the weight of this on your shoulders. It's more likely someone dosed her drink with it than she took it voluntarily. But what they hoped to accomplish, I'm not sure."

"None of this makes sense, Fortune."

"I know. But I'll figure it out. I promise you."

————

CARTER WALKED IN ABOUT AN HOUR AFTER DOROTHY HAD slunk out the back door. He looked ready to spit nails. Since I knew he would never waste that much energy being angry at me for doing things he knew I would do, I assumed it was the Calahan Effect.

"Rough day?"

He grabbed a beer out of the fridge and sank into a chair at the kitchen table. "You have no idea. Since you're back, I guess you got off the cross?"

"It was more of a consulting gig, but I have problems with the uniform."

"Especially when running through the woods."

"I have no idea what you're talking about."

"Uh-huh. Even considering the wardrobe, I'll bet you had a better time than me the past thirty-six hours."

"Hmmm. Well, let's see. Gertie deliberately took the bad cop role before Ida Belle could open her mouth. She was feisty, disgruntled, and generally insulting over most everything."

"Leaving Ida Belle to play the peacemaker role. I bet that stung."

"I had to play an innocent, naive girl ripe for the taking by a smarmy con man. That was much harder."

His lips quivered and the smile finally broke through. "You

also had to pretend that your primary method of helping people was praying. I'm surprise you didn't fire off an entire magazine in the bayou as soon as you got home."

"Oh, I did. Shot two speckled trout. I'm not even sure how that happens, but I sent Tiny out to fetch them. We're having grilled fish for dinner."

"The only bright spot in my day. Probably going to be the only bright spot in yours when I say what I have to say next."

"Calahan?"

He nodded. "The ME signed off on the suicide. Don't get me wrong, I can't see how it could be anything else, but I wanted to check the extenuating circumstances."

"Of course. But I'm guessing Calahan has other ideas."

"He's been harping for two days now about the waste of resources. That I need to close this file and move on to the next case. That I'm costing taxpayers money for no reason."

"Zion being a scammer is no reason?"

"When the person he potentially scammed is dead by their own hand, that's how Calahan sees it."

"But Mildred is bound by that same crappy contract if we can't figure out a way to get her rid of that leech."

"I know and I seriously doubt this is Zion's first time skirting ethics or the law, but Calahan said if I don't finish up the loose ends tomorrow and close the file, he's going to report me."

"My offer to shoot him is still on the table."

"Tempting, but I'm pretty sure they'd know where to look."

"I don't know. My guess is anyone who's ever met the man has felt the same way, so the pool of suspects is probably huge."

"True, but I still can't afford the additional scrutiny."

"Did you run Zion?"

"Yes. And came up empty. I mean really empty. There's no

trace of a Zion Gates before he appeared in New Orleans two years ago."

"Which in itself is sketchy but not remotely surprising. Did you run his prints?"

"Yep. Nothing."

"I refuse to believe that he's not guilty of something illegal somewhere. Otherwise, why change your name? And he's not from here. His accent says Midwest to me, not Southern. He's done a good job of adapting it to the region, but I can still tell this isn't his home turf."

Carter nodded. "I want to do a deeper dive, but the only way is to put out his photo on the wire and start working his identity backward. If I question him, he'll just relocate again."

"But that takes time, and working the phone talking to other law enforcement branches means you give Calahan ammunition. You know you can't afford to run the risk."

"I know." He cursed and slammed one hand on the table. "Zion is going to get away with something—I'm certain of it."

"Were the drugs you found in his cabin a match for what was in Eleanor's bloodstream?"

He stared. "How do you know I found anything?"

"I overheard Zion and Sapphire arguing about it. Both are denying ownership, by the way."

"Yeah, I know. There was no label, neither has a prescription on file for the med, and the prints on the bottle don't belong to either of them."

"Interesting. So someone goes to the trouble of handling the bottle with gloves but just leaves it in a nightstand instead of tossing it. You never answered my question, by the way."

I didn't really expect an answer, but Carter's frustration must have outweighed his rigid principles.

"It was a match. Extremely strong painkiller. Think palliative care."

"Phenobarbital. Mildred told me. I figured they belonged to Dora given how sick she was, but Mildred said she couldn't find anything in her mother's records."

He nodded. "I double-checked and she was never prescribed this particular drug."

"So someone provided Eleanor with the drugs, at minimum. On the more serious side of possibilities, they spiked something she drank and maybe fed her the idea of suicide."

"It's possible it went down that way, but I can't prove anything."

"What about the gun?" I asked, figuring I'd press my luck since he was being so forthcoming.

"Unregistered, serial number filed off. I can't prove it didn't belong to Eleanor but everything I found in her house was registered to either her, her father, or Jasper, and all numbers were intact."

I shook my head. "All of this is so wrong."

"I know. But what can I do about it? And when it comes down to it, the woman killed herself. There's no way around that. I'd love to figure out who Zion is and what he's been up to before coming here because I'd bet my career that law enforcement somewhere is looking for him to answer questions at a minimum. But my hands are tied."

"Mine aren't," I said, then sighed. "But if I find stuff that you didn't then it makes you look bad. And if I pass you the information and you claim it, then you were going against protocol and Calahan reports you. Crap."

"Yep. I've already gone rounds in my mind over all of it, and there's no way I can get Zion and come out a winner."

"Calahan won't be here forever."

"No, but I bet he outlasts Zion. And once he slips out of sight, he'll pop up somewhere else as a completely different person."

"So what are you going to do?"

He sighed. "Nothing else I can do. Calahan has left me no other option but to close the investigation tomorrow."

I frowned and stared out the window. Calahan was ruining everything. I was as certain as Carter—probably more so—that Zion was shady. But I also knew he was right. With Sapphire giving him the boot and Carter sniffing around over Eleanor's death, Zion was probably already planning his exit strategy. Maybe even to Florida, if he could convince Sister Britney to make a deal.

Something had to be done to stop him from preying on more women, but Carter's hands were tied. Which left me, but I lacked access to police databases and had no connections to other law enforcement branches, except Casey. And I couldn't ask a decorated homicide detective to put her own career on the line over a con man. Tracking down Zion's past was a job best suited for Carter, but with Calahan lurking behind every corner, Carter couldn't do his job.

I needed a plan.

And then one hit me.

"I suppose that idiot Calahan is taking up space at the café again this evening?" I asked.

"He was headed that way when we left the sheriff's department. He sits there for hours every night, blowholing to all the residents. Francine has already asked me if she can get a restraining order against him. I wish she could."

"She could just refuse service. That's her right."

"And give Calahan a reason to make her life miserable? You know he'd be petty enough to send every inspection agency to the café every day for a year."

I sighed, certain he was right. But there had to be some way around Calahan so that Zion didn't get away. Then it hit me.

I jumped up from my chair so quickly it startled Carter.

"I've got to go do something. Fish are marinating in the fridge and ready to toss on the grill. Asparagus is already wrapped with bacon. Don't wait on me."

He didn't utter a single word or even lift an eyebrow when I grabbed my keys and ran out of the house. Smart. Because the coup I was planning was something he didn't need to know anything about. Ever.

———

I HAD ALREADY DIALED HARRISON BEFORE I BACKED OUT OF the driveway.

"I need help on a case," I said when he answered.

"Oh no. Carter already told me what you're working on and has threatened me with unemployment and no invitation to deer hunt this year if I so much as stick one nostril hair in the mix."

"Well then, it's a good thing I don't need *your* help. I need your fiancée. Please tell me Cassidy is working the night shift at the ER."

"She'll be there until tomorrow morning."

"Has Calahan ever met her?"

"No. Why would he have? Wait—"

"Gotta go."

I hung up before he could ask anything he didn't need to know the answer to. My second call was to Gertie.

"I need some of Nora's brew," I said.

"Really? This is a surprise. What kind of high are you looking for?"

"I'm not. I need to make Calahan sick enough to check out of work for a bit but not kill him."

"Well, that's somewhat disappointing—the no killing part,

I mean—but I have something that should work. Had too much protein and cheese on a new diet back a few weeks ago. Thought I was going to need the jaws of life for a regular bowel movement—"

"I don't need details. I *really* don't need details. Can I disguise the taste in soda or beer? Or maybe water?"

"Yeah, it's got a tiny bit of flavor but otherwise, it's clear and deadly. Think Drano for your large intestine."

"Great. Grab it and some syringes if you have those. I'm headed to Ida Belle's to get her to drive. We'll pick you up in a few."

"Hot dog! I love a covert operation. Especially when we're taking out the bad guy and don't have to wear a habit."

I shook my head as I disconnected. What a shame the cop was the bad guy. Oh well, needs must, and I had a scammer to expose. I'd fill them in on what was happening with Carter and my conversation with Dorothy on the way.

Ida Belle didn't even hesitate when I burst in the front door and told her we had a job to do. Walter just gave me a nod and kept drinking his beer as though I hadn't said a word. Apparently, the smart gene ran in the family.

Gertie came out of her house with a huge tote slung over her shoulder, and whatever was in it was heavy because she was leaning to one side.

"This can't be good," Ida Belle said.

"I asked her to bring supplies," I said.

"Anvil? Anchor? Cannonball?"

"No. Some liquid and syringes. I don't want to know about the rest."

"I don't either."

I hopped out and grabbed the tote from Gertie because I wasn't sure she could climb into the SUV without falling, and I didn't want to damage the precious cargo she had with her.

"Where to?" Ida Belle asked as she pulled away.

"Bayou Inn. Now, let me tell you why."

I filled them in on the situation with Calahan first, feeling a tiny bit of relief when I saw his truck still parked in front of the sheriff's department when we pulled through downtown.

"I get it now," Gertie said. "You're hoping you can take Calahan out long enough for Carter to run down background on Zion. Brilliant."

Ida Belle nodded. "Do you think you can buy him enough time?"

"Trust me," Gertie said. "This stuff is lethal. I mean, not deadly lethal, but I-can't-leave-the-house lethal. Heck, I didn't leave the bathroom for two days. I thought—"

"No." Ida Belle held up one hand. "That's all I need to know."

"There's more," I said. "I had a surprise visitor this afternoon before Carter got home."

I told them about my conversation with Dorothy. When I was done, they both looked somewhat floored.

"I'm not sure whether to be more surprised that Dorothy came and talked to you or by the information she gave you," Ida Belle said.

"I know. It was a real eye-opener."

Gertie shook her head. "If Eleanor had something to do with Jasper's death and her own mother, all over trying to land that idiot Zion, and then he dumped her and it all came home to roost, that might have finally been enough for her to crack."

Ida Belle nodded. "Especially with some help from the drugs, assuming they would have skewed her thinking ability."

"But we still don't know where she got the drugs," Gertie said. "At first I thought it was Zion, but now that we know Sapphire followed him to the retreat that day, I'm not so sure."

"Sapphire could have slipped the drugs in something

Eleanor would drink," I said, "but there still had to be a catalyst to send all of it crashing down on Eleanor."

"Maybe Sapphire confronted her," Ida Belle said. "Told her that Zion was still very much her husband and just using Eleanor for the property. Might have even warned her off."

"Possible," I agreed. "But we know Eleanor and Zion were arguing before he left because Mildred saw them. There's also the problem with the gun."

"People don't file serial numbers off for no reason," Ida Belle said.

"If someone dosed Eleanor with barbiturates and gave her a gun, then surely that was a setup," Gertie said.

"It looks like it," I said. "But why give Eleanor a gun when she owns them?"

"Maybe she didn't have any at the retreat," Gertie said. "Maybe Zion didn't know if she owned guns and figured if he provided one—under some other pretense—and then worked her up, that she'd ingest the drugs and the whole problem of having to pretend he was into Eleanor would take care of itself."

I shook my head. "That's a lot of risk and even more hope."

"Nah," Ida Belle said. "More of a free throw. If it didn't work, then he could just bide his time until he could figure out a better way to manage it. This way was just quicker and gave him instant access to property, assuming that agreement holds up."

"Mildred is going to fight him tooth and nail on it," Gertie said. "And I don't blame her. Given the way the investigation is going, do you really think Zion will put up a fight for it?"

"No," I said. "I think if he can get a payout from Sapphire, he'll bail, which is the problem I'm trying to solve for tonight. If he clears out before Carter can run down his background, he might get away with everything here and become a problem for a whole new set of victims."

Ida Belle shook her head. "The thing I don't understand is why keep the drugs around? Seems really foolish to stick them in your nightstand when they could be at the bottom of the bayou."

"It bothers me too," I said. "It seems like a really dumb move from someone who's likely made their living off scheming, but then, if investigating has taught us anything, it's that criminals sometimes do really stupid things."

"Maybe the drugs really do belong to Sapphire," Gertie said. "He said they were in her nightstand. Maybe he used a few but couldn't afford for the entire bottle to come up missing since it wasn't his."

I nodded but I still wasn't convinced we'd hit on the right combination of answers. The whole deal with the drugs, Zion, and Sapphire wasn't lining up, but for the life of me, I couldn't figure out why.

When we pulled into the parking lot of the motel, I directed Ida Belle to park at the end of the motel on the other side of a moving truck, where she, of course, backed in like the getaway driver pro she was. I didn't think Calahan would recognize her SUV from the one that had been parked at the retreat, mostly because I thought he was really crappy at his job, but even an idiot can have a moment of clarity, so it was best to stay hidden. I grabbed Gertie's tote bag and we headed for the office, where I hoped we'd find our old friend Shadow Chaser running the desk. If not, we'd rent a room and figure out the rest.

Fortunately, Shadow Chaser was in his usual spot behind the computer watching a movie. He looked up when we walked in and his expression immediately shifted from boredom to sheer panic.

"Who's dead?" he asked.

"No one yet," I said.

He turned a shade paler than his usual ghost white. "You're not here to kill them, are you?"

"Not intentionally."

"If only I knew for sure that you were joking."

I just shrugged.

"Oh my God!" He grabbed a pad of paper off the desk and started fanning himself.

"Of course I'm not going to kill him," I said. "I just want to detain him."

"That sounds like stuff cops say before I see them on *Dateline*."

"I'm not a cop. Trust me, if I want to kill someone, I issue no warnings, and I'd never be sloppy enough to be featured on *Dateline*. But you might need to bill me for cleaning."

He stared. "You know what—fine. Whatever. You have a pass with the scary man I report to anyway. If anything goes sideways—who the heck am I kidding—*when* whatever you're up to goes sideways, I'm telling him exactly who did it."

"If this goes sideways, he'll already know who did it."

The scary man was Mannie, the strong arm for Big and Little Hebert, who'd turned out to be excellent at business and was now in charge of the Bayou Inn, one of Big and Little's recent acquisitions. Mannie was attempting to renovate the place and make it more attractive to the less seedy side of the population.

"How are your aunt and uncle doing?" I asked.

He relaxed and smiled. I'd helped his uncle out of a murder rap the month before when Shadow had begged for help. I was glad we'd been able to clear the cute older couple of any wrongdoing and save their bed-and-breakfast.

"They're great. Murder must be good for business because bookings are up so much they're turning people away."

"Fantastic. Tell them we said hello and are glad they're doing so well."

"We should plan a short girls' trip when they have an opening," Gertie said.

Ida Belle sighed. "The last girls' trip we were on, we had to dress like nuns, do yoga, and drink really crappy smoothies."

Shadow Chaser put his hands over his ears. "I am not hearing this. I am not hearing any of this. What criminal did I rent a room to this time?"

"Last name's Calahan."

"Huh?" he asked.

"Take your hands off your ears!" I yelled.

"Oh, yeah. Name?"

I told him the name again and his eyes widened. "The cop? Well, why didn't you say so. That guy is a total creep. Came in here and took a whole case of my bottled water from the storeroom then told me to 'bill it to the state.' Like that's really a thing. And he's wearing this grin when he says it like he's just challenging me to tell him no. Are you sure you can't kill him?"

Gertie snorted. "Oh how the wind changes when you know the target."

"Look, I've got one missing case of water to account for already, and he's left his stay open-ended. I'm afraid the scary man won't believe me when I say I was extorted by a cop."

"I'll let him know the cop's a huge problem. You won't be on the hook for anything."

His relief was apparent. "Thanks. The huge problem isn't here yet, by the way."

"Good. I'd prefer he didn't catch me in his room."

"That figures. He usually gets here about this time, so

whatever you're not doing that I know nothing about, you better hurry. Room 15."

He handed me a key.

I motioned to the tote and Gertie pulled out a bottle of clear liquid that looked suspiciously like water. I opened it and smelled. Definitely not water but not everyone had my nose either. Someone like Calahan wouldn't notice. Then she handed me the syringes.

"How much should I use?" I asked.

"Nora said dosage was a teaspoon and it lit up my behind for days," Gertie said.

Shadow Chaser let out a squeak and threw his hands back over his ears again.

"Okay," I said. "You two, head back to the SUV and play lookout. You should have a good view of the entrance from where we parked. Text me if you see Calahan pull in."

"He'll have a clear view of the door to his room as soon as he pulls in," Ida Belle said.

"I'll go out the bathroom window and run around the back of the motel to the SUV. At least he's on the first floor. Just be ready to haul it when I get there."

Ida Belle snorted. "As if I have ever *not* been ready to haul it."

I grinned as I pulled on my gloves, then hurried to Calahan's room and slipped inside. I went straight to the minifridge and was pleased to spot several bottles of water and cans of beer inside. I was guessing Calahan would go for the beer first thing, but since I couldn't be sure, I doctored up a couple beers and waters and placed them at the front of the fridge. Since I also couldn't be certain how much he would consume, I put the teaspoon dosage in each. If he came in and started chugging beers and chasing them with water, it was not going to be a good night for him.

I had just screwed the top back on the bottle when my phone buzzed, signaling an incoming text. I pulled it out.

Calahan here. Get out.

I jammed my phone and the bottle in my pocket and hurried to the bathroom. But when I went to shove up the window over the toilet, it didn't budge.

Holy crap!

CHAPTER FIFTEEN

WITH ALL THE RENOVATIONS THAT BIG AND LITTLE HAD agreed to, they'd been painting. But whoever had painted this room had painted the window shut. I had a knife on me, but there was no way to get it open and get out before Calahan barged in, so I rushed back into the bedroom and slid under the bed just as I heard the door open.

Window won't open. Need a diversion so I can get out.

I listened as Calahan walked inside and immediately went into the bathroom. If the shower fired up, I only had to bide my time, then hustle out, but unfortunately, it was just a fast relief and flush and he was back in the bedroom. He flopped on the end of the bed, and I said a silent prayer of thanks that Big and Little had sprung for new furniture. The old beds would have left me flat as a pancake.

I heard the minifridge open and smiled. Now if he'd just chug whatever he'd taken out and hit the bathroom, I might be able to flee.

I didn't have to wait that long.

The explosion outside wasn't as loud as the dynamite

Gertie usually set off, but I had no doubt where it had come from.

"What in the world!" The room door flew open and banged against the wall as Calahan rushed out.

I peered out from under the bed skirt and saw Calahan in the middle of the parking lot, staring at his truck, which was encased in a pillow of smoke. Unfortunately, he was still too close for me to make a run for it as there was nothing nearby to duck behind. I waited for the follow-up—because surely that wasn't all Gertie had in her handbag of tricks—when suddenly the metal wheels of a cart rolled into the room.

"Get in!" Shadow Chaser said in a sort of yell-whisper.

I slid out from under the bed and without a second's hesitation, flipped into the laundry cart, and he threw a comforter over me.

"What the hell is going on here?" Calahan's voice boomed from the doorway.

Shadow Chaser was humming and Calahan repeated his question.

"What?" Shadow Chaser asked. "Oh, wait. Earbuds. Sorry. You can't listen to AC/DC on low. Can I help you?"

"What are you doing in my room?"

"Baking a cake…laundry, of course. Virginia called in sick. We all know she's not—she just gets drunk and then can't make her shift, but management won't let me fire her and I've been dealing with the contractors all day so I couldn't get to the linens. I told them we needed to hire someone older and ugly who doesn't get invited to parties. Maybe even a diabetic since they should avoid too much drinking, but they said—"

"Are you mental? Did you not hear that explosion? Someone vandalized my truck."

"Oh. Sorry, the music was so loud and I was singing. Do you want me to call the police? Oh, you are the police."

"Did you hear me say someone vandalized my truck? They set off a bomb of pink glitter on it."

"Well, that's one I haven't heard yet. Usually they just smash windows and steal sunglasses or something. So I should call the police."

"You should start helping me question everyone here to see who saw something."

"Dude, this is the kind of place where no one sees anything. Besides, that's not in my job description and unless you want to sleep on a sketchy mattress tomorrow and dry off with toilet paper, I have laundry to do. I'll just call the cops."

"Forget it!"

I heard stomping as Calahan left and then the cart began to roll so quickly that I wondered if Shadow Chaser was jogging it down the walkway. We made a sharp turn where I was pretty sure the breezeway to the back of the hotel was and then I heard him open a door and push the cart inside.

"Get out and go hide somewhere else before I have a heart attack."

I popped out of the cart and realized we were in the laundry room.

"Good call," I said. "Thanks for the assist."

"Gertie painted a penis in white glue on that cop's windshield and then set off a pink glitter bomb on the hood of his truck, which almost makes the heart attack I'm going to have worth it. Still, I might need to start drinking now and stop maybe sometime in October."

I grinned. "I owe you."

He grimaced. "Since I already owed you, can we just call it even and you stop coming here?"

"As soon as the bad guys stay somewhere else, I'll be happy to. But you'd probably miss me."

His look of dismay was so apparent that I couldn't help

laughing as I rushed to the door and peeked out. The breezeway was clear, so I sprinted for the back of the motel and then skirted the back side and circled around to the end where the SUV was parked. I jumped inside and found Gertie doubled over laughing. Even Ida Belle was chuckling.

"You really did it, didn't you?" I asked. "You painted a glue penis on Calahan's windshield and blew up a glitter bomb on it."

"Not just any glue—superglue. That thing isn't coming off, even with a chisel."

"All amusement aside," Ida Belle said, "the downside is that if Calahan calls the cops, who knows when he'll get around to drinking something."

"He won't call the cops," I said.

I told them about his interaction with Shadow Chaser and my escape, and they started laughing again.

"I get it," Gertie said. "If the cops come out, they'll see that Pink Pretty on his windshield. And no way Calahan is letting that story get out. He'll take a sledgehammer to his windshield and claim a rock hit it before he lets cops know."

Ida Belle nodded. "That's the kind of story that will follow you your entire career. Well then, I hope he goes back in soon to stew over a cold bottle of something and doesn't just keep standing there staring at it."

"Me too," Gertie said. "I want to get a picture now that the smoke has cleared."

"I'll go peek around the corner," Ida Belle said.

"I can do it," Gertie said. "I'm the one who wants the picture."

"We all want a picture, but I move faster than you."

"I moved pretty fast when I was running away from Calahan's truck."

"Uh-huh. And how does your knee feel now?"

Gertie huffed. "Fine. But I want a close-up *and* a distance shot so we can identify the truck."

Ida Belle slipped out of the vehicle and peered around the corner of the moving van. Calahan must have cleared the scene because she took out her phone and took some pictures. When she climbed back in she pulled them up to show us. Sure enough, there was a bright, glittery, neon-pink penis across the entire windshield of Calahan's truck.

"Good Lord," I said, choking as I laughed. "That thing is huge."

"Said no one to Calahan ever," Gertie said. "He ought to be thanking me."

"That was a big risk," I said. "He could have seen you drawing it on."

"He was hurrying inside like a man who had to take a big pee," she said. "And I've been practicing."

"I'm not even going to ask. Well, hopefully, he decides to decompress with a beer or water. I figured I'd dose both since I wasn't sure. Whenever he clears out, we'll replace the ones he didn't drink and the empties with clean containers. We'll have to get some cheap beer at the store on the corner. I don't figure he was counting the water since he took an entire case from Shadow Chaser. I'll just restock any water from that."

"You know he's going to blame Francine for this," Gertie said.

I nodded. "I called on the way to pick you up. Calahan had the shrimp gumbo along with a bunch of other customers eating from that same pot. He won't have a leg to stand on."

"That might be a literal description if he chugs more than one," Gertie said. "My whole left leg went numb. I was vacuuming when it hit me and had to use the darn thing as a crutch to make it to the bathroom."

Ida Belle stared at her in dismay. "Why must you overshare?"

"Because I'm me. You either get oversharing and pink glitter penises or watching old Westerns and griping at Walter about eating an entire bag of chips."

Ida Belle just sighed.

IT WAS A LONG BORING FORTY MINUTES BEFORE WE SAW ANY activity. Shadow Chaser had already sent twelve texts, worried about what was coming next and giving Gertie kudos for the glitter bomb. I kept telling him no one knew what was next, but I don't think he believed me.

Then he called. "That fool just asked me to drive him to the hospital. What did you give him—you know what, don't answer that. I told him that our liability insurance would drop us cold if I was driving guests around on my moped, and that even if I had a car, I wouldn't let him in it sick."

"Good. Stay out of it."

"Like that's possible. I'm already in this up to the top of my laundry bin. Then he demands that I go drape a sheet over the windshield of his truck. I told him that I'd have to bill him for the sheet since no way I'm laundering anything with glitter here, and that would be an extra thirty dollars. The cheapskate refused to pay it."

"Maybe you should stop answering your phone."

"Already forwarded to the answering service."

"Good. Hang tight. I think we're about to get an answer to your what's-next question."

Ten minutes later, I heard an ambulance in the distance.

"I think we're up," I said.

Ida Belle grinned. "I should have figured Calahan would

call the paramedics. God forbid he drive himself to the hospital with Gertie's artwork on his windshield."

"In all fairness," Gertie said, "he probably shouldn't drive after drinking that stuff. It does weird things to your muscles."

"And you keep drinking Nora's random cocktails, why exactly?"

Gertie shrugged. "They work."

We watched as the ambulance turned into the motel and I jumped out so I could monitor them. They parked in front of Calahan's door and rushed inside. Then they came back out for the stretcher and a couple minutes later, they had Calahan strapped down and were pushing him out to the ambulance. Since I could hear him complaining the whole time, following his complaints up with 'do you know who I am,' I assumed I hadn't killed him.

As soon as the ambulance left, I pulled on a new set of gloves and, due to Gertie's horror stories, donned a mask. Then I hurried inside to check the fridge. We'd lucked out and he'd only gone for the water so no beer run required. But he'd drunk two, so it was probably going to be a long night for our favorite cop.

I emptied two bottles of clean water in the sink and tossed one in the trash can and the other on the floor where I'd found the tainted ones. Then I hurried to the SUV with the tainted bottles, and we set off for the hospital. Shadow Chaser was standing outside the office and gave us a relieved wave as we headed out.

"What if Calahan sees us at the hospital?" Ida Belle asked.

"Unless we're standing in the bathroom with him, he won't see us," Gertie said. "After two doses he might not even be able to see."

I nodded. "And besides, I'm sure there's someone at the hospital that you know. There's no laws against visiting."

"Beatrice Paulson just had her corns removed," Gertie said.

I pulled out my phone and called Cassidy.

"I've been waiting to hear from you," she said when she answered.

"Harrison tipped you off."

"He did...well, as much as he could. But all I needed to hear was this was about Calahan and I was on board. Harrison had me on speaker when Carter came in the Mudbug office with that arrogant moron. He let me listen in and it was all I could do to keep my mouth shut the way he disrespected everyone. What do you need from me?"

"He's on his way there now with the paramedics."

"Did you shoot him?" she asked, now sounding a bit concerned.

"Why does everyone assume I shot someone? You know what, never mind. I dosed him with some homemade laxative."

"What's in it?"

"Undetermined. But Gertie tried it so it probably won't kill him. However, he had double her dosage, so it's going to be rough."

"Got it. I assume he ate at Francine's as I got an earful from her yesterday as well about him, so I won't go with food poisoning. I think maybe a suspected parasite of some sort—who knows where he picked it up."

"Probably touched something gross then picked his nose," Gertie said. "He looks the type."

Cassidy laughed. "I'll have to see the results of your handiwork before I know what tests I can order and how long I can hold him up, but dehydration alone buys you several hours in the ER since it's not a priority. And since you don't know what's in the doses, I should run some tests anyway. That adds hours of waiting onto things. Then the paperwork bureaucracy and sheer lack of employees with a work ethic should get you at least until noon tomorrow. I can probably get a couple more hours out of discharge paperwork."

"Can't he choose to just leave?" Ida Belle said.

"Sure. But if he does so against doctor's orders, the state police can not only refuse to allow him back on the job until proper discharge, they can also refuse to pay the bill. And to be honest, since you don't even know what was in the doses, I need to give him a thorough checkup anyway."

"Perfect," I said. "We're on our way now."

"Here? Isn't that risky?"

"Of course, but we want to see the show—the opening act at least."

"I get it. The paramedics will be bringing him through the back entrance, so get a move on and come in the front. I'll tuck you in the janitor's closet—they just finished our area and won't be back for a while—and make sure I put him in the room across the hall. I can't guarantee you'll hear anything though."

"We'll hear," Gertie said. "He'll be yelling."

"Well, then I'll threaten him with sedation, and he'll be here even longer."

Ida Belle passed the paramedics on the way to the hospital. No surprise there. Cassidy met us at the entrance and escorted us to the janitor's closet. It was a bit of a squeeze with all three of us and the supplies, but it wasn't as though we were taking up residence. We all leaned against the door, waiting.

We'd only been there for a few minutes when Cassidy walked by and said, "Showtime."

We heard the paramedics come in at the end of the hallway and Cassidy gave them instructions. Calahan was whining and complaining the entire time.

"Let's get him cleaned up so I can see what's going on," Cassidy said.

"What's going on is that woman poisoned me!" Calahan raged.

"What woman?"

"That woman who owns the café in Sinful."

"Francine? We've never had anyone here because of eating there. What did you have?"

"Shrimp gumbo."

"If it was food poisoning from the gumbo, we'd have people lined up and down the hallway. Francine always sells out on the gumbo. Do you have reason to believe you were personally targeted?"

"She doesn't like me. I can tell."

"I imagine she doesn't like a lot of customers, but they don't wind up in my ER."

"Well, how the heck else do you explain this? I think I crapped out an ear. I've never had something this bad."

"Did you consume anything after the gumbo?"

"Only bottled water."

"Hmmm. Then it could be a parasite or something you ate set off an underlying condition. We'll need to get you some fluids and run some tests."

"What kind of tests?"

"Bloodwork, sonogram, and MRI to start, and I'll get you scheduled for a colonoscopy tomorrow morning."

"What? No way! Just give me some Gatorade and let me out of here."

"I'm sorry. I can't do that."

"You're holding me hostage?"

"Of course not. You're free to leave, but it will be against doctor's orders."

"Then I want to see another doctor."

"Great. He'll be on shift tomorrow morning at seven. But since I'm the head of this department, I assure you, he's going to follow the exact same protocol I'm recommending because I'm the one who wrote our protocols and I give out the raises."

"Whatever. Then just give me my clothes back and I'll leave."

"Your clothes are being laundered. You're welcome to leave in the hospital gown but we'll be billing you fifty bucks for it."

"Fifty bucks? That's outrageous!"

"Complain to insurance companies. It's their fault. I also need to inform you that without a doctor's release, you can't return to work. Until we know exactly what caused you to be so ill you sent for an ambulance, you put others at risk. It could be a parasite...something you could spread, and trust me, I do not want to become famous for being at the center of some outbreak of a new strain of Cajun malaria."

"You can't keep me from working."

"Technically, no. But I'll report you to your commander and they will put you on leave until you receive medical clearance."

"This is bull—"

"Excuse me. I need to take this."

I cracked the door and saw Cassidy in the hallway, looking at her phone. She gave me a thumbs-up and headed back in.

"That was the clerk at the motel," she said. "After seeing your room, he shares the same concerns I do and is now in a panic about his own health. You're not welcome to return there until you receive clearance. He said he'll wrap your belongings in plastic and maybe call the EPA. Now, if you still want to leave, you're welcome to walk out in your gown, but it's going to be quite a hike back to the motel for your vehicle. There's no Uber out this way at this hour and even if there was, I couldn't in good conscience allow you in one. If you have a friend that would be willing to risk picking you up, that's always an option, or I can provide you another ambulance ride for about five thousand. How would you like to proceed?"

"This is unbelievable. Where the hell would I have picked up some parasite?"

"You work in and around the bayous, correct? I've seen all kinds of things in this hospital that attached themselves to humans. It's always best to be safe, but it's your call."

"Whatever. Do the tests, but make them quick."

"Of course. I'll put you in the express lane and in the meantime, we'll move you to a room with a private bathroom. You're going to need it."

I heard a door close and then Cassidy gave some instructions to the nurses. The door opened and closed again and then the door to the janitor's closet opened and she waved us out.

"Hurry," she said as she took off for the lobby. "I wouldn't put it past that idiot to try to leave."

"Thanks, Cassidy," I said. "I owe you huge."

Gertie nodded. "You should be an actress."

"Oh, that wasn't acting. Whatever you gave him already has his eyes sunk in. I really do need to check him out. And I have to admit to a certain level of curiosity about something so obviously potent. In smaller doses, it might really help chronic pain patients with the side effects of the opioids we prescribe."

She grinned and headed off in the other direction, probably to get Calahan on the schedule for the bevy of tests he was about to undergo.

We hurried down the hall, practically jog-walking, and jumped into the SUV. We barely got the doors closed before we started laughing.

"That was epic and brutal," Gertie said. "But it sounds like we bought Carter some time."

I nodded. "Let's hope it was enough."

Carter was sprawled out on the couch when I got back. There were two empty beer bottles on the table and a plate with one remaining stalk of asparagus next to it.

"How was the fish?" I asked.

"Great. I left yours in the microwave."

"Good, because I'm starving."

I warmed my dinner up, grabbed a beer for myself, and headed back to the living room, where I dropped into my recliner.

"I bought you some time," I said.

He sat up. "What?"

"Time. From Calahan. Not sure how much but maybe a day."

"Did you kill him?"

I threw my hands up. "Why is that everyone's first thought? Of course I didn't kill him. He's alive and maybe not so well but being attended by Cassidy at the ER."

"Should I even ask?"

I shrugged. "She's afraid he might have contracted some sort of intestinal parasite working in the bayous. Even if he's released tomorrow, he might not be getting too far from a bathroom for a while."

"Good. God."

"You're welcome."

I pulled out my cell phone. "And he might want to report some vandalism, but I'm guessing not."

I passed him the phone and his eyes widened, then he started laughing so hard he began choking.

"Take a drink of something," I said. "I'm not putting this fish down to give you CPR."

He finally regained control and rose from the couch and leaned over to take my plate and put it on the table.

"How about putting it down so I can give you a kiss."

He leaned in and kissed me gently on the lips, then smiled. "I love you, Fortune Redding."

I grinned. "I know."

CHAPTER SIXTEEN

CARTER PRACTICALLY RAN THROUGH THE SHOWER AND OUT of the house the next morning, anxious to get to work on tracking down Zion's identity. Since I hadn't decided yet what was on the agenda that morning, I took my time over coffee and cooked up eggs and bacon that I shared with a grateful Merlin and Tiny.

I polished off the half pot that Carter had left me and decided to go for a second. Despite my glee over our successful takedown of Calahan, I hadn't slept well. All the information I'd collected had whirled around in my mind all night and every time I'd drift off, I'd jolt back awake, thinking I'd figured something out but disappointed when it was all still as big a mess as before.

Ida Belle and Gertie wandered in about eight, Gertie still looking pleased with herself. Not that I blamed her. As far as pranks went, the one she'd played on Calahan was one of the funniest and the most appropriate I'd ever seen, and I'd worked with CIA assassins. We were creative and mercenary when it came to pranks.

"When I told Jeb about what I did to Calahan last night,

he laughed so hard, he threw his back out again," she said as they sat. "Sexy time is definitely off the table this weekend, but Jeb said he wanted to do something special to reward my creativity, so he's taking me to that new steakhouse in NOLA Saturday night."

"I heard reservations were booked six months out," Ida Belle said.

"A childhood friend of his is the owner and they had a last-minute cancellation. So he bumped the next on the waiting list and slotted us in."

"Nice," Ida Belle said. "If it's good, I might have to try to get Walter and me in for our anniversary next year."

"Have you heard anything from Cassidy?" Gertie asked.

I nodded. "She texted this morning. She said to tell Carter she'd ordered the parts for the plumbing repair, but they couldn't deliver until this afternoon."

"Ha," Gertie said. "Plumbing repair. Cassidy is one smart cookie."

Ida Belle nodded. "All the information we needed and yet nothing that can blow back on her. So what's on the agenda for today?"

"I don't know."

Ida Belle frowned. "It's not like you to be without a plan."

I sighed. "I know. And yet, here I am...planless. I mean, what is our objective anymore? Carter will run down Zion through law enforcement channels and hopefully get something to arrest him on."

"Hopefully, before he bolts," Gertie said.

"I suppose we could kidnap him and hold him hostage somewhere to prevent that from happening, but it seems problematic."

Ida Belle snorted. "Understatement of the year."

"The truth is, what do we have left to discover? We know

Zion is shady and there's no sense pursuing the Sister Britney angle because we got what we went for with that."

"And we now know that he scammed Sapphire as well and had Kim dangling," Gertie said.

I nodded. "But no matter how much unsavory stuff we uncover, we still come back to the same thing, and that's the fact that Eleanor committed suicide."

Ida Belle looked over at Gertie. "You're absolutely positive there was no other way in that cabin?"

Gertie gave her an indignant look. "Why would I shoot open the door if there was another way in?"

"Because you like shooting stuff, especially in situations where you're not normally supposed to?"

"That's true, but in this case, there really wasn't another way in. That door was dead-bolted from the inside. All the windows were locked."

I frowned. "Let's pretend for a minute that there was another way in. As a thought experiment. Who had opportunity to commit the crime?"

"Zion and Sapphire, of course," Gertie said. "Kim, potentially. She could have been coming from the cabin instead of going to. When I saw her she was stopped and looking at a flower, so we only have her word as to what she was doing. And I guess now that I think of it, anyone at the retreat could have gone through the woods to Eleanor's cabin."

"Is there a trail?"

"No idea. But if it's a thought experiment then I had to throw it out there."

"Well, hell," Ida Belle said, "Jack the Ripper could have strolled through the woods as well."

"Okay," I said, "So next step—who has the most to gain from Eleanor's death?"

"Financially, Zion and Mildred," Ida Belle said. "Emotionally, Sapphire, Kim, and taking into account the things Dorothy said, maybe Mildred as well."

"But there was no way Mildred could have done it," Gertie said. "Kim said Mildred was in her office doing tax stuff when she left to go get Eleanor and besides, it would have taken Mildred forever to get down there and back."

I nodded. "So financially, Zion still has the strongest motive, assuming this questionable agreement holds up and Carter doesn't find a reason to arrest him. Those cabins would probably bring a good amount. But on the emotional side, Sapphire was trying to save her marriage. An effort in futility, but she's young and clearly not all that bright when it comes to men."

"And she has a temper, as indicated by her treatment of guests, her argument with Zion, and her driving."

I nodded. "And then there's Kim, who was poised to be Zion's newest target. Young, lonely, and probably still grieving her mother's passing."

"Just the way Zion likes them," Gertie said, clearly disgusted.

"So the question is, what was the bigger motivator—money or love?"

Gertie shook her head. "I don't think we can make that call as people have killed for both and often with even less at stake."

"The drugs are still an angle that might narrow the suspect list down," Ida Belle said. "If we can prove Zion or Sapphire gave Eleanor the drugs, then the ADA might be able to make a case for contribution to her death on their part."

"But how do we prove it was one or the other?" I asked. "They both have motive."

"My money is on Sapphire slipping Eleanor the drugs—probably in her water like you did Calahan with the laxative,"

Ida Belle said. "Zion sounded sincere when he accused her of having them."

"And with Zion being Eleanor's business partner, I assume he had keys to the place," Gertie said. "Sapphire could have accessed them at some point and made a copy. The dead bolt to the cabin wouldn't have been pulled when Eleanor and Zion were both conducting the class. All Sapphire had to do was follow him to the retreat and then wait for Eleanor to clear out of the cabin."

"I agree the opportunity was there," I said, "but what would Sapphire hope to accomplish by drugging Eleanor? She wasn't supposed to know Zion was romancing Eleanor much less going to dump her. And if that 'breakup'—assuming that's what happened—was the final straw that shifted Eleanor's mental state to ending her own life, how would Sapphire have known to coordinate drugging Eleanor with Zion's actions?"

"They definitely weren't in cahoots on it," Ida Belle said. "Or he wouldn't have been checking her car and accusing her of following him."

"Exactly," I said.

"Maybe Sapphire thought she'd given Eleanor enough to kill her," Gertie said.

"Possible," I agreed. "But then there's the gun. So Sapphire decides to drug Eleanor and leaves an untraceable gun in case the drugs don't work? Or did Zion just happen to provide Eleanor with an untraceable gun before breaking up with her, hoping to push her to suicide on the exact same afternoon as his wife drugged her?"

"Yeah, that's way too much coincidence," Gertie said. "Even for me, and I love a good conspiracy."

"And that's what I wrestled with all night long. Plenty of motive. Plenty of opportunity, per se. But no way to pin it on one particular person. And the key players are too fragmented for me to believe any of them are working together."

"Not to mention, their desired outcomes are somewhat at odds," Ida Belle said.

"So where do we go from here?" Gertie asked.

I shook my head. "I wish I knew."

My cell phone rang.

"It's Purple," I said as I answered.

"Fortune, I did some poking around on that shady Zion. Don't worry, my story was that he'd approached me about an investment, but I didn't get a good feeling and wanted some insider info. Well, my network came through in glorious fashion and with a resounding 'don't you dare' on going into business with him."

"That's great. What did you get?"

"First off, Zion started putting feelers out about selling your client's cabins on Tuesday."

"The woman died on Monday!" Gertie yelled, clearly outraged.

"I know," Purple said. "I hope you don't mind but I checked into that whole thing. The police aren't saying a lot, but I got enough basics to know that the body wasn't even cold before he started making phone calls."

"Good. God." Even the normally stoic Ida Belle looked offended.

"But that's not the worst of it," Purple said.

"What's worse than peddling someone's belongings before the funeral?" Gertie asked.

"My attorney is friends with Sapphire's attorney, and of course, this is all confidential and we shouldn't know and he shouldn't have said and blah, blah, blah, but the long and short is Sapphire is filing for divorce."

"We figured that was coming," I said.

"After seeing her expression when those cops showed up at dinner, so did I, but I figured he'd fight it tooth and nail to get every dime he could out of her."

"You're saying he's not?"

"Nope. Sapphire offered him twenty thousand to go away and he agreed."

"He's panicking," I said.

"Definitely panicking. Because Sapphire is worth a pretty penny. Given who her attorney is, I'm sure there was a great prenuptial, but they can all be worked around. Part of the reason I'll never get married, but that's another story."

"So instead of sticking around to contest the prenuptial and potentially make out with way more money, Zion is taking a low payout," I said. "He's getting ready to pull a runner."

"That's what I'm thinking," Purple said. "And since none of us believe that's his real name, my guess is he'll pop up somewhere else as a completely different person with the same old scam. And please excuse me for poking my nose all the way in your business, but when I checked the website for your friend's retreat, I did a bit of a deep dive into the sister and the assistant."

"Did you come up with anything?"

"Nothing on the sister. She was an accountant living in Colorado. Never married. Didn't own any property. Rented the apartment above the CPA firm she worked for. It's nice, but not extravagant. There was nothing about her life that raised any flags, and I couldn't find any assets to speak of. Only her name as one of the beneficiaries of her father's trust."

"Good."

"But Kim is another story. She's loaded. I mean so loaded she's almost out of my league and my family are no slouches. Her dad died years back—heart attack, which is no surprise in the finance realm. Her mother died recently though—complications with epilepsy—and Kim inherited everything as she's an only child. And everything is *very* substantial."

"I read an article on her and it alluded to significant money."

"It's significant all right. She sold the family home in NOLA, which isn't surprising. It's old and historic but who wants to live in the place you watched your mother die in, right? And it's too much and too rigid for a younger person to want anyway. Aside from that, she has a villa in Italy and a penthouse in Bahrain, but the most interesting item is the recent purchase of 100 acres on Horn Island."

"Where is that?" I asked.

"Mississippi Gulf Coast. Most of the island is national seashore, but there are private parcels and she scooped up well over half of them."

"When was this?"

"Two weeks ago. I'm not trying to cast aspersions or anything, but the girl I saw in the pictures was pale as a ghost with what looked like natural red hair. I don't see her lounging on a beach all day long."

"Me either. I really appreciate the intel. I might have to put you on as a consultant when we have anything real estate related."

"I'm happy to help. I did a little research on you as well. You've quite the track record for nabbing the bad guys and helping out good people in the process. I'm happy to consult, but I'd rather be your friend. I'll let you know if I hear anything else. Have to run into a meeting. I'm looking at a hotel in Turks and Caicos."

She disconnected and I looked over at Ida Belle and Gertie.

"So Zion's about to pull a runner to an island off the coast of Mississippi."

"I don't get it," Gertie said. "Why not head to that villa in Italy or the penthouse in Bahrain? Seems like it would be easier to disappear that way. It's not like he's on the FBI's most wanted list and they'll be combing the world for him."

I smiled. "Because he can't get out of the country without using his valid passport, and I guarantee you someone is looking for our friend Zion under his real name. His passport is probably flagged. And there's something else she said—about Kim's mom."

I grabbed my phone and dialed Cassidy. "I hope I didn't wake you," I said when she answered.

"Haven't gone to bed yet, but I'm on my way. Your friend Calahan drove me to morning drinking, but he's easily booked until tonight. Depending on what tests reveal, I probably can't hold him any longer than that though."

"One day is a lot of time for Carter to work. I don't want you risking your job over someone like Calahan. If he even gets an inkling of your connection to me, he'll be making a stink."

Cassidy chuckled. "Oh, he's already making a stink. The overnights wore masks the entire shift. If we were allowed, we would have fired up enough candles for an exorcism."

"That sounds right," Gertie said.

"Did you need something else?" she asked.

"Yeah, I had a quick question for you about phenobarbital. Would you prescribe it to someone with epilepsy?"

"Sure, and it's common for late stages. It's helpful for managing seizures due to the relaxation effect."

"Thanks, Cassidy. Go get some rest."

I dialed Carter next.

"You know that fingerprint you pulled off the meds that didn't match Zion or Sapphire?"

"Yeah."

"Try Kim."

"Eleanor's assistant?"

"And Zion's latest target. Her mother died due to complications from epilepsy. Phenobarbital is a common drug given to epilepsy patients."

"On it."

He disconnected before I could ask if he was making headway on running down Zion's true identity, but it didn't matter. The walls were closing fast and even if Zion fled, we knew where he was going.

"You think Kim lifted her mom's drugs?" Gertie asked.

I nodded. "Remember when we talked to her, she said she was looking everywhere for her sleeping pills but must have left them at the retreat?"

Ida Belle nodded. "And then she said her doctor refused to refill her Ambien. So you think she improvised with her mom's meds."

"That's exactly what I think."

"And she didn't lose them," Ida Belle said. "Zion lifted them."

"Then why was he accusing Sapphire of having the drugs?" Gertie asked.

I shook my head. "Maybe to pretend he wasn't involved and because he'd already told the cops that wasn't his nightstand."

"When he's probably the one who put them there," Gertie said.

"I don't know. It still doesn't make sense to me. If you were going to drug someone and try to make it look like they'd taken them of their own accord and then killed themselves, you'd leave the drugs at the scene. And if you weren't smart enough to do so, why on earth would you bring them back to your own home? Pitch them in the bayou for Christ's sake."

"That's true," Ida Belle said. "It would be one thing if

either of them were prescribed the meds. Then it would look stranger if they *weren't* in their possession."

"Most criminals think they're the smartest person in the room," Gertie said. "We've seen it before. If this whole retreat scam is Zion's MO, then maybe he figured he'd hold on to the meds in case he needed them again. Maybe he was planning on using them on Sapphire once things settled down."

I frowned. "Maybe."

But somehow, none of the scenarios we'd come up with felt quite right.

My phone rang and I saw it was Mildred.

"The motion detector at the retreat's office sent an alert," she said.

"Do you have cameras?"

"No. Just the motion detectors on the front wall of the main building and the cabins. I turn them on when it's vacant, mostly to let us know if bears are wandering around. We had one take a door off one time and stroll inside. They're up too high for smaller animals to set them off."

I looked at Ida Belle and Gertie. "Anyone want to bet on whether or not it's a bear?"

"Not a chance in hell," Ida Belle said.

"Do you have a security system?" I asked.

"The office door does but not the windows. They were all locked, though, and the system hasn't been tripped or disarmed."

"Interesting. Is the retreat still a crime scene?"

"I think so—Eleanor's cabin anyway. But the motion detector isn't working there. Hasn't been for weeks. I kept telling Eleanor that we needed to get someone out to fix it, but she said it was low priority. If the police were going back out there, wouldn't they let me know?"

"They should," Ida Belle said. "Too easy to get shot trespassing in these parts."

"We're on our way to pick you up," I said. "If we get caught out there without you, it might look bad. Plus we'll need you to determine if anything has been disturbed."

Mildred was waiting on the front porch when we pulled up. She clutched the railing and made her way down the three steps and over to Ida Belle's SUV. I hopped out and helped her into the front seat.

"Have you received any more alerts?" I asked.

She shook her head. "Maybe it was nothing. I'm going to feel foolish having you drive all the way out there if it turns out a bird flew by or the sensor is malfunctioning."

"Better safe than sorry given the circumstances," I said. "Have you heard anything else from Carter?"

"No. But my attorney called while I was waiting on you."

She angled a bit in her seat, and I could see her face was flushed with excitement. "Apparently, Zion is relinquishing any claim to the cabins and has asked to void his agreement with Eleanor altogether and dissolve the retreat business. He said he'd be happy to sign whatever my attorney drew up. My attorney already had a couple documents ready to go, hoping Zion would go for that option, so he got a signature right there."

Ida Belle, Gertie, and I gave one another knowing glances.

"What?" Mildred asked. "You don't seem surprised."

"We think Zion is about to make a run for it," Gertie said. "With Carter investigating, the last thing he can afford to do is stick around here for a prolonged legal fight with you."

"And I definitely would have given him one."

"Carter is trying to run down exactly who he really is," I said. "And we're betting that he's wanted for something somewhere."

"But wouldn't his fingerprints have come up when Carter ran them?"

"Not unless he'd been arrested. If he fled before cops could pin him down on something, then he's still wanted for questioning but hadn't been charged."

"Doesn't mean he's not guilty though," Ida Belle said. "In fact, I'm betting on fraud charges being forthcoming as soon as he's exposed."

She huffed. "That explains it. Here I thought maybe he'd finally acquired a shred of decency since a woman probably died over him, but I should have known better. Well, at least I won't have to deal with fighting him for the cabins."

"Have you thought about what you're going to do with them?" Gertie asked.

"Good Lord, the woman just found out they're hers for sure," Ida Belle said. "You might want to give her a minute to process. We haven't even had a service for Eleanor yet."

Guilt flashed across Mildred's face. "I feel bad about that. People keep asking or hinting…but I just couldn't work myself up to planning something with so much unanswered. I know people will be asking questions about her death and Zion and who knows what else, and I don't think I can take standing in a church for hours on end, saying 'I don't know.'"

She sighed. "I guess I was hoping Carter would come up with some explanation—something that would explain the choice. Maybe then Eleanor wouldn't look as bad as she does right now. People are already talking about Zion and saying it was inappropriate because he was so much younger and she took up with him right after Jasper's death. They'd have a stroke if they knew she was carrying on with him before Jasper died."

"We can't be sure of that," Gertie said in what I assumed was an attempt to make Mildred feel better.

Mildred gave her a sad look. "I can. I was going through the desk in her room this morning, trying to find the paperwork on that darned microwave that keeps cutting out. I found credit card statements. She went to Zion's retreat nine months ago. And then again three weeks later, then every two weeks after that."

"I'm surprised Jasper didn't say anything," Gertie said. "That couldn't have been cheap."

"They had separate finances," Mildred said. "Well, that's not exactly correct. According to Mom, Eleanor's money—which was basically trust money—was *her* money and Jasper's money was *their* money. She always had her own bank account and credit cards in addition to their joint stuff."

Ida Belle snorted. "I guess that's a good deal if you can get it. Although I'm not sure how great the relationship would be."

"I'm not either," Mildred said and sighed again. "The more I learn about my sister, the less I think of her. That doesn't mean I wanted her to die—"

"Of course not," Gertie said. "You've just had an enormous amount to absorb and all while you're still grieving your mom."

Mildred shook her head and her eyes got misty. "I shouldn't have stayed away. After my father passed, I should have moved back here."

"To what end?" I asked. "Eleanor had control over the trust and therefore the purse strings. Given that, she also had the final say in everything to do with your mom."

Ida Belle nodded. "And it's not like good accounting jobs grow on trees around here. Besides, you had already made another life for yourself, and it was good for you to get out from under your father's shadow. He cast a long one."

"That he did," Mildred said, her voice sad.

She was silent for a long time, then finally shook her head. "I'm not going to get anywhere dwelling on all this sadness and negativity. I can still mourn my loss but make plans to move forward with the rest of my life, right?"

"You not only can, but you should," Gertie said. "Looking to the future, and keeping busy with the plans you're making, is what will keep you from falling apart. Sitting and dwelling on things you can't change and couldn't control is the pathway to deep depression."

She gave Gertie a strong nod, then straightened a bit as she looked over at Ida Belle. "According to Eleanor, you were interested in buying the cabins at one time. If that's still the case, we can talk about it. I'm going to sell the house as well. My life isn't here anymore—hasn't been for a long, long time. And staying... Well, it would put me right back under that shadow. That's not something I want to do."

Gertie nodded. "I don't blame you. But where will you go?"

Mildred's eyes widened and she smiled as she shook her head. "Lord, I don't know. My old job in Colorado's already been filled and to be honest, I was starting to get restless. Fifteen years doing the same thing can either make you feel secure or restless. It did both for me, but restless was what I mostly felt before I moved in with Eleanor."

"What about your surgery?" I asked.

"I'll have to talk to my surgeon in New Orleans and see what the progression rate is. I know it makes more sense to have it done here where I've got friends to help, but after everything that's happened, I would feel bad taking charity from people. And not to offend present company, but I don't want to deal with all the whispering behind my back. All this stuff about Eleanor and Zion is going to come out eventually, and I don't want it to land on me. I know that sounds selfish and probably reckless but that's how I feel."

"You do what you need to do," Gertie said. "Your mental health plays a big role in your recovery. And you can always hire help until you are able to do things yourself. I know it's probably crass to say but the reality is, once you sell the cabins and the house, you'll have the resources to not only have your surgery and get some help, but to take your time getting into another job."

Mildred blinked. "You're right. I know that... At least I think I did, but it's still hard to wrap my mind around."

She gave Gertie a smile. "Who knows—maybe I'll do one of those medical tourism things and jet off to some sunny, beautiful beach to take care of everything."

"That sounds like a plan to me," Ida Belle said. "And if you're serious about selling the cabins, then I'd love to talk to you about them. But I'll be making a fair offer. We can save some on the Realtor's fees by dealing direct but I'm not looking for a discount. That's just taking advantage. We'll have an appraisal done and I'll offer market."

"What in the world are you going to do with the cabins?" Gertie asked.

Ida Belle raised one eyebrow. "Maybe I'll open a yoga retreat."

Gertie snorted. "The heck you will."

"Fishing and target shooting?"

I grinned. "That sounds more like it."

"And no habits required," Gertie said.

CHAPTER SEVENTEEN

IDA BELLE TURNED OFF THE ROAD AND INTO THE DRIVE FOR the cabins. I scanned the woods as we drove, looking for any sign of movement, but the only thing I saw was birds. The parking lot in front of the office was empty as well.

"There's no police tape here," Ida Belle said.

Mildred nodded. "I called and asked. Carter wasn't in but Deputy Breaux said the only area off-limits is Eleanor's cabin. We're okay to check the office, although I don't see what we would find. The alarm is on and hasn't tripped."

"Let's take a look anyway," I said. "I didn't get to see any of the property before, and I'd like to get the lay of the land."

"Sure," Mildred said and pulled out her phone. She disarmed the alarm and pulled out a set of keys. "This a full set to everything. Usually, I keep the cabin and outbuilding keys in the office, but given the situation..."

I helped Mildred out of the SUV and we headed into the office. The front room was a small lobby with a counter in the middle with a desk forming an L on the left side and a hallway beyond with two doors on each side. On the left wall was another door. We headed that way first.

"This is the dining area," Mildred said as she pushed it open.

I peered in and saw five tables with seating in a large sitting area and a long bar with an open kitchen behind it. There were no other entries or exits to the room except for the windows, which all appeared to be closed and latched save for one door in the far corner.

"What's that lead to?"

"A half bath to serve the dining area."

"Does it have a window?"

"No."

"Okay," I said and stepped back into the lobby.

"This is where everyone checks in." Mildred waved at the counter before moving around it. "This is Kim's desk behind it."

We followed her down the hall and she pushed open the first door on the right. "This is the office supplies, janitor's closet, and maintenance storage, I guess you'd say."

She pushed the door open and flipped on the light. "It's all cleaning supplies and things to make repairs, air filters, all of that."

"And who did the repairs?"

"Eleanor did a lot of them. She was pretty handy. We had a local guy for things she couldn't or didn't want to handle herself. Across the hall is the bathroom," she said and pushed open the door. "Got a full one with walk-in shower since this was a family cabin at one time. Came in handy for me as my cabin only had a small tub."

We continued down the hall and she pushed open the door on the right. "This was Eleanor's office."

We walked in and I looked around. It contained a nice desk in the center with a credenza behind. Two chairs in front of the desk and a couch on the inside wall shared with the storeroom. A big painting of sunrise over the bayou hung on the wall behind the couch. A large window on the back wall opened to a view of the forest, where I saw the smallest hint of water glimmering through the trees.

"Nice," I said. "Does anything look out of place?"

Mildred frowned and walked around behind the desk. She pulled open the drawers and peered inside, then shook her head.

"I don't know why I'm looking," she said. "It's not like I had an inventory of Eleanor's office, but it all looks the same to me. The same as when the cops were here anyway."

I nodded. "I assume your office is across the hall?"

"Yes," she said as we exited and headed over to it.

Mildred's office was easily 30 percent smaller with no room for a cushy couch or even guest chairs. A single folded metal chair stood in between the filing cabinet and the wall, and a sturdy desk sat just inside the door, providing a side view out the window on the back wall that mirrored Eleanor's.

Gertie frowned. "One would think you'd get the bigger office as you were spending the most time here and doing all the paperwork."

"Oh, Eleanor had to meet with people and she had to plan all the classes and work on advertising and stuff with Kim. As long as I have a good office chair and reliable computer, I'm fine. And the view is the same."

"It's definitely pretty," I agreed. "And everything in here looks good?"

"Same as before. I'm really sorry I dragged you out here. It was probably nothing."

"It's not a problem," I said. "And like I said, I wanted to put everything in perspective anyway."

"And I'm getting another look at my future purchase," Ida Belle said.

"Yes, I guess there's that," Mildred agreed.

"Let's take a look at Eleanor's cabin next," I said. "I know we can't go inside, but if someone was here then the only two places that make sense to go are the office or Eleanor's cabin. How far is it?"

"To be honest, I haven't been down there since I was a kid," she said.

"Less than a quarter mile," Gertie said. "But it's a decent hike. Nice wide path though. Three cabins are off that path but much closer in than Eleanor's, and the others are on the other side of the parking lot down a different path altogether."

"Can we drive any closer?" I asked.

"I'm afraid not," Mildred said. "Eleanor kept saying she was going to buy a UTV so that I could get around the property, but I didn't see the point as I really didn't need to go anywhere but my office and my cabin, which is the closest one on the other side."

"Do you want to wait here while we check?"

She looked conflicted but finally nodded. "If I had my walker with me, I'd give it a go, but I don't think I can make it there and back without a good sit in between. And I'm assuming her porch is off-limits as well?"

"Probably so," Ida Belle said. "Do you feel safe here alone or would you prefer one of us stays with you?"

"Oh! I guess I hadn't thought... I don't see any reason to feel unsafe, I suppose."

"How about you lock yourself in the office and turn the alarm system back on. It's got an audible signal as well as being monitored, right?"

She nodded.

"And you have my cell phone. Call if you hear or see anything."

Gertie reached in her purse and pulled out a nine-millimeter. "You can borrow this. I have more."

Mildred stared for a moment, then took the gun, giving Gertie's purse a sideways glance. I understood her apprehension.

"Okay, we'll just take a look around the cabin and be right back. It shouldn't take long."

We headed out and I heard the front door lock behind us as Gertie pointed to the path.

"At least it's wide and hard packed," Ida Belle said.

"And there hasn't been rain lately," Gertie said. "I heard Eleanor saying something about paving all the sidewalks. I know it wouldn't be as natural but a good ole Louisiana downpour would turn this into a mud walk in a minute."

"Unfortunately, a hard path means no footprints," I said.

"Heck, I didn't even think about that," Gertie said. "Do you really think someone was out here?"

I shrugged. "I don't know but I think it's strange that the motion detector went off. Surely, if it was so easily tripped by birds or bugs or whatever, Mildred would be getting notices all the time."

"That's true," Ida Belle said.

"There's my cabin," Gertie said, and pointed to a small cabin about twenty yards off the path. "Ronald was just beyond me. I spotted Kim on the trail just up from me when I was headed out."

We continued on the path as it wound through the woods. I had to admit it was pretty and peaceful, but it was definitely a ways back. I wondered if Eleanor had deliberately selected the most remote cabin so people were less likely to see what she was up to with Zion.

Finally, we rounded a corner and Gertie pointed. "There's the roof of Eleanor's cabin."

I saw the roofline through the trees and made another ninety-degree turn. The path opened to a clearing and the cabin came into full view, police tape draped across the front porch like Christmas lights.

"It has decent-sized rooms from what I saw," Gertie said. "It would be a great camp, but there's only one bedroom."

"I could turn the sauna into a bunk room," Ida Belle said.

Gertie stared at her in dismay. "I'm not sleeping where someone died."

"I'll change the flooring."

"Well, that makes all the difference in the world."

I stared at the front door as we approached. Since Gertie had blown the lock off, I assumed one of Carter's deputies had put a latch with a padlock on it to secure the scene, but as we got closer, it looked as if the door was open a crack.

Maybe it was shadows or the police tape was distorting my view, but as I stepped up to the porch, all doubt was removed. The door was cracked open an inch, a latch with a padlock hanging from the side where it had been pried off.

I pointed to the door and put my finger to my mouth. Ida Belle and Gertie nodded as I directed them to flank me on each side of the porch. I was going in.

I said a prayer that the porch was sound and the hinges on the door oiled, pulled on gloves, pulled out my nine, and crept up the steps. I peered in the crack and listened for the sound of anything inside, but it was quiet. Then I heard something rustling. It sounded as though it was coming from the back of the cabin.

I inched the door open and slipped inside into a sitting area with a hallway on the right side of the room. The door was off center toward the right side of the cabin, but not so far right that I had a clear view down the hallway. Which was good, because it meant if someone was back there, they didn't have a clear view of me either.

I scanned the room, looking for potential places to take cover. A leather couch stood against the wall just inside the door to the left. A coat rack on the right. A love seat stood on the far wall, and two chairs and a table on the back wall. The coffee table in front of the couch was wicker and wouldn't even slow down a bullet by a millisecond. The couch and love seat weren't much better.

I'd just have to avoid being shot.

I eased over toward the hallway and flattened myself against the living room wall listening for any sound that whoever had broken in was still in residence. I still wasn't certain that the sound I'd heard was coming from inside the cabin. It could have been brush rubbing against the outside.

Then I heard a floorboard creak and a thud. Someone was definitely inside.

I peered around the opening and saw that the hallway was clear. I remember Gertie saying the sauna was toward the back of the cabin next to Eleanor's bedroom. That meant the door at the end of the hall, facing the living room, must be hers. I eased down the hall, listening at each closed door as I passed, but couldn't pick up any sound inside. The sauna had a glass window in the door, and I ducked down below it, then inched up to peer into the room. It was clear, so I knew the intruder must be in the bedroom.

I crept to the bedroom door and crouched down because when most people fired through a door, they aimed high. Then I reached up with my left hand and slowly twisted the knob. When the latch had completely released, I gently pushed the door open, my nine ready to return fire.

The curtain at the back window fluttered in the breeze, the window wide open. I ran across the room and looked into the woods that crept almost right up to the back of the cabin. The brush was so dense that I didn't see anything at first, but then I made out a break in the tree line and what looked like a trail.

As I pulled myself through the window, a shot rang out and the window shattered, sending glass down on top of me. I threw my hands over my head and rolled, then dashed to the corner of the cabin where Ida Belle was crouched.

"Take cover, Gertie," I yelled because I was pretty sure the shot had come from the other side.

A couple seconds later, Gertie rounded the side of the cabin from the front, her face red and breath ragged.

"Got to add sprints to my workout," she huffed. "I saw someone in the woods, just behind the cabin. The bayou is west of here, I think."

I nodded. "I'm going after whoever that is. Get back to the office and make sure Mildred is covered."

They took off running down the path, and I peered around the corner and into the woods, Nothing. It was only twenty feet to the tree line, so I had to go for it. I dashed across the open area, praying that whoever had taken that shot was on the move and not poised like a sniper, and pushed out a breath of relief when I hit the woods and drew up behind a huge cypress tree.

There was no sound except the gentle rustle of trees and foliage. The shooter was either hiding, ready to take a shot, or fleeing and well ahead of me. Neither was a great option, but I'd worked with worse. I sprang around the tree and pushed through the brush, headed for where I'd seen the trail. When I found it, I saw that it was nothing more than a narrow strip of dirt that led straight into the woods, but that had to be where the shooter had gone.

I ticked my pace up to a slow jog, figuring the shooter had

a car or other transportation stashed on a road nearby. If they got to it before I got to them, it was over. I'd gone a good way when I rounded a corner, then slid to a stop where the path split. One continued straight and another veered off to the left. The hard-packed ground and dense, lush foliage left no indication which way the shooter had taken. With time, I probably could have found a sign, but I didn't have time.

I was just about to continue straight when I heard a crashing in the woods to the left. In a split second, I pivoted and took off down the alternative path. I was still at a slow jog when, ahead of me, I heard noise again and started to run.

And just when I thought I was going to apprehend the shooter, I ran into the bear.

CHAPTER EIGHTEEN

I'm not sure who was more surprised, but I'm going with me. I sprang back from the giant wall of fur as if I'd hit a trampoline and vaulted into a tree faster than you could say Yogi. The bear, who'd been standing on his hind legs and apparently scratching his back on a tree, stared at me, eyes wide, then whirled around faster than I figured anything of that size could manage and ran off through the brush.

I looked down and realized that the bear had probably saved my life. The tree he was scratching on was perched on the edge of a bank with a twenty-foot drop. Directly below it were cypress roots pointing up like giant stakes.

A boat motor fired up in the distance and I realized I'd miscalculated. There was a chance that the shooter and the boat operator were two completely different people, but I wasn't betting on it. I jumped out of the tree I was in and grabbed on to the bear's tree, then leaned as far as I could over the water. Downstream, I saw someone in a black hoodie push a flat-bottom aluminum boat away from a dock that by my calculation was directly behind the office.

Since it was ninety degrees and a thousand percent humidity, I would bet my last bullet that was the shooter. And there was absolutely no way I could get to the dock before they got away, nor could I make a leap from the embankment into the water without impaling myself on the cypress knees. I lifted my nine, figuring I could try to shoot out the engine when they passed, when I saw the rope swing dangling off the embankment just a bit down from me.

Without bothering with a risk assessment, I ran down the embankment as the boat drew nearer and leaped onto the rope like Tarzan. I swung out over the bayou and when the boat was almost below me, I let go and dropped.

Bull's-eye!

In a perfectly executed Jackie Chan move, I landed right in the bow of the boat with both feet firmly planted and facing the startled driver, whose hoodie had blown back.

Kim!

She moved for her pocket and I launched, tackling her out of the boat and into the bayou. When we hit the water, I wrapped the hoodie around my hand and yanked her up to the surface when she emerged sputtering.

"Put your hands up or I drown you right here."

I heard cheering down the bank and saw Ida Belle and Gertie standing on the dock. I glanced behind me as I treaded water and saw the boat was only a couple feet away. I tucked one arm under Kim and pulled her toward the boat. When I reached it, I grabbed a cleat and spun her around, slamming her into the side of the boat.

"Grab on, and so help me God, if you reach below the water for that gun, I will shoot you."

She burst into tears and started blubbering. "I dropped the gun when you knocked me over. I swear. I wasn't trying to kill you."

"You'll have to excuse me if I don't believe you."

"I just wanted to scare you so I could get away."

"And you thought shooting at a CIA assassin was the way to do that?"

Her eyes widened and she started shaking her head. "I didn't know. I swear. I just thought you were a regular detective. Oh my God. Please don't kill me. I swear I wasn't trying to kill you. I'm just not a good shot. I only learned how to shoot yesterday. Oh my God."

I shook my head and pulled myself over the side and into the boat, then reached down and pulled her up and over, dropping her into the bottom. She'd gone completely limp and was now collapsed in a dripping heap, sobbing like a baby.

The boat was still running, so I grabbed the throttle and gave it some gas, turning it around. When we got to the dock, Ida Belle and Gertie stared down at the crying lump in the bottom of the boat.

"Who is it?" Gertie asked.

I reached down and pulled her up.

"Zion's latest victim."

———

WITH THE HELP OF IDA BELLE AND GERTIE, I PUSHED KIM onto the dock where she slumped like a corpse, leaning against a piling.

"Search her," I directed. "I want to make sure she doesn't still have that gun."

I started my search in the boat, lifting seats and digging in cubbies to try to find something—anything—that indicated why Kim had broken into Eleanor's cabin.

"Well?" I asked when I came up with nothing.

Ida Belle and Gertie both shook their heads.

"Nothing on her," Ida Belle said. "And she's zoned out like she's drugged."

"Maybe she's in shock," Gertie said.

"I'm the one who got shot at," I pointed out.

"But you're used to it."

It took both Ida Belle and me to carry/drag Kim up the trail toward the office. We ran into Mildred halfway there, struggling down the path with a cane.

"I called the police when I heard gunfire," she said. "Then I saw Ida Belle and Gertie go running by and I couldn't stand waiting any longer. I had to see if you were all right."

"We're fine," I said. "And we caught your intruder."

Mildred peered at Kim, who had her head dropped so low she couldn't see her face, but she must have recognized enough to place her because her expression shifted from fear to shock.

"Kim? What on earth?"

Kim didn't even acknowledge she had spoken, just kept looking down, half standing there.

"Let's get her inside and secured until the cops get here," I said. "I'm sure you have some rope or cord in that supply room."

"I have handcuffs in my purse," Gertie said.

"Do you have the key?" I asked.

"Hmmmm."

Ida Belle rolled her eyes. "Handcuff her to herself and tie her to something heavy. Let the cops figure it out."

"Sounds like a plan."

We got her inside the office and I pushed her onto a metal folding chair Ida Belle had grabbed from the janitor's closet. No sense getting the good furniture wet. We were both already dripping on the rug. I snapped Gertie's hand-cuffs on her and tied a rope from the handcuffs around a post on the front desk, but I had serious doubts she was going anywhere. Her shoulders were slumped and her expression vacant. Whatever rush had prompted Kim to take the actions she had was completely drained from her system now.

"What were you doing in Eleanor's cabin?" I asked.

She didn't even flinch. Just continued to stare down at the floor.

"Did you use your drugs on Eleanor?"

I saw her jaw flex so I'd clearly struck a nerve, but that could have meant she had provided the drugs or had no idea that Zion had lifted the drugs from her and used them on Eleanor. I had a feeling as soon as Carter announced that fingerprint on the drug bottle was a match for Kim, she might be more cooperative. And I was more certain than ever that match was forthcoming.

"Phenobarbital—that's what was found in Eleanor's system," I continued to push. "That's what your mother took for her epilepsy. What you lifted to use for sleeping when your doctor wouldn't refill your Ambien."

She stiffened slightly and I knew I was right.

"You had to know a forensic team had already combed Eleanor's cabin, so why were you in there? What were you looking for?"

Nothing.

"Kim, I don't understand why you would cover for someone like Zion. Do you realize how much trouble you're in? A woman is dead. A woman you worked for. The cops can make a case for the supplier of the drugs to be contributory in her death. And Zion is not the person you think he is. He's a con artist and you were his next target."

My phone rang and I saw Cassidy's number in the display.

"I have to take this," I said and jumped up and headed outside.

"I'm so sorry, Fortune," she said when I answered. "But that fool Calahan went AWOL."

"What? He left the hospital?"

"The front desk nurse said she saw him get into an Uber. The tech was coming in to do the colonoscopy and Calahan was no longer in the procedure room."

"What time was this?"

"About an hour ago. I'm so sorry I didn't notify you sooner, but I was asleep and didn't hear my phone."

"No apologies necessary. It was a long shot anyway and I appreciate the help. Calahan is a loose cannon, so there was no predicting how this would turn out."

"Well, I'm not letting it drop. My next call is to his commanding officer. He's supposed to be the person investigating rule-breakers, so he should be holding himself to a higher standard."

"And yet they rarely do."

"Harrison and Carter do, and that's what has me so peeved. Anyway, sorry I couldn't buy you more than the morning."

She disconnected just as Carter's truck pulled up in front of the office. I let out a breath of relief when I saw he was alone. He jumped out and hurried over when he caught sight of me.

"What happened? Was anyone hit?"

"No. But not from lack of trying."

His eyes widened. "You took a shot at someone?"

"You need more coffee. If I'd fired, someone would have been hit."

He shook his head. "Right. Sorry. So what's going on?"

As we walked inside, I told him about the motion sensor and Mildred's phone call and our trip here to ensure the cabins were secure. I left out the part where I'd gone into the cabin and instead, told him I'd walked around to the back to see if it was secure when Kim fired the shot. If she wanted to correct my statement, then she'd have to talk. At that point it would be her word against mine, and I was betting on mine being the one believed. At least by a jury. Carter knew good and well I'd gone in but no way he was letting that cat out of the bag.

He stepped inside and gave everyone a nod before going to stand in front of Kim. She never even acknowledged he'd walked inside.

"Ms. Barnes," he said. "Why did you trespass onto a crime scene?"

No answer.

"She's refusing to talk," Gertie said.

"Shock?" he asked.

Ida Belle shook her head. "Maybe at first, but now it's deliberate."

He nodded. "Fine, then Kim Barnes, I'm arresting you for trespassing onto a crime scene and attempted murder. I'm sure I'll figure out some others on the way to the sheriff's department."

I untied her from the counter as Carter recited her rights. Kim paled as he talked but her jaw was firmly locked. And I suspected Ida Belle was right. The initial shock had passed and common sense had finally returned to the building. My guess was Kim's mouth would remain clamped shut until her attorney arrived.

As Carter was hauling her out, a white minivan pulled up. I looked over at Mildred, who shook her head, looking as bewildered as I was. Then I caught sight of the Uber sticker on the window and groaned as Calahan jumped out of the van, still wearing a hospital gown.

"You have got to be kidding me," Carter said.

"Sorry. Cassidy just called and told me he pulled a runner. I didn't think he'd turn up here though."

The Uber driver must have enjoyed Calahan as much as the rest of us because he hadn't even gotten the door closed before the driver floored it, spinning the tires on the gravel, before finally taking off without so much as a backward glance.

Calahan stomped over to us, glaring as he approached.

"Why are you in a hospital gown?" Carter asked.

"Because I was in the hospital, you moron," Calahan said.

"They don't steal your clothes at the hospital," Carter said. "Did you leave without being discharged?"

"That's none of your business!"

"It's my business if you were under a doctor's care and haven't been discharged. You can't be on the job. And quite frankly, you can't be on the job when you're not properly clothed either. Didn't they have a larger size?"

"They're one size fits all."

Gertie rolled her eyes. "Well, your all is hanging out the back. Please do us a favor and grab the bottom of that thing. The breeze is picking up and we're not interested in seeing more."

Calahan pointed a finger at Carter. "I told you to close this case this morning, and instead, I find you here wasting taxpayer's money. I'm putting all of this in my report."

"Feel free," Carter said. "But I'm not here investigating. I'm here arresting someone for trespassing and attempted murder. Call came in shots were fired and here we are."

Calahan blinked and looked at all of us, finally resting on Mildred, who nodded.

"The motion sensor went off," she said. "These ladies were kind enough to bring me out here to check on things and they caught Kim breaking into Eleanor's cabin. Then she tried to kill Fortune and stole my sister's boat trying to get away. Lucky for us, Fortune caught her before she managed to or we might have never known who it was."

Calahan looked taken aback, and I could see the wheels spinning in his mind, trying to figure out how to reroute this to be a problem for us again. Finally, he narrowed his eyes at me.

"You went into a crime scene?"

"Nope. I went *around* a crime scene. Kim was the one inside and she won't say why. But since it was a good enough reason for her to take a shot at me, I'm guessing you'll want to figure it out. And since it was Eleanor's cabin, I'm going to say it's probably related to her death. But what do I know?"

"You're not supposed to know anything," he said. "And my report will clearly state that you're interfering with a police investigation. Carter will go down for this. Just like I figured."

I threw my hands in the air. "I'm not involved with anything but helping my client out. And I hardly think charges can be pressed against me for taking down an intruder who tried to kill me. Good luck making that one stick."

"If you'll excuse me," Carter said, "I need to get this woman booked. Calahan, you're welcome to hang out here and resecure the crime scene if you'd like. Or I can send a deputy to do it. Your choice."

"I'm not doing construction work like some handyman. I'm not your employee."

"Got that right. I would never hire someone as inept as you."

Carter pulled Kim toward his truck. "Let's go. Apparently, I get to add boat theft to your charges. They just keep piling up."

"You're not going to arrest your girlfriend?" Calahan demanded.

"For what?" Carter asked.

"Trespassing on a crime scene."

"She already said she wasn't in the cabin."

"But she's on the property."

"*My* property," Mildred said and took a step forward, hands on her hips. "And I've heard about enough from you. Are you telling me I have no right to be here? Because I've got a good friend down at the *Picayune*. I'm happy to give her a call and tell her the state police have forbidden me access to my own property. I think it's because you have a problem with disabled people."

Calahan blanched and his jaw dropped. "I didn't say anything like that," he said, putting his hands up.

But it was too late. Mildred was full-on mad.

She took another step forward and poked her finger at him. "Then you show up here, in front of me and these other women, downright indecent. I'll have you up on sexual predator charges before I'm done."

Calahan took a fearful step back and his foot slammed into one of the rocks lining the parking area. He struggled to maintain his balance, flapping his arms like a bird, but finally lost the battle and fell over backward and crashed onto the ground.

"Good. God," Gertie said, covering her eyes. "Now we've seen it all. I'm not a fan."

Mildred turned her head. "I'm going to need therapy."

Ida Belle grimaced, her eyes clenched shut. "Maybe an eye bleaching."

I just grinned. "Well, it confirms some things I already knew. So Mildred, let's go lock up and get you back home. I think we all need a detox—maybe with some sweet tea and one of those pies, assuming I'm okay to drip on your kitchen floor."

Ida Belle whirled around, eyes still closed, and stalked back to the office. "Maybe some whiskey in that tea. Good Lord, it's barely noon and I'm ready to call it a day."

Gertie nodded and followed. "Heck, I'm the racy one and even I was offended."

Carter blew the horn on his truck and leaned out the window. "You got five seconds to get your naked butt off the ground, *covered*, and in the truck, or I'm leaving and sending a deputy here to arrest you and take a report from your victims."

Calahan jumped up and hurried to the truck, holding the gown from behind. I was still laughing when they drove away.

"Poor Carter," Ida Belle said, shaking her head. "Having Calahan's bare butt on his seats...he's going to have to reupholster."

Mildred started laughing, then choking, then fell into a chair on the front porch. "Oh my God. I haven't laughed this hard in—well, ever. Is this what your work is like all the time?"

"Thank God no!" Ida Belle said. "I'm a fan of catching the bad guys, and exposing and embarrassing fools, but not when I have to see business I don't want to see. I'm not going to eat hot dogs for a month at least."

"Vienna sausage," Gertie said, and Mildred started laughing all over again.

We all sat and laughed until we were gasping for air. When we finally came back to sanity, Mildred gave me a serious look.

"What was Kim doing in Eleanor's cabin?" she asked. "Surely she wasn't looking for the drugs."

I shook my head. "Kim's in cahoots with Zion, and I'm sure she already knows Carter found the drugs in his possession."

"Then it begs the question, what could be worth the risk?" Ida Belle said.

"There wasn't anything valuable to speak of in her cabin," Mildred said.

"Kim doesn't need money," I said. "I think we have to assume she was looking for something for Zion. She claimed she just learned how to shoot a gun yesterday. Who do you think taught her?"

"But what could she possibly be looking for?" Mildred asked. "It's not like the cabin was Eleanor's real home. It's just where she stayed when we were holding a retreat."

I nodded. "Did Eleanor have any other visitors while you were holding the retreat—anyone you didn't know?"

Mildred frowned, considering, then finally shook her head. "If she did, I didn't see them."

"What about packages? Did she receive anything with a return address you didn't recognize?"

"I don't think so—wait. There was an envelope. It came FedEx, which is unusual. That's why I remember it. Return address was New Orleans but there was no name. I guess I figured it was probably legal stuff although looking back, the name of the firm was usually on documents they sent."

"Is that envelope in Eleanor's office?"

"Let's check."

We headed inside and combed Eleanor's office top to bottom, even checking under the rug and couch and the underside of the desk, just in case it was hidden there.

"Does Kim have a key to the office and know the security code?" Ida Belle asked.

"Sure, all three of us do...did."

"But she didn't come in the office to look or you would have gotten a notice that the system was disarmed," Ida Belle said. "Which means whatever she's looking for was so important that she didn't think Eleanor would have hidden it in her office."

"But she could have accessed Eleanor's cabin when she was teaching class," Mildred said.

"Maybe she didn't know about the envelope until after Eleanor's death," I said.

"If that envelope contained information that Zion didn't want anyone to know then why didn't the forensics team find it?" Mildred asked.

"It must be well hidden," I said.

"But we searched Kim and the boat," Ida Belle said. "There's nothing there."

"Maybe we interrupted her," Gertie said. "We were talking on the way up the path. She might have heard us and bailed before she found what she was looking for."

"Or maybe it was no longer there," Ida Belle said.

"Could it be at your house?" I asked Mildred.

"I mean, it's possible if it's hidden, but I dug through all the paperwork pretty good, looking for all the trust documents and the legal stuff to do with the retreat, bank statements, all of it. I never came across it anywhere."

I nodded. Instinct told me that envelope was important and also that it had never left the retreat, but there was only one way to be sure.

"We have to check Eleanor's cabin," I said. "I know it's a crime scene and blah, blah, blah but I think the chances of Calahan returning are slim to none at this point. And it's small. We can go through the entire thing before Calahan could even get dressed and drive back."

I looked at Mildred. "But it's your call. It's against the law, and I'm not going to make you part of that unless you're okay with it."

"Good Lord, what are you waiting for?" she said. "I want this whole mess cleared up and put to bed. I can't live with all this uncertainty."

I nodded.

"If you don't mind," Mildred said, "I'll hold down the fort here."

"It's better that way," I said. "Then you have plausible deniability if a deputy shows up to seal the scene again and we get caught. You can and *should* claim you had no idea what we were up to."

"I'll keep watch," Mildred said. "If anyone shows, I'll text you. You'll have time to clear out before anyone gets there."

We practically jogged back to Eleanor's cabin, Gertie huffing as we went, but there wasn't one word of complaint. We donned gloves and headed inside.

"I doubt anything would be in the living room as I'm told the sauna people used it as a sort of lounge," Gertie said.

"I agree," I said. "Let's start in the bedroom. If we don't find anything, then we'll check the rest of the rooms just to be certain. It won't be somewhere obvious or the cops would have found it."

Ida Belle nodded and crouched down, checking the planks on the floor. Gertie started checking under furniture and tapping the walls while I climbed on the dresser and removed the air vent. The vent was clear and the furniture revealed nothing. I was just about to suggest we head to another room when Ida Belle peered up from the other side of the bed.

"I think I have something here. There's a piece of flooring just under the bed that's loose. Pass me a screwdriver."

I handed her the screwdriver and crouched down as she worked up a plank of the flooring and pulled it away.

"It's definitely a hiding place," I said.

"But it's empty," Gertie said.

"There's a screw here," Ida Belle said. "It was meant to hold the plank down but it's just sitting loose next to the foot of the bedframe."

"Maybe Kim did find the envelope," I said.

"Then where is it?" Gertie asked.

"Maybe she chunked it in the woods," I said. "Running

with it would have slowed her down. She might have figured she could come back for it, or worse case, it's paper, right?"

Ida Belle nodded. "Storms would have eventually disintegrated it."

She pulled out her phone and dialed. "Walter, get Scooter to mind the store. I need you to bring Rambo out to Mildred's cabins. Yes, now. You think I'm calling to schedule an appointment?"

She disconnected and shook her head. "No sense of urgency with that man."

"To be fair, he doesn't know we're on the trail of a potential killer," Gertie said.

Ida Belle stared. "To be fair, when are we not?"

CHAPTER NINETEEN

WALTER MUST HAVE FINALLY REALIZED WHAT WE WERE UP to because he arrived quicker than I figured he would. Rambo was excited to see Ida Belle but even more excited to see a new place to sniff. I'd already asked Mildred if she had something of Kim's for him to lock in on and she'd pulled out a pair of fuzzy socks from the front desk drawer.

"That girl always had cold feet," Mildred said.

"Lucky for us," I said. "Mildred, I know your back has got to be killing you. I'm sure Walter would be happy to give you a ride home. That is, if you don't mind leaving us the keys to lock up. We might need a bathroom and potentially medical supplies before we're done."

"It would be my pleasure," Walter said.

"Oh!" Mildred said. "Are you sure you don't need me to stay then?"

"We can handle it," Ida Belle assured her. "No one is coming back here except the police at some point to secure the cabin."

I nodded. "Even if Zion had a whole collection of silly

women to do his bidding, he's not foolish enough to send anyone back after what went down here."

"Do you think he knows?" Mildred said. "Surely Kim wasn't stupid enough to use her phone call on Zion."

"I'm sure Kim used her phone call on her attorney, but she could have asked her attorney to call him."

"Oh, right. Well, I certainly can't help you search the woods and I guess there's no point sitting here wringing my hands. If I'm being honest, I'd feel better back at home all the way around."

"If we find anything, we'll let you know," I said and gave Walter a nod.

We headed back to Eleanor's cabin with the excited Rambo, who dodged from one side of the path to the other, smelling as he went, his tail wagging the entire time. The front door to the cabin was still cracked, but there was no sign that anyone else had been there. We headed to the back, and I located the entrance to the path I'd spotted from the bedroom window.

Ida Belle pulled out Kim's socks and gave Rambo a sniff. Then she indicated direction so he wouldn't head back to the cabin, and he set out.

"Isn't he just going to follow her path all the way to the dock?" Gertie asked. "If she tossed something into the woods, why would he break off the path versus following where she walked?"

"If Kim threw something in the woods, the smell will be stationary, and therefore stronger than the one she left merely by passing," Ida Belle said. "A good scent dog should direct to the strongest odor."

"And if he never veers off the path?"

"Then there's either nothing in the woods to find or

Rambo's not a good scent dog. Guess which one I'm going with?"

Gertie snorted.

"If Rambo doesn't find anything, I think we'll have to assume that Kim tossed whatever she found in the water," I said.

"She'd have to have done it when she first got to the dock," Gertie said. "Because she wasn't too far away when Ida Belle and I got there and there was no paper in the air or on the water."

"I got your takedown on video, by the way," Ida Belle said.

"You did?"

"Yep. I figured if the shooter got away, at least I'd have video of them stealing the boat and maybe the size and frame could narrow down the suspects."

"That leap was spectacular," Gertie said. "I think you should put it on your website. For advertising purposes."

"I'm not sure if that would be advertising or issuing a challenge," I said.

"Hey, if that was Eleanor's boat that Kim stole to try to get away, how did she get here?" Gertie asked.

"I assume she drove," I said. "The cops will probably find her car stashed somewhere nearby."

Rambo paused momentarily at the split in the trail then continued straight—the direction I didn't go.

"I wonder if he smells the bear," I mused.

"What bear?" Ida Belle asked.

In all the excitement, I hadn't even told them about my literal run-in with the bear, so I did it now. They both looked surprised, then started chuckling.

"I wish I could have gotten the bear's face on video," Ida Belle said. "He must have been so startled he forgot to do bear things."

"Good news for me," I said. "He could have easily shaken me out of that tree. It wasn't the sturdiest."

Rambo came to a complete halt and we drew up. He sniffed the air to the right of the trail, then whined and launched into the bushes, pulling Ida Belle along with him. The little hound had a much easier time navigating the dense foliage than we did, and Ida Belle kept having to check him to slow down. Not that it did much good. He strained at the leash, now baying as he went.

Then he stopped suddenly again, right in front of a giant thorn bush.

Ida Belle sighed. "It had to be thorns."

"Walk the edges and see if you can see anything in it or under it," I said. "I'll find a good limb to use."

I found a solid eight-foot stick with a burnt end, signaling it had likely been struck by lightning. But it wasn't rotted and was sturdy enough for what I needed.

"I think maybe I see something over there," Ida Belle said, peering into a section of the thorns directly facing the path. "There's some broken thorns at the top where something might have entered from above. And on the ground, I see a straight line when there shouldn't be any. But it's so dark, I can't tell what's making it."

I took a look and spotted the anomaly, then crouched and stuck my branch in. "Tell me when I'm over it."

"About two inches back and a couple to the right. Okay, now."

I dropped the far end of the branch and put pressure on it, then slowly pulled it toward me.

"It's moving!" Ida Belle said.

It took a few more lift and drops to get the object within safe arm distance but finally, I pulled a FedEx envelope out of the bush.

"Addressed to Eleanor!" Gertie said and clapped her hands.

The envelope was already open with just a small piece of tape sealing it again at the top. I tore it off and pulled out the papers inside. Ida Belle and Gertie both leaned over me and we all stared.

"Eleanor was having Zion investigated," Ida Belle said. "Of all the things we might have found, that one wasn't anywhere on the list."

"I can't say I'd thought of it, but it does make sense," I said. "It seems that Eleanor was starting to question Zion's sincerity in the relationship. If she thought he was lying to her, especially about his marriage, then hiring a PI would be the way to go."

"That might be what they fought about," Ida Belle said. "This PI states clearly that Zion and Sapphire show every sign of living together as husband and wife and that he found no indication that either had filed or talked to an attorney about filing for separation or divorce."

I flipped the page and felt my pulse tick up a notch.

"He found Zion's most recent alias," I said. "And it says right here that the cops in North Carolina want him for questioning."

"Jackpot!" Gertie said. "Are you going to tell Carter?"

"Of course she is," Ida Belle said. "He's got to get that man in handcuffs before he flees and becomes Santa Claus or whoever else he has lined up."

"What about Calahan and his 'you're interfering with an investigation' nonsense?" Gertie asked.

"We were using a scent hound to determine if Kim stole anything," I said. "And since the owner of the property asked us to do so and we didn't enter the crime scene, what's he going to say—arrest them for turning over evidence?"

"Probably," Gertie said. "He's like the male version of Celia."

"Well, he doesn't have a good argument on this one. We'll call the sheriff's department on the way and see if Carter is there and we'll officially turn over what we found, like the good little citizens we are."

Ida Belle snorted and started to say something, but her phone rang.

"It's Myrtle," she said as she answered.

"Good Lord, you won't believe what's happened down here," she said.

"Down here where?" Ida Belle asked.

"The sheriff's department. That new guy had a doctor's appointment, so I switched with him and am working days today and tomorrow. I knew there would be problems when that idiot Calahan called, demanding to know where Carter was. Carter had already told me that I had to give him that kind of information when he asked, so I just clenched my butt and told him. I've done so much butt clenching this week it might affect my regularity."

"I have something for that," Gertie said.

"Might need it," Myrtle said. "Anyway, I tried to call Carter and warn him about Calahan, but he didn't answer. I know why now of course, and I know you guys were there because I heard an earful of complaining about it from that fool. I just knew he was going to show up there and make trouble."

"He did show up but he wasn't able to make trouble," Ida Belle said. "He just showed his butt...in more ways than one."

"You're serious? Good Lord, the man's a menace *and* a slow learner. Carter pulled up in front of the sheriff's department, and I could see Calahan in the passenger's seat, just a-jawing, and since Carter had already told me he had a prisoner to be processed, I headed outside to see if I could help. Calahan opened the door, griping like there's no tomorrow, and Fortune's name was in his mouth every other word. Then he jumped out of the truck and his hospital gown got caught on the door. Ripped the ties clean off the middle, and there it all was, flapping in the wind. The man mooned the entire downtown."

We all looked at each other, grinning.

"Were there a lot of people out?" Ida Belle asked.

"Good Lord, yes. Had the lunch crowd headed out of the café, and a baby shower at the Catholic church just finishing up. I'm telling you, a bunch of those church women got the vapors. I think some others might have got some ideas but that's too sad to contemplate. Anyway, Carter starts yelling at Calahan about him flashing the whole danged universe, and then a man stepped out of a car that had just pulled up after Carter did. And it was Calahan's commander."

Now we all hooted.

"Calahan flashed his commander?" Gertie asked.

"I'd say given the height of the car, the commander got a full frontal, and he was not impressed. He got out, and Calahan was scrambling to find the ties that were dangling from Carter's truck door. The commander yelled at him and he froze like he was in some sci-fi movie. Then he realized who it was and twisted his arm up behind his back so hard he yelped trying to hold that gown together."

"I would have given up my stash of Nora's weed to see that," Gertie said.

"It's all on the department camera, but I have a feeling the commander is going to demand we hand it over as soon as he realizes his department is bucking up against a lawsuit from a bunch of distressed diners and an entire religion."

"So what happened with the commander?" I asked.

"He demanded to know why Calahan was wearing a

hospital gown. He sputtered some excuse about the hospital laundering his clothes, but the commander wasn't buying it. I mean, come on, go back to your hotel and dress before you come to work. Or for the love of Pete, he had to have passed at least one Walmart on the way out there to accost Carter. I was just about to say all of that when Carter stepped on my foot."

"He knows you too well," Ida Belle said.

"Got that right, and I have to admit, he made the right call on this one. If I'd have gone off then the commander might have felt obligated to defend Calahan, as he is, after all, the state police's employee. But we all just stood there in silence and the commander let loose on him. Said he'd gotten a call from the hospital that Calahan had basically snuck out and was working without proper release, which set them up for huge legal problems. So if you can believe it, Calahan gets indignant and then tells the commander that Carter is the real problem that needs to be addressed and the commander is *not* taking him off this case."

"I can believe it," Ida Belle said, and Gertie and I nodded.

"Well, the commander turned red as a beet and told Calahan that not only was he being suspended, but he was being placed under investigation himself. Then he looked over at Carter and asked if he'd like to press charges on behalf of everyone downtown. Carter just shook his head and said that wouldn't be necessary as long as Calahan removed himself permanently and never returned."

I smiled. "Well played."

"Agreed, so Calahan was just about to blow his top and launch into a tirade when the commander told him that he needed to pack up his belongings, go home, and forget he'd ever heard of Sinful or Sheriff LeBlanc, and if he ever so much as breathed a word of anything to do with this investigation that he'd have him up on charges faster than he could disrobe. Well, that last sentence is where I finally lost it. I'd been holding it in all that time, and I just couldn't anymore. I laughed until I collapsed in a heap right there on the sidewalk. Took Carter and Deputy Breaux both to get me up."

"I think you deserve a medal for keeping it in that long," Gertie said. "So what about Kim? Is she talking?"

"Not a peep except to ask for her phone call."

"Tell Carter we're on our way with evidence," I said. "I think what we have to show him is going to make him almost as happy as Calahan getting his due."

"I'll let him know."

Gertie grinned. "Best. News. Ever."

———

CARTER MUST HAVE BEEN WATCHING FOR US BECAUSE HE WAS waiting at the front door when we pulled up. He waved us in and back to his office.

"You heard about Calahan?" he asked.

We all nodded.

"I think Myrtle called as soon as she could breathe again," I said. "It couldn't have happened to a better person."

"I have you guys to thank for it—you and Cassidy."

"I'm sure we have no idea what you're talking about."

He grinned. "Of course you don't. Myrtle said you have some evidence for me? I can't wait to see what you're willingly turning over to a police investigation."

"Hey, I'm a law-abiding citizen."

"You're a citizen."

I pushed the envelope across the desk. "Rambo tracked that off Kim's scent. It had been thrown into a thorn bush just off the trail I chased her down. We're certain it's what she lifted from Mildred's cabin."

He pulled out the paperwork and his eyebrows lifted when he saw it was a PI report. Then he started to read. He seemed to find the first page—the one about Zion's marriage—only mildly interesting, but when he got to the second page, he jumped up and yelled.

"Yes!" He shook his fist. "I'm calling the North Carolina police now. If they don't have enough to arrest him, I can still detain him for questioning for forty-eight hours. If this PI came up with this much information that quickly, then I think it's just the tip of the iceberg. A couple more days, and his entire life will unravel."

He pressed his phone. "Myrtle, get Breaux back from lunch. We need to pick up Zion Gates for questioning."

"What about Kim?"

"She can talk to her lawyer when he gets here, but I'm not releasing her. She racked up a bunch of charges—felony charges—in a short amount of time. I'll be sending her to New Orleans tomorrow and the ADA can figure out what he wants to do with her."

"Her attorney is going to want to speak to you—try the whole naive, taken-advantage-of route to work up sympathy," Myrtle pointed out.

"Tell him the person she tried to kill was my fiancée and he'll know not to bother."

"Perfect! I'm so glad I'm on the clock today. If I was working tonight, I would have missed all this fun."

We all rose and walked out with Carter, giving Myrtle a thumbs-up before we left. Deputy Breaux was just walking up, and he jumped in Carter's truck and they headed off.

"We better go fill Mildred in," I said.

WE'D JUST LEFT A VERY SURPRISED AND RELIEVED MILDRED when Carter called.

"Zion is gone. No personal belongings at the cabin, and Sapphire swears she has no idea where he is and that she hasn't heard anything about him since yesterday, when her attorney handed him a duffel bag with twenty thousand in cash. What the heck is wrong with these people?"

"Got me," I said. "If she'd just waited a day or two, she could have gotten rid of him for free via the penal code. But don't worry. I have a good idea where he might be."

I told him about Kim's new purchase on Horn Island.

"Jesus. Did they really think they could hide on an island a couple hours away for the rest of their lives?"

"I'm sure that's what Zion told Kim. But I have no doubt he was going to use that cash to get a fake passport and leave the country. Things were starting to snowball."

"You're sure this information is accurate?"

"Yes."

"And you came by it, how exactly?"

"A new source connected to the NOLA wealthy and the real estate community. It's where I'd be going right now if I hadn't given you all my good intel."

"Guess I'm off on a road trip then. I'll leave Breaux to handle Sinful and tap Harrison for the takedown."

"I mean, Gertie took him down with a bad knee."

"Gertie is as big a menace as Zion, just in a different way," he said and disconnected.

"What now?" Gertie asked.

"I think we've wrapped this one up," I said. "As much as it can be wrapped anyway. We've pulled together evidence, motive, and opportunity for drugging Eleanor. It's up to the ADA if he wants to pursue that angle at all, but my guess is Zion will have plenty of charges once they start unraveling his past."

Gertie smiled. "So...hot tub and champagne to celebrate? You are technically a bachelor tonight and Lord knows my body could use it. Amazing how something that is supposed to be so Zen wrecked my body and mind."

"Murder is never Zen," Ida Belle said.

"I meant the yoga and meditation."

"There is nothing Zen about twisting your body like a pretzel. And there darn sure isn't anything Zen about sitting still for an hour and trying to get your brain to think of nothing. It's far more relaxing for me to rebuild a carburetor, and it accomplishes something useful."

"Walter might appreciate some of those pretzel moves. A couple weeks ago, Jeb and I—"

"No!"

I smiled. It was good to be back to normal.

———

IT WAS AFTER MIDNIGHT BEFORE CARTER CAME IN, completely exhausted. I had spent the entire afternoon in the hot tub consuming far too much champagne, so I was half watching TV, half dozing on the couch when he arrived.

"Shower before anything," he said before shuffling upstairs.

Since I knew exactly how it felt to have the adrenaline rush course out of your body as quickly as it arrived, I just nodded and waited. I wasn't worried. If they hadn't found Zion, he would still be out there looking. I just had to wait on the story.

Thirty minutes later, he walked back into the living room and sank into my recliner.

"You hungry?" I asked. "I can fix you a sandwich."

"No. Harrison made us pick something up on the way back."

"So can you tell me how you took him down? Or do I have to finagle it out of Harrison tomorrow?"

"How do you know we took him down?"

I raised one eyebrow and he smiled.

"Yeah, we got him. He was right where you said he'd be. It was a huge parcel, though, and took us some time to locate where he was hiding. Found him in a closet clutching a Bible and a bottle of whiskey."

"I guess all that meditation didn't work. Boy, that was anti-climactic."

"Were you hoping for a gunfight?"

I shrugged. "I was figuring more on a footrace, but I guess he just gave up."

"He was definitely a weak opponent. I guess I was expecting more. Harrison was disappointed. Said going on a call to the Swamp Bar was more dangerous."

"Naturally. Zion was a bully and he intentionally picked victims who were at their weakest point. He would have never made it past a savvy woman with no trauma. The three other women at his retreat got his number quickly and were playing his game back on him for discounts."

"Really? Good for them."

"Not good for Eleanor."

"No. But she will be the last of his victims."

"There's still Kim."

He sighed. "Oh yeah. That's going to be a tough one. Given her money and family name, I'm going to bet the ADA offers her a plea deal as long as she gives information on Zion. I know he's already talked to Sapphire. I don't think they know anything about his previous life, but I passed that PI's file over to Blanchet and he's working it for me."

"Blanchet's a good call."

Andy Blanchet was a retired cop who filled in at the sheriff's department and did some consulting when Carter needed help. He was excellent at his job and was always willing to pretend he saw nothing where I was concerned. I think Carter was still on the fence as to whether that was a good thing or a bad thing.

"So I guess that's it," I said. "You'll close the file tomorrow and pass it all to the ADA. Then he'll decide if he wants to add any charges regarding Eleanor's suicide."

He nodded. "I'll be glad to have this one behind me. Everything about it made me feel like I needed to shower."

"Well, you did spend most of the week with Calahan on your heels. But hey, at least we saved the next guy from his reign of terror. Celia's going to be disappointed that the guy who was supposed to be investigating you for lacking is now under investigation himself."

"Given that Celia was one of the people who saw his, um... true character today, I think she might be willing to concede this one."

I laughed. "Myrtle didn't tell us that."

"She didn't know. Celia had left before the rest of the shower attendees and was already in her car. I guess I need to talk to Myrtle about telling you police business again."

"Is it really police business if it happens right there on Main Street? I mean, does the sheriff's department get to claim everything as confidential just because it happens in the parking spaces in front of your building?"

"Good point. I'm going to head up. I'm beat. You coming?"

"I've been waiting on you."

CHAPTER TWENTY

Carter slept in a bit the next morning, but that just meant it was 8:00 a.m. before he tapped lightly on my office door. I called for him to come in and gave him a curious look.

"You knock now?"

"I heard the typing and thought you might be working."

I shut my laptop and the noise ceased. "Nope. Just got a movie running on my laptop while I sit here and ponder. You must still be half asleep."

"Why is that?"

Because you're leaping to bad conclusions. I watch horror movies all the time. When you step onto the porch and hear people screaming, do you assume I'm killing people inside?"

He raised one eyebrow.

"Fair," I said. "How did you sleep?"

He shrugged. "I dropped off quick but about midway through I started dreaming. Those crazy, frantic kind of dreams."

"Probably PTSD from Calahan."

"That's a good possibility."

"Are you headed to the office?"

He nodded. "I know it's my day off, but I want to get those reports filed and Kim transferred to New Orleans. What are you up to today? You might have worn out the motor in the hot tub yesterday. You definitely emptied the liquor cabinet."

"Well then, I guess a trip to the liquor store is in order. Beyond that, I have a big day of reading in my hammock planned. Merlin and Tiny asked for some quality quiet time."

"Uh-huh. Wish I could join you."

"Get that paperwork wrapped up and that silly woman shipped out of your jail and you can this afternoon. I'll pull some steaks out of the freezer and we can fire up the grill."

"You mean *I* can fire up the grill."

"I'm picking up more beer. And I made a full pot of coffee."

He smiled and leaned over to kiss me. "Sounds fair. I'm going to fill a mug and head out. The sooner I get started, the sooner I finish."

A knock at the front door had us both freezing, then looking at each other.

"Don't look at me," I said. "My friends have keys or come in the back door. Except Mannie. I'm not sure how he gets in. Maybe he materializes."

"Ha. Guess I better go see."

Curiosity had me following him to the front door. After all, it was my house. There was always the chance that a potential client had come looking for me in person. Plenty of people didn't like talking on the phone about extremely personal things.

But neither of us knew the anxious-looking young woman standing there.

Five foot three. A hundred ten pounds. Excellent muscle mass indicative of martial arts training. Threat level undetermined on her turf. On mine, we were probably good.

"Carter LeBlanc?" the woman asked.

"Yes. Can I help you?"

"My name is Angela Tran. I'm a scientist with a lab in New Orleans. I need to talk to you about Dora Matte."

"Please come inside," he said.

The woman stepped inside and I waved at her to take a seat.

"I assume this is a private matter, so I'll leave you to it," I said. "Can I get you something to drink?"

"No, thank you," Angela said as she perched on the edge of the couch.

I headed down the hallway to my office, closed the door, popped in my earbuds, and pulled up the living room camera on my computer. I figured if Carter didn't want me to hear what Angela said, he would have taken her down to the sheriff's department. It wasn't as if he didn't know who he was living with.

"I have to apologize straight off for coming to you with this so late," Angela said. She pulled a folder out of her bag, and I could tell she was nervous as she handed it to Carter.

"What is this?" he asked as he opened it.

"The results of hair and blood tests done on Mrs. Matte. We were supposed to send the result to Mr. Jasper Stout."

"Jasper?" Carter asked, clearly surprised.

"Yes. He's the one who brought her in for the tests in January. My understanding is that Mrs. Matte had chronic health issues and she and Mr. Stout were unsatisfied with the doctor's lack of solutions. Mr. Stout encouraged her to have the tests run to either pin down or eliminate possibilities."

"So I take it you weren't able to get the results to Mr. Stout before he passed."

She gave him a pained look. "I'm afraid it's a bit deeper than that. We were installing a new computer system at the lab, and

I'm both embarrassed and horrified to say that Mrs. Matte's file got corrupted, and the samples sat in storage until someone noticed the dates on the labels. At the same time, I went out early on a four-month-long maternity leave. I can't begin to tell you how sorry I am for our mistake. When I found out Mrs. Matte and Mr. Stout were both deceased, I was sick over it."

"Mistakes happen, Dr. Tran. And it doesn't sound like this one was on you."

"Perhaps not, but this mistake might have cost Mrs. Matte her life."

Carter straightened. "What?"

"She was being poisoned. Heavy metal poisoning. And given the amount of concentration in her body and the length of time since symptoms had begun, there was no way it was environmental in nature."

"You're saying someone was poisoning Mrs. Matte and that's what killed her?"

"I have no way of knowing for certain. I contacted the ME but with no autopsy and a cremation, I have no way to prove that was the case."

"But that's what you believe."

She nodded and swiped at her right eye. "I am struggling greatly with the knowledge that if we hadn't messed up Mrs. Matte might still be alive."

"You can't blame yourself, although I understand how you'd feel that way. Did Mrs. Matte give any indication that she suspected something like this?"

"No. I got the impression that she had only requested the tests due to Mr. Stout's urging. But he was very specific about contact—only wanting us to speak with him directly. He said others had access to Mrs. Matte's phone and mail and it wouldn't be confidential. Mrs. Matte agreed. So I have to think he had his suspicions even though he wasn't sharing them."

"But he didn't give you any indication what he was thinking?"

She shook her head. "Mr. Stout was her son-in-law, correct?"

"Yes."

"I'm not a cop, Sheriff LeBlanc, or a psychiatrist, but I'd bet my medical license that Mr. Stout was afraid we'd find exactly what we did. He was antsy and asked some leading questions about poisoning, trying to make it sound like he was concerned about something nondeliberate."

"But you didn't buy it."

"No. When I learned he'd died only a week after that visit and then Mrs. Matte a week after that, I couldn't help but worry that whoever was poisoning Mrs. Matte had gotten to both of them. That was the moment I became positively ill over the entire thing."

"The only person who had a motive and opportunity to kill them both was Mrs. Matte's daughter—Mr. Stout's wife."

She nodded. "I figured as much. And when the ME told me she'd died recently of a self- inflicted gunshot wound, it all seemed to fit. But I couldn't let you close the file on Mrs. Matte's or Mr. Stout's death without this information. I think both need further investigation, because the dead deserve justice as much as the living. I know no one can pay, but the truth is its own form of restitution."

"I agree," Carter said as Angela stood.

He rose with her and took her hand. "Please allow yourself to grieve this and then let it go. You couldn't have saved them. If someone is hell-bent on committing murder they will find a way."

Angela looked down at the floor and sniffed, then looked back at Carter and nodded. "Thank you."

He closed the front door behind her, then sank onto the couch. I walked into the living room and sat next to him.

"You know Walter never felt Jasper's death was right," I said quietly.

He nodded.

"Do you think Eleanor killed them both?"

"Yeah." He wrapped his arm around me and pulled me in close. "Yeah. I do."

"What are you going to do about it?"

"I'm going to make a copy of these records tomorrow and turn them over to the ME. I'll see what I can do about changing cause of death to suspicious for both Jasper and Dora. Given that the person most likely responsible is already gone, there's nothing more that can be done. But I'll ask my questions about Jasper's boat and talk to Dora's doctors. At the very least, it will be on record. Maybe then Jasper and Dora can rest in peace."

"I hope Eleanor doesn't."

"That makes two of us."

"You're going to have to tell Mildred."

"I know. But I need to do things in the proper order." He shook his head. "Good God, what a mess. Poor Mildred. I hope she can live with the weight of all of this."

"It's not on her."

"No. But survivor's guilt is real, and if she thinks there's something she could have done to prevent it, well..."

"Yeah."

CHAPTER TWENTY-ONE

THREE WEEKS LATER, WE WERE OVER AT MILDRED'S HOUSE, helping her with a few minor repairs she had to complete before closing the next morning. Ida Belle had inked a deal for the cabins the week before and was already deliberating on plans for them. The house had sold just as quickly to the neighbor across the street who wanted it for an elderly aunt who was going to move to Mudbug. Since Mildred had already decided she was not only leaving Mudbug, but the country, she was selling it furnished.

"You'll be off to Costa Rica tomorrow afternoon," I said.

I passed Ida Belle a suitcase down from the attic, then a second one.

"Are you really only taking two suitcases of stuff?" Ida Belle asked.

"I didn't come here with much and aside from a few of my mother's personal items, there was nothing else I wanted," Mildred said. "I shipped a few boxes ahead. They'll hold them at the rental agency. So all I really need is my clothes that I'm taking."

"Hey, you only need a bathing suit anyway, right?" Gertie said.

Mildred smiled. "I think it will be a while until I attempt the ocean. But once I get settled in, I'll start making arrangements for my surgery."

"You let us know if you need anything," Ida Belle said. "We're never opposed to a road trip."

"I can't tell you how much I appreciate everything you've done for me. This whole thing has been a nightmare wrapped in a whirlwind. If you hadn't investigated, Zion might have gotten away with stealing the cabins and my sister... Well, let's just say no one would have ever known."

"Eleanor paid for her sins," Ida Belle said.

I nodded. "And with all the dirt Blanchet and Carter dug up on Zion, I don't think he'll see sunlight outside of a prison yard for a very long time."

Mildred shook her head. "I can't believe he scammed so many women, and that there were two other deaths in his wake. I know they were elderly and it's possible he picked them because he figured they were close to it, but it doesn't paint a pretty picture."

"And after the situation with Eleanor, the authorities will be taking a closer look at both of those deaths," I said. "Maybe they won't turn up anything, but you never know."

"Have you heard anything on Kim?"

"Not much," I said. "Her attorney is still trying to make a deal for her to basically skate entirely if she testifies against Zion. Carter doesn't seem to think she knows anything of real value."

"But she tried to kill you," Mildred said. "Surely they won't just let her walk on that."

I shrugged. "Her attorney will say she was manipulated by a professional in her deficient mental state after her mother's death and that she accidentally fired the gun. Her never having shot one until the day before will weigh in. She claims she didn't even know what was in the envelope and never opened it. That one, I actually believe her on because it wasn't until the ADA showed her everything they had on Zion that she broke down and started talking."

"Please," Gertie said. "So her defense is that she did it all for love? Pathetic."

"But workable with a young, fragile woman," Ida Belle said. "They'll paint her as a victim and she'll probably get off."

Mildred shook her head. "I can agree that Zion played her, and I know better than most that Kim wasn't an emotionally strong person. And she had zero street smarts. But I don't believe for a minute she accidentally did anything. All this playing innocent makes me angry. She had to have known about Eleanor and Zion before she took up with him. She was around Eleanor more than I was. If I'd already clued in, I don't see how she could have missed it, especially when she was bucking to take Sapphire's place."

"I think she knew," I said. "But she'll never admit it because then it gives her motive to have conspired with Zion. She needs to be his victim as well or she goes down with him for setting up Eleanor."

Mildred sighed. "I know I probably shouldn't, but I almost feel sorry for her. If Zion managed to fool my sister, a girl like Kim must have been child's play."

"I don't think he fooled Eleanor for long or she wouldn't have hired that PI," Ida Belle said.

"Long enough to ruin people's lives," Mildred said. "Literally."

We headed back to the kitchen and Mildred sank into a chair, rubbing her back with her right hand. Finally she looked up at us, her expression sad.

"I hope you ladies don't think I'm a coward, running away like this," she said. "Even though I know it's true."

"You're not a coward!" Gertie said. "No one can possibly understand what you've been through. Whatever is best for *you* is the right way to handle things, and anyone who thinks differently can go pound bayou mud."

"I appreciate that. I know I could have probably gotten more if I'd taken the time to sell the contents of the house individually. Or if I'd done a few minor updates, I could have listed it for more. But donating and giving away personal stuff to old friends of Mom's and selling the house furnished made cutting ties faster and easier."

She sighed. "The truth is I just couldn't be here any longer. All the looks and whispers. And it never would have ended. I'd always be poor disabled Mildred, whose sister stole her inheritance and murdered her mother. And poor Jasper. It hurts my heart that he was trying to save Mom and that Eleanor's infatuation with that creep Zion is probably what got him killed. Jasper was a good man."

We all nodded and Mildred sniffed.

"Okay, so what's next?" I asked, changing the subject because that one led nowhere but depression and sadness.

"You've done everything on the closing list," she said. "The walk-through tomorrow morning should be quick, and I'll sign the papers a couple blocks away."

"What about that microwave you were complaining about a few weeks back?"

"Oh. It wasn't on the list and to be honest, I'd forgotten all about it as it's been working lately. It was an intermittent problem. I tried to get Eleanor to replace it, but she could be incredibly cheap with some things and insisted it could be repaired. I think she ordered a part for it but never got around to replacing it."

"Do you think you still have it?" Ida Belle asked. "I could probably make the repair."

"Maybe. If she ordered it and it's still here, then it would be on the shelf in the garage above the work counter. That's usually where she kept project stuff. When some people helped me go through that stuff, I told them to leave any maintenance items for the home on those shelves for the new owner."

"Let's go check," I said to Ida Belle, and we headed through the tiny laundry room and into the garage. The room was cleared out except for the freezer, a ladder, some gardening tools, and a couple of boxes and air filters on a shelf. I grabbed the ladder and climbed up to lift the first box.

"Good Lord, this is heavy," I said. "Feels more like a carburetor than a part for a microwave."

I carried it down so we could check it out. Sure enough, it sorta looked like a carburetor as well, but it wasn't a real part.

"Oh," Ida Belle said as she used both hands to lift it out. "Nice."

"What the heck is it?"

"A trophy. Jasper's to be exact. Walter said he had an old Chevy that he hopped up years ago. Apparently, he won the big drag race at the fair in it one year. If those church ladies were helping Mildred in here, they probably just peeked in the box and thought it was a part to something. Oh well, put it back up there. Someone might want to use it for a doorstop. Check the other box."

I climbed back up and slipped the box with the trophy back into place and grabbed the other box.

"Jackpot," Ida Belle said when she pulled it open. "This won't take any time at all to replace. Hopefully, that will fix it and then the new owner doesn't have to deal with it."

Gertie and I helped Mildred clear out the last of the food

she'd collected from her refrigerator while Ida Belle worked on the microwave.

"I hate us taking everything," Gertie said. "Don't you want to keep something for dinner tonight?"

Mildred laughed. "It's 11:00 p.m. I ate dinner while you were delivering that lawn equipment for me."

"Good grief," Gertie said. "I had no idea it was that late. It's a wonder I haven't starved to death myself."

Ida Belle stared. "You snacked the entire time we were delivering stuff. I'll be vacuuming crumbs out of my SUV for a week at least."

"Oh yeah."

Mildred chuckled. "I don't want it to go to waste. Besides, I have a piece of pecan pie in the fridge for breakfast tomorrow morning. It may not be healthy, but I thought it was fitting that it would be the last thing I ate in southern Louisiana."

"Well, I'm all finished here," Ida Belle said. "That should take care of the microwave. Are you sure there's nothing else?"

"Positive. You ladies have gone above and beyond, and seriously, I can get an Uber to the airport tomorrow. You don't need to taxi me around on top of everything else you've done."

"We don't mind," Gertie said. "We're headed to Mother's for lunch after we drop you off. I might even talk them into shopping."

"Doubt it," Ida Belle said.

"We could stop at the boat shop on the way back."

"Maybe."

"Then let's call it a night," I said, rising from the table. "We'll be back in the morning for the walk-through in case there's anything else to be handled."

"Good night, ladies. And again, I appreciate everything."

We grabbed our stack of leftovers and headed for the SUV.

Come tomorrow, we'd see Mildred off and officially close this chapter of her life.

———

The next morning we were all moving a little slower but were all excited for Mildred and her new adventure. The home inspector did his walk-through and had no complaints, then Mildred asked Gertie if she would snap some photos of each room for her estate attorney while Ida Belle took Mildred to the closing.

"The attorney said we should have photos to prove how things were when I left," she said, looking flustered as she dug in her purse to ensure her ID was in it. "I told him the inspector was coming this morning, but he still insisted. Then I forgot completely."

"It's always best to cover yourself," Ida Belle said.

Gertie nodded. "And it's no problem. We'll be ready to go when you get back."

So I walked the rooms with Gertie while she snapped away with her phone. Then we sat on the back porch in the nice breeze. We weren't there long before Ida Belle and Mildred returned.

Mildred was practically glowing as we loaded her two suitcases in the SUV and headed off. She was beaming when we said our goodbyes at the airport after flagging a valet to assist her.

"You're sure you'll be okay flying alone?" Gertie asked.

"I've already asked for assistance," she said. "They'll bring me a wheelchair at check-in and they'll have one at the gate when I get there. I've hired a car service, and he'll meet me at baggage claim. I'll be fine. The rental company already has a house manager who will take care of groceries and the like, at least until I get my footing."

She gave us all hugs and headed inside, turning for a final wave before the door slid closed behind her.

"She looked happy," Gertie said. "I'm really glad. I was scared for her...especially after that scientist brought that lab report to Carter."

"It's definitely a lot to live with," Ida Belle said. "She's doing the right thing leaving. Staying here would be a constant reminder and even the well-intentioned would bring it back constantly."

I nodded. "So...Mother's?"

———

A WEEK LATER, I WAS IN MY HAMMOCK PRETENDING TO READ a book but was mostly staring out at the water, trying to figure out why my mind was still unsettled. Mildred had made it to Costa Rica and sent pictures of the view from the beach cabin she was renting until she decided whether or not to look for a permanent situation. The ADA had put his own people onto Zion and information kept flowing in from other law enforcement agencies. So far, they couldn't pin a homicide on him, but there were so many good cases for fraud that Zion would likely spend the next thirty years or better shuffling from one state's prison to another's.

Kim had made some sort of deal—no real surprise there—and had gotten off with five years of probation. The judge had issued a restraining order against her for both me and Sapphire, just to be safe. Not that it mattered. I figured the next thing her attorney would get to work on was permission for her to leave the country. My guess was she'd head to one of her family's other properties and probably wouldn't step foot in Louisiana again. Hopefully, she'd find a good psychiatrist wherever she landed.

Ida Belle was already making noise about turning the cabins into a gun range and training camp for scent hounds, much to Walter's dismay. I had a feeling he'd had his eye more on retirement than starting a new business venture. But once Ida Belle's mind was made up, there was no stopping her. Which Walter knew better than anyone.

The files on Jasper's and Dora's deaths had been amended to contain the new evidence and Carter's thoughts on the matter, and they were both now listed as suspicious. But since the person responsible was also deceased, that was really all that could be done.

So everything that could happen had happened. And all the bad guys who were still living were going to pay in some way. But still, I wasn't satisfied. I just wasn't sure why.

"You've been on that same page all morning," Carter said as he stepped up.

He placed a bottle of water on the table next to me to replace the empty one and sat in the lawn chair nearby.

"Something bothering you?" he asked.

"Yes. But I don't know what."

He nodded in understanding. "You'll figure it out eventually. Meanwhile, I'm thinking about breaking out the fryer and cooking up some fish."

"Sounds great."

I reached for the water and almost lost my grip as it slid from my hand.

"Sweet potatoes or regular?" he asked.

I wiped the sweating bottle on my shirt and took a drink. Then I froze.

"Fortune?"

"Huh?"

"Sweet potatoes or regular?"

I stared at the bottle of water, then dug my phone out of my pocket and pulled up the picture that Gertie had taken of the sauna. Then I sent her a text.

Send me the photos you took of Mildred's house.

"I'll just go with regular," Carter said, and wandered off.

I waited until the pictures rolled in and pulled them up, flipping through them until I got to the one I was looking for.

Bingo!

That's what had been bothering me.

I jumped out of the hammock and hurried inside. Carter looked up as the door slammed behind me and sighed.

"I shouldn't wait on you for dinner, I suppose," he said.

"Not unless you want to eat two- or three-day-old fish."

"Two or three days? Where are you going?"

I shook my head. "If I'm right, you don't ever want to know."

He held up one hand. "I'll see you in a few days. Are you taking the Trouble Twosome with you?"

"Not this time. It's just a quick in and out, and I'm going to call in a favor to make it happen."

"Be careful."

"Don't worry. It's not that kind of trip."

"With you, it's *always* that kind of trip."

"I'm leaving Gertie behind. Technically, you're at more risk than me."

CHAPTER TWENTY-TWO

I SAT IN THE LOUNGE CHAIR ON A PERFECTLY GORGEOUS DAY on a particularly incredible stretch of Costa Rican beach and watched the couple frolicking in the ocean. They weren't young—on the contrary, most would say their best years were behind them, physically anyway. But the extra weight, emerging gray hair, and the bits of sagging skin didn't deter them.

And they were clearly in love. Even a staunch realist like me could see it.

I could hear their laughter as it drifted over the surf and up the beach and I lay back and enjoyed the cool breeze on my skin. I was in no hurry. After all, there was nothing to accomplish here besides assuaging my own curiosity.

When the couple finally tired of water play, they trudged out and headed up the beach toward the rented bungalow just behind me. They didn't even notice me sitting there until they were only feet away.

I sat up and smiled. "Afternoon, Mildred. And this is Jasper, I presume."

Mildred's jaw dropped and Jasper gave her a panicked look.

"How did you know?" she asked.

"It's what I do. And I wasn't certain, so I came here to find out."

"Are you going to tell Carter?"

"Tell him what? That you're cavorting with a dead man in Costa Rica? Last time I checked, that's not against the law. To fake your own death, maybe, especially if there's insurance payouts and the like. But I'm guessing Jasper didn't have any part in his narrow miss with the Grim Reaper."

Mildred looked at Jasper, who sighed.

"We might as well tell her," he said. "If we don't, she'll just keep poking at it and that will only keep the spotlight on the whole mess."

He gave me an apologetic look. "My uncle was an FBI agent. I have some experience with the type."

Mildred nodded. "Then we might as well move over to the table. The least we can do is hash it out over margaritas and a charcuterie plate."

"Fine by me."

I headed over to the small dining area on the porch and took a seat. Mildred and Jasper came out a few minutes later with drinks and a plate of cheese, crackers, and sliced meats.

"We've been living like bachelors," she said as she sat the tray down.

"You get no judgment from me," I said as I popped a piece of pepper jack cheese into my mouth and tested the margarita. "This is great."

"A local gave me her recipe," Mildred said. She stared at me for a couple seconds, then blew out a breath. "I don't even know where to start."

"In the movies, they always say 'at the beginning,' but I don't plan on staying long enough to hear about the past twenty-plus years of your life. And I have pretty good guesses for most of it, so maybe just the highlights."

"Okay, but it's still going to take a while. You've already heard about my father and mother and my childhood—at least enough to know why I left as soon as I could."

I nodded. "And I know why Jasper stayed behind, and I credit him for taking those responsibilities on despite what it cost him. I figure Eleanor stayed because she had the upper hand with your father and then she didn't have to pursue a career to support herself. Plus it gave her the opportunity to edge you and your mother all the way out and leave her with complete control. What I don't understand is why you ended up married to her, Jasper. I heard there was a pregnancy, so I get it from that angle, but why get involved with Eleanor in the first place?"

Jasper frowned. "I'm pretty sure I didn't. Not in the beginning. We were at a party together and I was drunk. I blacked out completely. Woke up the next day at the cabins, in bed with Eleanor. She was going on about how great the night was and how she was glad I'd finally come to my senses and picked the right sister. I just wanted to get out of there."

"But then she claimed she was pregnant."

He looked miserable. "I guess I could have washed my hands of it all. Said I'd pay support and that was it, but I'm just not made that way."

Mildred nodded. "Responsibility is Jasper's religion."

"Anyway, Eleanor had been feeding me a bunch of lies—at least, I know they are lies now—about how Mildred had moved on and had found a new guy that she was serious with. And how she was never coming back to Mudbug."

"When Eleanor told me about her and Jasper, that's when I decided I was never coming back," Mildred said.

"You both played right into her hands," I said.

They nodded.

"So I had a rushed marriage to Eleanor, and her father bought us a house," Jasper continued. "Then about four months in, Eleanor started complaining about stomach cramps. She made an appointment with the doctor and when she came home, she said she'd miscarried."

"Then why not end the marriage then?"

"Because by then her father had bailed out my dad's business. It was written up as a loan, but he'd claimed it was a gift and that when it came time for payments to start years down the road, he'd just tear up the contract and we'd be solid."

I shook my head. "So you went from being leashed by Eleanor to being led by her father."

"Yes. The years went on and eventually, he kept his word and tore up that contract, but by then, Mildred had graduated and started her career. She'd never once set foot back in Mudbug. I'd tried to contact her a couple times hoping to apologize and explain, but she wouldn't take my calls."

"If only I would have," Mildred said sadly. "Maybe all of this would have turned out differently."

"But why stay with Eleanor all those years?" I asked. "Even if Mildred was no longer in your life, you could have divorced Eleanor after the debt was forgiven and made a new life for yourself."

He shrugged. "Guilt maybe. I guess I felt like I had gotten what I deserved for cheating on Mildred. I mean, I broke up with her before she left because I didn't want to hold her back and I couldn't see any way for myself to get out. But it was still wrong to marry Eleanor. I should have just agreed to child support and tried to get on with my life."

I nodded. "But Eleanor was never pregnant, was she?"

Mildred's eyes widened. "No, she wasn't. But neither Jasper nor I knew that at the time."

"How did you find out?"

"My mother sent me a letter," she said. "She was so sick there toward the end and felt guilty that she'd never told me. But apparently, way back, she figured out somehow that Eleanor had faked the entire thing just to get Jasper to marry her. But by the time she figured it out, Jasper's dad had already taken the loan. So she saw no point in telling either of us. It just would have caused more damage and I'd already made my decision to stay away."

Jasper nodded. "But when Dora got ill, it kept weighing on her, I guess. She wrote the letter and asked me to mail it to Mildred. That was a couple days after I took Dora to that lab for the bloodwork."

"I'm sorry the lab fumbled Dora's bloodwork," I said.

"I will admit that I was angry about that when Mildred told me," he said. "But after I calmed down, I realized that even if they'd done everything they were supposed to, they still wouldn't have gotten it completed before I 'died.' So to speak. The truth is, Eleanor was hell-bent on getting rid of both of us because she thought she was about to get the life she deserved with that phony yoga guy."

"Tell me about your death," I said.

"I needed to get away to think. I had my suspicions about what was going on with Dora, and truth be told, I think Dora did as well. I was dreading having those suspicions confirmed and trying to figure out how to handle it all. Mind you, even if we'd known what was happening, I don't know that Dora could have been saved. There was so much damage by then. And to be honest, even though I'm certain she suspected, I don't know if she could have handled it all laid out. Her heart was weak and I think suspecting but remaining in denial and having the proof right there in front of you are two different things."

He took a moment to draw in a deep breath. "I took my boat out, thinking that getting out on the water would bring me some sort of wisdom, I guess. I was so distracted, I didn't notice the leak and that's on me. When I started up the boat to leave my fishing spot, I realized I hadn't latched my cooler properly and headed up to the front of the boat to do so. I opened it to make sure the ice was covering all the fish, and that's when it blew."

His voice shook as he continued. "If I hadn't been hunched behind that lid—the cooler was practically a deck box, so it took the blast without shredding. I was blown clean out of the boat and into a piling, but that lid saved my life. I fell into the water and drifted down a little until I hit the bank. I barely managed to crawl up and then blacked out. A bit later, I came to. I was sore but didn't feel like anything was broken. I was pretty skinned up and had some burns though."

"How did you get back to town?" I asked. "And how did you disappear after that?"

"I started walking up the bank. There's an old hermit that lives off that bayou. He keeps to himself, but I've talked to him a time or two when I was out. I made it to his place, and he helped patch me up—let me stay several days until I was stable. Then I asked him to take me to Mudbug late one night. I hid in the shed next to the garage until the next day when Eleanor left with Dora."

His eyes teared up. "I could see Dora had been crying and it about killed me that I couldn't console her. But exposing myself wouldn't do either of us any good because I had no doubt that Eleanor had rigged my engine. I maintained that boat myself, and two things can't go that fast at the same time. Not with someone like me as an owner."

"Walter said as much. He was troubled over the whole

thing. He didn't say outright that someone had killed you, but I'm sure that's what he thought."

"I imagine he's not the only one, but what could anyone do about it? Anyway, we had a hidden key on the back porch, so I let myself in. I'd lost my phone in the blast, but I used my iPad to call my uncle."

"The former FBI agent."

He nodded. "Then I grabbed the cash I kept stashed in the garage and hid back in the shed until dark. My uncle drove all day and picked me up late that night. I told him everything that had happened and what I suspected."

"Why didn't you just go to the police?"

"And tell them what? I had no proof of anything. My boat sank and anything that might have been evidence was carried away by the tide. The lab had already told us they were weeks, maybe a month out on getting those tests on Dora done. I thought the best thing to do was let Eleanor think I was dead until the lab results came back. And if they proved what I thought, I'd go to the police then. I didn't think Dora would pass the next day."

"Maybe your death was too much of a strain," Mildred said.

"Maybe. And that thought still makes me sick. I hate thinking that my waiting might have sent her to an early grave."

Mildred reached over and squeezed his hand. "You're not to blame for any of this. You were doing the best you could. Hindsight is always twenty-twenty."

"She's right," I said. "And for all you know, Eleanor ramped up the poisoning after you died, figuring your death could easily explain the quick decline. Regardless, those lab tests prove that Dora was probably well beyond the point of saving. I hate to say it, but even if she'd lived, it would have been in extreme pain."

"So death was a mercy?" he asked.

"At that point, maybe. So what did you do after your uncle picked you up?"

"I contacted Mildred that next morning and laid it all out for her. That's when she told me Dora had passed that morning. I couldn't believe it. Everything had been for nothing. I hadn't been able to save her. When I told my uncle what I suspected, he wanted me to go to the police right then with everything."

"But you didn't want to."

"No. I still didn't have any proof."

"And you both wanted Eleanor to pay," I said.

They glanced at each other, then nodded.

"Yes, we did," Mildred said. "So we cooked up a plan. I was going to head to Louisiana and see if I could get proof of what Eleanor had done. I didn't know how I was going to do it, but I knew the only way I'd be able to catch her slipping was to be on-site."

"So Jasper had his uncle help him acquire a fake passport and you had your back surgery done here in Costa Rica. You did a great job of faking your disability, but then I guess you had years of real-life experience. I bought it right there until the end."

"What gave me away?"

"The trophy."

"Huh?"

"Jasper's trophy that looked like a carburetor. It was on that shelf in the garage with the microwave part I took down for Ida Belle. We opened that box first and Ida Belle told me what it was. But when Gertie took pictures the next morning for your attorney, that box was gone. I just didn't realize it until later. That trophy was heavy and on a shelf you needed a ladder to get to. There's no way someone with a condition as bad as yours could have managed it. And since we didn't leave until midnight and came back early that morning, there was no way anyone else handled it for you."

I shrugged. "And why would you even want the trophy unless Jasper was still alive?"

Jasper shook his head. "I told you to leave that thing."

"I wanted you to have something you were proud of," Mildred said. "Something you'd earned that Eleanor couldn't take away."

Jasper reached over and took her hand. "I have you."

Mildred sniffed.

"Since the door to the garage was open, I heard you and Ida Belle talking about the trophy. I didn't even realize it was up there, but once I did, I just couldn't live with myself, leaving it behind. Guess I should have left the empty box up there."

I shrugged. "I still would have gotten around to it eventually. So when you were past the critical healing for your back," I continued, "you called Eleanor and convinced her to let you move back home because of your claimed health issues."

"You're right except the convincing part. Eleanor jumped to offer me a place."

I sighed as the pieces came together. "Because she wanted you out of the way as well."

Mildred nodded. "I think she figured that if I came down with the same mysterious illness as our mother that everyone would think it was genetic."

"That's a big risk—so much death in one family at the same time."

"I think Eleanor was too far gone at that point to weigh the risks. She wanted Zion all to herself and her moral compass—assuming she ever had one—was completely gone."

"And she didn't want either you or your mother draining

even a small part of the estate because she needed it to keep Zion on the line." I shook my head. "I wish I could say I understand but the truth is, I just don't."

"I don't think decent people can ever understand something like that," Mildred said.

"I assume you never acquired the evidence you wanted before it all fell apart."

"Yes and no. I had the water in the fridge in my office tested. It had high levels of metal in it."

"But you hadn't been drinking it."

"No. The bottles looked fine, but I didn't trust anything that Eleanor had access to. I kept my own stash and just dumped a bottle or two out every day so she'd think I was drinking it."

"So if you had the proof, why didn't you expose her?"

"Because I got those results the day after she killed herself. I drank tap water at home and we both drank the coffee and tea. I never drank anything she poured that I didn't see it happening, so there was no opportunity for her to get to me at home. I even had a tube of toothpaste hidden away."

"I still haven't quite wrapped my mind around why she killed herself," I said. "I didn't know her, but with what I do know, I find it hard to believe she had any remorse."

"Maybe the drugs Zion or Kim gave her brought it all on her," Jasper said.

"Perhaps," I said, looking straight at Mildred. "So much death and destruction in her wake. Maybe it all finally hit home. Everything she'd done and then finding out that Zion had been playing her the entire time. Maybe it all slammed into her like a freight train, and it was too much to live with."

Mildred looked straight back at me, never wavering. "Maybe it was."

I nodded and rose. "Well, now that I have my answers, I guess I'll head back to Sinful."

Mildred and Jasper gave each other nervous glances.

"Are you going to tell Carter?" she asked.

"Tell him what? That you're finally living the life you deserve? That Jasper opted to stay away from a woman who tried to kill him? What good would that do? There's no sense burdening Carter with knowledge he can't do anything about."

I looked at Jasper. "Do you plan on letting people back home know that you're still alive?"

Jasper stared down at the table before looking back up and shaking his head. "I don't have any family left to speak of, except my uncle. He knows the score and has no issue with the way I want to leave things. And I'm sad to say that I had more acquaintances than friends. Eleanor made it hard on people to hang around. She wasn't a pleasant woman and I wasn't the type to push back. I know that makes me a coward, and I'm sorry good people like Walter are troubled over my passing, but the truth is, I wasn't close enough to any of them for it to bother them for long."

I gave him a nod. "I'll tell Ida Belle and Gertie, of course. But they'll take it to the grave."

"I know they will," Mildred said. "I can't tell you how much I appreciate everything you did. If you hadn't pushed the issue on Zion, Carter would have been forced to close the file on Eleanor's death right away and that man would have continued to scam women indefinitely. But I'm sorry I wasn't honest with you from the beginning."

I shrugged. "Everyone is hiding something. The thing I have to figure out is whether or not their secrets matter to my investigation. In the case of taking Zion down, they ultimately didn't. I hope you and Jasper have a happy life here."

Mildred gave me an enthusiastic hug, and I could tell she would be crying before I ever stepped off the porch. Jasper grasped my hand, then gave me an awkward pat on the shoulder before thanking me.

Then I headed back to Sinful for a long conversation with Ida Belle and Gertie.

CHAPTER TWENTY-THREE

Ida Belle must have had spies watching downtown to see when I rolled through because I'd barely made it inside my house before she and Gertie came barging in.

"Carter's at work so you have plenty of time to fill us in," Ida Belle said.

Gertie nodded. "I baked a casserole earlier in case you were hungry, so we don't lose any time foraging for food. And Ida Belle picked up cookies at Ally's. We checked with Carter on the beer supply, so everything's ready for you."

I smiled. "Can I use the bathroom first?"

Gertie threw her hands in the air. "Hurry up! We've been waiting forever."

"I was gone two days."

"And if you'd taken us with you, you'd be headed to bed for a nap instead of to the kitchen for the Spanish Inquisition."

"I called in a favor with a Costa Rican informant I used to work with and got a private flight. I wasn't allowed any baggage—especially the human kind."

Twenty minutes later, I was halfway through a hefty serving

of casserole and completely through with my story. Ida Belle and Gertie stared at me, then each other, then back at me.

"That's incredible," Gertie said. "The whole thing is like something out of a movie."

"I can't believe Jasper is alive," Ida Belle said. "I'm glad, of course, but that was a twist I did not see coming."

"I didn't see any of this coming," Gertie said. "And don't you go saying you did."

"No. I'm definitely floored by all of it."

She looked at me. "I didn't realize you were still processing all of this. It's been a couple weeks. I figured you'd put it to bed like we had."

"I tried to, but something kept bothering me. I just couldn't put my finger on it. Then I almost dropped a bottle of water and asked Gertie to send me those pictures of the house that she took. And that's when it all made sense. But I couldn't be certain until I verified it."

They both looked confused.

"I get how the picture of the garage gave away Mildred's back being okay," Ida Belle said, "but what does almost dropping a bottle of water have to do with it?"

I put down my fork and leaned forward. "The day I left, Carter brought me a bottle of water outside and set it on the table. When I reached for it a couple minutes later, it was covered in condensation and I almost dropped it."

"Sure," Ida Belle said. "Because the water in the bottle was cold but it was hot outside."

"Exactly."

I pulled up the picture Gertie had taken of Eleanor in the sauna. "Look at the water bottle."

They both peered at the phone.

"It's sweating," Gertie said. "But it's in the sauna. Of course it's sweating."

"Except Eleanor took the bottle of water with her into the sauna, and she'd been in there for over forty-five minutes based on the timer, right?"

Gertie nodded and then both their eyes widened.

"The temperature of the water in the bottle should have matched the room by then," Ida Belle said. "It wouldn't have still been sweating."

I nodded. "Exactly."

"You think someone switched the bottle?" Gertie asked. "But who? And why?"

"Remember, the water bottle in the sauna didn't have any of the drugs in it," I said. "Which was convenient because then it didn't allow for someone to have doctored her water beforehand and just waited her out. We assumed that Zion had slipped her the meds before she went into the cabin or that Eleanor had deliberately taken them when offered. But what I think happened is that someone dosed Eleanor's water, knowing she'd go into the sauna after class like she always did, and then replaced it with a fresh bottle before the cops got there, just like I did with Calahan."

"But why the need to replace the drugged water with a new one?" Ida Belle asked.

"To make sure it looked like taking the drugs wasn't her choice, which was most likely to cast suspicion on Zion. He was the last person to see Eleanor alive—that anyone knew of. And he was getting involved with Kim, whom the drugs belonged to. If Eleanor had taken the drugs voluntarily, then they would still be in the cabin."

"Wait," Gertie said. "Are you saying Zion didn't drug Eleanor?"

"I don't think so. Putting the drugs in the cabin he lived in with Sapphire was just to tighten the noose on Zion. But I believe that since the real poisoner didn't know whose nightstand was whose, they got it wrong and put the drugs in Sapphire's side."

"Which is why Zion accused Sapphire of drugging Eleanor," Ida Belle said. "So you don't think Sapphire was the poisoner either."

"No. As soon as Sapphire heard Eleanor had died, she bounced, filed for divorce, and paid Zion off to get rid of him. Those actions don't jibe with a woman killing to keep her man. If Sapphire had done it and Zion accidentally got caught in the cross fire, she would have told him to shut up and lawyered him up. Plus, even though she has horrible taste in men, I doubt she would have been foolish enough to keep stolen drugs in her own nightstand."

"Well, who do you think did it then?" Ida Belle asked. "Kim?"

I shook my head.

Ida Belle looked at Gertie, both of them clearly confused.

"But there's a limited number of people that would have even known Kim had the drugs," Ida Belle said. "And more importantly, how did they get the water into the sauna, and then there's— Good. God. If someone switched the water bottles, then they also killed Eleanor."

I nodded.

They both looked at each other then back at me.

Gertie's jaw dropped. "There's only one other person who could have..."

"You think Mildred killed her sister?" Ida Belle asked.

"Yes."

"But how?" Gertie asked. "I mean, I'll give you that since her back was actually fine, she could have climbed out her office window and taken the trail to Eleanor's cabin. There would be no record of the open window because they didn't have sensors. The trail's a harder walk but half the distance that way, and everyone knew Kim never got in a rush. But Kim said she heard Mildred in her office working around the same time we all heard the gunshot."

"But did she?" I asked. "Or could she have heard Mildred's computer playing a recording of her typing? Remember how Mildred turned off the alarm with her phone? She could just as easily set a video to play in case Kim came down the hallway. If she had control of her desktop through her phone, she could have easily turned off the video after Kim left to go find Eleanor."

"And she would have known when Kim left because the motion detector would have sent her an alert when she passed by," Ida Belle said.

"But with the motion sensor at Eleanor's cabin broken, the system wouldn't have a log of anyone passing that way," I said. "Mildred could have easily sneaked into the cabin and there would have been no indication that she'd ever been there."

Gertie shook her head. "That cabin was dead-bolted from the inside. And all the windows were locked. I don't care how good Mildred's back was, she couldn't walk through walls. And there is no way to draw that dead bolt or latch those windows from the outside."

"I agree," I said. "I think Mildred was still in the cabin when you shot the dead bolt off the door."

"What?"

"No way!"

They both yelled at once.

I nodded. "I think she waited until Eleanor was half conscious because of the drugs, went in there and placed the gun in her hand and pulled the trigger. Then since she'd broken the blender, she waited for Kim to come get Eleanor and hid behind the couch nearest the door when she saw her coming."

"So you think she was crouched behind the couch when Kim and I came in?" Gertie asked.

"Yes. I noticed when I went into the cabin that the front door wasn't visible beyond the first couple feet of the hallway. When you and Kim went to the sauna, I believe Mildred sneaked out and took the trail back to the office. Remember you said that you'd never seen someone go from flushed to pale that quickly? But why would Mildred be flushed if all she'd been doing was paperwork in her office?"

"I was so flustered myself I didn't even think about it," Gertie said.

"Despite a successful surgery, I'm sure that run through the woods cost her," I said.

Gertie frowned. "She did seem even slower after the retreat than she was while we were there."

Ida Belle leaned back in her chair, shaking her head. "That was a huge, huge risk."

"Yes."

"What if Kim had run from the sauna without going in and saw Mildred in the living room or on the porch?" Gertie asked.

I shrugged. "I'll assume she was wearing a hoodie, so she probably would have taken off into the woods. Kim wasn't likely to chase her, especially after seeing Eleanor that way. Her lack of urgency with any form of exercise was common knowledge and she didn't know the trails like Mildred did. And I think we can assume Mildred had been practicing that run as often as she could. But Mildred was really hoping Kim would do exactly what she did—fall apart, maybe even pass out—because it would give her time to get away."

"What if I'd just shot her while she was running off?" Gertie asked.

"You coming along with Kim and shooting the dead bolt off the door was probably something Mildred didn't consider,"

I said. "That's where she got very lucky that you were both in the sauna long enough for her to get away. And that Dorothy didn't arrive any sooner."

"But how did Mildred think Kim would get into the cabin since the dead bolt was drawn? She's hardly the type to shoot off locks or walk around with a crowbar."

"She probably assumed Kim would break the window nearest the door and reach in and pull the dead bolt back. That would have been the easiest way in."

"Oh," Gertie said.

"Your way had more flair," I said. "The dead bolt was the tricky part. It had to be drawn or Eleanor's death would have first been considered a homicide, and the prime suspect would have been Kim, especially since it was her mother's drugs in Eleanor's system. And her desired relationship with Zion would have come out as well."

"But that's not what Mildred wanted," Ida Belle said.

I shook my head. "I'm sure Mildred is happy for Kim to have some problems to sort because it might teach her a valuable lesson, but it was Zion that Mildred wanted the police focused on. She was certain he was shady and that Eleanor wasn't his first and wouldn't be his last victim. She wanted justice for her mother and Jasper but also to prevent Zion from taking advantage of another vulnerable woman."

Ida Belle shook her head. "I can't believe she took all that risk. I get why but it's such a huge gamble."

"I'm still confused," Gertie said. "Kim wasn't missing her pills until that day, so how did Mildred lift them and use them to drug Eleanor that day but manage to get them into Zion's cabin afterward? There were eyes on Mildred all day long, and Zion probably didn't leave his retreat after he heard about Eleanor's death. Oh! Jasper."

"That would be my guess. He was probably planting the

drugs in Sapphire's nightstand at the same time Zion was teaching the class at Eleanor's retreat."

"And Sapphire had followed him," Ida Belle said. "So their place was empty."

I nodded.

"Genius," Ida Belle said. "And diabolical."

"Are you going to tell Carter?" Gertie asked.

"Tell him what? A bunch of suspicions that I don't have any evidence to prove? That would just put a dark cloud above him that he had to carry around and couldn't do anything about. I don't want that for him."

"*You* have to carry it around," Ida Belle said.

I shrugged. "I'm not as invested in the justice system as Carter."

"You really don't have a problem with what Mildred did?" Gertie asked.

I thought about this for a moment.

"Ultimately, I don't think that I do. I might have until I heard that Eleanor had already tried to poison Mildred. She wasn't going to stop until she had no resistance and all the money. She'd already killed her own mother and tried to kill her husband—in fact, thought she had. Even if the lab had gotten back to Jasper, they still couldn't have proved Eleanor was the one poisoning her mother. They'd have had to put cameras in the house, hoping to catch her dosing Dora's food or drink. If they'd brought the lab report to the cops, Eleanor would have been just as likely to accuse Jasper of doing it. And who would they believe?"

"And with Jasper dead," Ida Belle said, "if any questions were ever raised about Dora's death, then it would be easy to shift all the blame to him. I wonder if Eleanor sensed Jasper was onto her and that's why she moved on him first."

"It's all downright evil," Gertie said. "And Eleanor would

have gotten away with all of it if Mildred hadn't set her up. I guess you're right. There's no point in telling anyone else your theory, although I believe it's dead-on. It won't change anything, and the last thing I want is to see Jasper and Mildred suffer more than they already have."

"If the cops could have built a successful case against Eleanor for Dora's death and Jasper's attempted murder, it's highly possible she would have gotten the death penalty," Ida Belle said. "Maybe that factored into Mildred's decision."

"Maybe," I agreed. "Either way, they have to live with it. And despite appearing happy, I could see the burden of what they'd done weighed on them. Maybe that's enough."

———

I WAS BACK IN MY HAMMOCK WHEN CARTER GOT HOME. HE headed out back, plopped into the lawn chair, and gave me a long searching look.

"How was the trip?"

"Productive."

"Did you find out what you wanted to know?"

"Yes."

He nodded. "Are you satisfied now?"

"I think so."

He raised one eyebrow. "Anything you want to tell me?"

Yes was what I wanted to say because I hated keeping something this big from him. But at the same time, it wasn't fair to put the burden of that knowledge on him when there was nothing he could do. Even if by some miracle, Carter could scrape enough evidence together to get the ADA to pursue a case, I had no doubt that when they went to look for Mildred and Jasper in Costa Rica, they'd be long gone. They'd probably started packing the minute I left.

I rose from the hammock and leaned over to give him a kiss. "I thawed some steaks."

He smiled and pulled me down into his lap and wrapped his arms around me.

"Good. We can celebrate."

"What are we celebrating?"

"Zion is up on sixteen charges across six states now, Calahan has been demoted back down to traffic cop, and Marie just had me review permits submitted for a production company. Apparently, they want to film a reality TV show in Sinful. Looks like it's going to bring in quite a bit of revenue."

"What kind of reality show?"

"I have no idea. But I bet Gertie tries to be in it, no matter what."

I laughed. "I'm not taking that bet."

Another Swamp Team 3 mystery coming this year!

www.ingramcontent.com/pod-product-compliance
Lightning Source LLC
Chambersburg PA
CBHW071534030726
47598CB00001B/126